Ethan Andrews never saw Justin Halstead coming. A broody jock with a propensity for studying. A hot-mess conundrum who, for some reason, continues to show up at Ethan's dorm room door.

Something is happening between them, but one particular sport stands in the way. Ethan never imagined falling for an overbearing, overprotective athlete with a Hall of Fame future and a secret heart of gold.

Taking the giant leap out of the closet nearly killed Ethan, and no one seems to understand his desire to close that door and stay inside his safe place. Strangely, Ethan finds he's not alone, and it's with the last person he ever expected to be his biggest supporter...

Future NFL Quarterback—Justin F**king Halstead.

(A trope-bending love story)

JFH:

JUSTIN F**KING

HALSTEAD

GiGi DeGraham

A NineStar Press Publication
www.ninestarpress.com

JFH: Justin F**king Halstead

© 2024 GiGi DeGraham

Cover Art © 2024 Jaycee DeLorenzo

Edited by Elizabetta McKay

First Edition, July 2024

ISBN: 978-1-64890-781-4

Also available in eBook, ISBN: 978-1-64890-780-7

CONTENT WARNING:

This book contains sexually explicit content, which may only be suitable for mature readers. Discussion of sexual assault/rape on a university campus (off page; past) and trauma from past assault.

For Ethan

Chapter One

Justin

JUSTIN RAN HIS hand over his jean-covered thigh and brought the other up to his forehead, shielding his eyes as he focused on his textbook, seeing nothing. *Don't look, don't look*, he told himself as his knee began to bounce. His fingers pulled the curved and frayed brim of his ballcap lower as if it could camouflage him. Justin pinched the bridge of his nose, and he knew he was going to do it. Down to his soul, he couldn't *not* look. He couldn't resist it—this undeniable urge. It happened *every* time.

And he looked.

It was the guy.

Ethan Andrews was supposed to be studying for an end-of-the-first-week fall quiz just like Justin, but currently, he joked around with his study group, who all shushed one another through their bouts of laughter in the library. Ethan grinned, nodding convincingly through his fight, gripping his side as if in pain. His shoulders shook, his head moving back and forth in what seemed like a desperate plea to make it stop. The others in the group were nearly goners, too, as they tried to abide by the library aide, who warned them once again. This was her third trek back to their table. Something over there was beyond funny. The entire group was on the verge of getting kicked out of the fourth-floor study lounge.

Justin's cheek pinched as he tried not to smile himself. He'd seen Ethan Andrews in action like this before. He was just funny, or so Justin thought, though he'd never actually been in on the joke since he didn't even know the guy. When Justin would see him on campus, Ethan was always with others: a friend or someone from a class. Justin rarely saw him alone. There never seemed to be an opportunity to strike up a conversation or accidentally bump into him. Not that Justin would.

But he'd turned this strange obsession into a terrible habit, this expert-level Ethan-watching. So, Justin wasn't buying it, not when he caught the brief moments that made him wonder. The ones overlooked by others when Justin saw those barely there glimpses of sadness concealed behind brave smiles and mixed in with the guffaws. He peeked between his fingers. And *there*, that little swallow, the quick glance downward, and Justin waited for it. The telltale subconscious rub of fingers across the forehead before Ethan went right back to laughing.

The girl working as an aide approached the table again. This time, her firm fists were pissed-off-planted on her hips. She waved around at the other students trying to study, and Justin quickly looked down again. The entire table turned to take in the only other student on the floor: *him*.

Justin flipped the geology lab workbook page so he wouldn't look suspicious, but he hadn't read a damn thing since Ethan had arrived and joined the group. This guy was everywhere, all the time. At the Coffee Stop, in the science lab, in his geology class, running around the track, in the gym, and now, in one of the last places Justin thought he'd see him, in the library. The one place Justin thought he'd be safe from his one-and-only distraction and the constantly nagging question: Which was the real Ethan?

Realizing he couldn't do it, not with Ethan-ology overshadowing geology, Justin packed up his things, slipped out, and headed back to his dorm. He'd have to try to study there. Though it was nearly impossible to concentrate in his room, with all the testosterone and adrenaline-driven antics in the hallways, a football always flying, or someone knocking on the door every five minutes to see if he wanted to join them or go to a party.

Despite the chaos, at least he'd be free from the close proximity of Ethan Andrews in the library. Justin sighed; his reaction to the guy confused him more every time. Yeah, he knew what his mind and body were trying to tell him, but it was also something he could never pursue. Sure, the world had changed in leaps and bounds, but if he wanted to play ball, he had to keep that shit locked down. Oh, the NHL had tried it with "Pride Night" and special jerseys, but even they'd skated that back faster than a five-hole slap shot.

The media vultures were waiting for someone else to get outed in any sport, not just football, and it wouldn't be Justin. At least two big leaguers had come out, but still. Not when he was only in his second year of college ball. Not when he didn't even know for himself. And his parents, he didn't think they would care. They weren't the problem. Justin knew exactly who the problem was.

Justin unlocked the door to his dorm room, dodging bodies rough-housing, and dropped his backpack on the bed. Frustrated with himself, he pulled out his books and began again. He was a good twenty minutes into preparing for the quiz the next day when he realized he'd left his phone and some of his notes at the library. Justin squeezed his eyes closed tight for a moment.

I can be such a dumbass sometimes.

Justin knocked on his suitemate's door. He used Shawn's phone to call himself, hoping someone, the aide—he prayed—would hear it buzzing on the plastic seat. That hope died, swirled a few times, and went right down the drain when someone else answered his phone.

"This is Justin Halstead's phone," a guy said, and Justin ran a frustrated hand over his face, already knowing who had his phone.

"This is Justin," he said.

"Oh, hey, *Justin*, this is Ethan Andrews," Ethan said.

Of course, it is.

Justin could only shake his head. This is what he got for being so distracted, a lurker—an Ethan-watcher—and here came karma. Maybe not a lurker since that was creepy, but Justin was…well, very aware of Ethan, like, *constantly* aware. Yeah, he was going with that word choice and steering clear of anything sounding more stalkerish. He definitely wasn't *that guy*.

Ethan's bright and teasing tone didn't falter. "Yeah, I guess you figured out you left your phone in the library. And who knew you took such copious notes, Justin Halstead." Then, he laughed.

Justin was momentarily distracted by the sound of Ethan's great laugh. He could hear papers shuffling in the background and then a pen being intentionally clicked several times.

"Nice pen, too," Ethan said.

"Uh…" Justin had no words, hoping Ethan would keep talking. Keep laughing. And *holy shit*, Ethan knew his name, his full name.

"It's really smooth; the ink just glides. No wonder your notes are so neat," Ethan said.

Justin silently agreed. It was a great pen, a wide-point TUL, and it was like writing with soft butter. Justin liked it because it felt faster than most, and he could get everything down before his professor moved on.

"Yeah, um, I like it," Justin said, sounding like an idiot. He shook his head; *Jesus*, he could do better than this.

Ethan belted out a laugh. "Tell me how you really feel."

There was a pause Justin didn't fill.

"All right," Ethan continued, "down to business, it seems. Where are you? I'll swing by and drop off your things. I'm about to leave the library now."

"Yeah, I'm at the football dorm." Justin's knee was at it again, and he pressed his heel to the floor to make it stop. He glanced at Shawn's phone screen when there was no response.

Ethan let out a nervous laugh. "Eh, maybe you come pick it up from me, then?"

"Nah, man, it's cool. You guys were studying for the quiz, right?" Justin asked, slightly panicked as his suitemate walked into his room and glanced at him.

"'It's cool,' he says. *Me* in the football dorm," Ethan said slowly, questioningly.

"It is. Just come up the stairs, and I'm in 214. And thanks for finding my things."

"Yep. Anything good on here I can snoop through?"

Justin thought for a moment. "Hardly, but, hey, thanks again."

"Yeah," Ethan said and hung up.

Justin thanked Shawn as he handed the phone back to him. "I left mine at the library."

Glancing around, Justin made sure his shit was squared away in his room after Shawn left. His heart hammered, and the shirt beneath his armpits began to feel sweaty.

Holy shit.

Ethan Andrews was coming to his room. Justin could finally get his answer. He frowned. Maybe getting his answers wasn't the greatest idea because then Justin would have no reason to continue keeping an eye on Ethan.

Chapter Two

Ethan

ETHAN SINGSONGED TO himself, "Going to the football dorm," as he swiped the screen of Justin's phone.

No password.

What a dumb ass.

Ethan frowned, disappointed by the factory wallpaper and lack of intriguing or hopefully implicating apps. The photo gallery only contained images of school notes, snapshots of what looked like football plays on a whiteboard, and a few random pictures of Justin with his teammates. Nothing shocking or questionable.

No pics that fulfilled Ethan's jockish expectations—because he *so* would have forwarded that shit to himself had there been. Ethan walked slower, searching. Not even a compelling Google search history. The last thing the guy had searched was: *Is it farther or further?* And *okay*, he realized he shouldn't snoop too deeply into the phone belonging to a guy who could absolutely kick his ass. Resigned, Ethan locked it back and held it with the notes.

He was keeping the badass pen because—*That's the price you pay, Justin Fucking Halstead.*

Ethan walked in the opposite direction of his own dorm and wondered about Justin. They'd had a few classes together; *Halstead*, as everyone else called him, was a somewhat popular football player. And he was a hot one compared to some of the intimidating brutes he hung out with or who were always around him. Ethan recalled reading Justin's essay last year about his love of football.

Ethan sighed.

For a guy like Ethan, the football dorm was either the stuff of really great fantasy or absolute nightmare. He stopped on the path and stared at the building housing football jocks and the subjects of a few naughty daydreams and a good healthy dose of fear. Ethan headed for the door as one of the very giants was coming out.

"Hey, can you hold that for me?" Ethan called, lifting his free hand.

"Yeah, man, who are you looking for?" the linebacker-like guy asked suspiciously, eyeing Ethan as if he knew him.

"Justin Halstead." Ethan held up the notes and phone. "He lost his stuff."

The big guy chuckled. "Typical. He's in room 214." He pointed inside. "Use those stairs; don't take the elevator."

Ethan thanked him as he let him in.

"Yeah, man, are you good?" linebacker guy asked.

Ethan nodded and headed up, so used to these responses to him now. It no longer bothered him when people got weird and overprotective around him. It happened constantly, even with people like this guy, who didn't even know him. They just knew *of him*.

Ethan knocked on the door of 214, and Justin opened it and stepped back to let him in. Justin had on the same thing he'd been wearing in the library but was now barefoot. Ethan forced his eyes to Justin's face. But Justin just stood there, holding on to the open door and unblinking.

Deer in the headlights.

Justin was acting a bit strange. Ethan assessed him as Justin let out a nervous-sounding laugh, swiped a hand across his forehead, and wiped it on his thigh.

"Thanks for bringing them," Justin said and motioned to a couch in front of a television and game system. "You want to come in?"

Okay, Justin *was* being weird. Ethan waved the notes and phone and then extended his hand, holding them out expectantly.

"Uh, yeah," Justin said, not taking them. "I thought you might want to go over the practice quiz questions?" Then he pointed inside with two shakes of his finger at the couch.

Ethan frowned; it seemed as if Justin wasn't breathing normally. Knowing it was likely the stupidest thing he could do—crossing *this* particular threshold—Ethan found himself standing in front of Justin's couch as directed.

"Are you all right?" Ethan asked.

Justin shut and locked the door. He sucked in a breath, let it out, and then laughed awkwardly.

"Yeah, sorry." Justin indicated the couch and table again, where books and more notes were strewn about as if he'd been trying to study.

With another glance at the solo study session happening on the coffee table, Ethan pulled off his backpack, sat down, and laid the papers and phone on the table. Suddenly, he felt guilty about his behavior in the library as his eyes took in the array and uncapped highlighters. He'd seen and could hear just how noisy Justin's dorm was beyond the locked door.

"Sorry we were being so loud, and you had to leave the library. We felt bad—well, for at least a second. It's really loud here. Now, I do feel bad."

"Nah, it's no big deal," Justin said. "I'm glad you heard my phone."

"You know, you should password-protect it." Ethan unzipped his bag and pulled out his notes from study group. Maybe if he ran through what the group had come up with and helped Justin, he could eliminate the guilty feeling.

"There's nothing on that thing; that's, like, my fourth one." Justin laughed nervously and didn't make eye contact, which was even weirder. "They don't last long with me." Justin sat and held out his hand for Ethan's notes.

Ethan handed them over, and Justin spread the notes out, leaning over to compare answers. Ethan took the opportunity while Justin was distracted to look around. Everything was neat and tidy, but there wasn't much in the guy's room—a lame mass-produced football equipment poster on the wall and a framed picture of Justin with his parents at his graduation. What did impress Ethan was a bookshelf jammed tight with books.

"Mind if I look at your books?" Ethan asked and stood so Justin wouldn't say no. Justin only nodded as he copied down something from

Ethan's pages.

"Yeah, man, and the bathroom is there, and there's water and beer in the fridge," Justin said.

Ethan grabbed himself and Justin water and set Justin's down on the coffee table. He headed for the bookshelf and drank as he eyed each row, tilting his head at the sideways crammed-in titles. He was impressed by several classics, some high fantasy, sports memoirs, and the many literature textbooks. Those looked well-worn and older. A few banned titles also stood out—definitely not reads currently available on the campus bookstore shelves.

"Are you a lit major?" Ethan asked.

"Yeah," Justin said, seeming slightly less strange now. "Those were my mom's. She teaches English and literature in high school back home." Justin turned back to copying notes.

"Huh." Ethan continued to study each shelf. Satisfied that this guy was not what he'd imagined, Ethan returned and sat down. He remembered Justin's essay had been well-written, with few errors, making Ethan's editing work easy. It had been one of those "swap essays and workshop your classmate's story" assignments.

"I got a different answer for twenty-three," Justin said, pointing it out but still not making eye contact. "I think this one is 'sedimentary.'"

Ethan checked it and then reached into his bag for his textbook. "Let's see."

And that's how he spent the next two hours in Justin Halstead's room. They found several other questions with issues and conflicting answers but worked through them. Over those two hours, Justin somewhat relaxed, but something was off about the guy to Ethan. He couldn't put his finger on it and hoped the dude wasn't on Adderall or illegal script drugs students sometimes took. He came across as fidgety and uncomfortable.

Justin seemed to have several repetitive nervous habits. He'd rub a single finger behind his ear, scratch back and forth lightly at the hairline on his forehead, and crack his neck and knuckles. The red spot behind his ear had now seeped down the side of his neck in a faint streak. Ethan briefly wondered if Justin was nervous. But, no, that couldn't be it.

"I'll send out a text to the group since we got these wrong," Ethan said. He swiped his screen and tapped a text. He hit send, leaned in, and stared at Justin to *make* him look back at him. "Want me to add you to our study group text chain?"

"Sure," Justin said with a single quick glance, still avoiding, and told Ethan his number.

Justin picked up his phone as it buzzed, tapped in Ethan's name, and saved the new contact. Sensing the study sesh was about to conclude, Ethan closed his book and reclined on Justin's couch.

"Seriously, how do you study here?" Ethan asked, voicing his previous concern. "Damn, now I'm genuinely sorry we were so loud in the library."

"Nah, man, it's fine. It's not like this in your dorm?" Justin fidgeted with a pen similar to the one Ethan had stolen. So, no, Ethan wouldn't feel an ounce of guilt over the minor transfer of ownership.

"No, not at all. I'm in Lawson; it's super quiet. Come study there if you want." Ethan scribbled down his room number on the corner of Justin's notebook page. "We have a study lounge, and it's all single suites."

"Yeah, how'd you manage that?" Justin asked, but Ethan was sure he already knew; *everyone* knew.

"The university decided it was best to put me there, in the graduate dorm," Ethan said and swallowed. "After what happened last year."

Justin nodded as if he remembered the incident. "I'm sorry that happened to you." This time, he did look at Ethan. Now, Ethan could see Justin's eyes weren't red, and the pupils weren't dilated, but they held a "look." It wasn't pity he saw staring back at him. Ethan blinked, then allowed his mental Zamboni to clean that ice and those impossible ideas flooding his mind right out of his rink.

Ethan shrugged it off. "It's done. They're gone—I got outed—and they gave me a private room."

Justin narrowed his eyes at the evident scar that ran from the corner of Ethan's eyebrow to his ear, and Justin's jaw clenched; the skin on his left cheek ticked.

Ethan reached up and rubbed at the scar that disappeared into his hair a few more inches. "They got charged. It's all over now."

"I'm still sorry that happened to you. I wish…" Justin shook his head. "Yeah, so, the next quiz. It *is* tough to study here." Justin snapped a picture of the room number Ethan had written on the paper. He glanced at the wall clock and then at his door.

Ethan knew this dorm had major curfew rules and began gathering his things; it was time to go.

"Hey man, did you get your phone back?" asked Shawn from the suite's shared bathroom door. "Oh hey, man." He gave Ethan a dude-bro head nod. Everyone knew Shawn, an eye-candy ladies' man who undoubtedly had a few homecoming king crowns under his belt. Though glancing again at Justin, Ethan knew who he would have voted for—the quiet prince over a rowdy king.

"Yeah, Ethan found it at the library," Justin said, and he and Shawn waited as Ethan put his books and notes in his bag and zipped it up.

"Thanks again for sharing the notes," Justin said, standing from the couch.

"No problem." Ethan shouldered his backpack and turned for the door.

"Hang on, I'll walk you out," Justin offered.

"That's okay. I'm good." Ethan nodded at Shawn as he passed by.

"You doing all right?" Shawn asked him.

"Yeah, I am. Thanks for asking. See ya." And Ethan was out and down the stairs.

Chapter Three

Justin

JUSTIN STOOD IN his doorway and watched Ethan leave until he went down the stairs and was out of sight. He headed across his room to the windows and parted the blinds to look at the sidewalk below.

Shawn came in and flopped down where Ethan had been. "Lucky that dude found it and not some clinger."

"Yeah," Justin said, still at the window.

He leaned in and stared below until Ethan exited the dorm's front door and made his way, headed for Lawson. He stayed there until he could no longer see him. Justin ignored the demanding urge to rush out and walk with him, getting him safely to his dorm. He wanted more time to listen to him talk or at least get to know him, more time to figure Ethan out. Instead,

Justin returned to the couch and sank down.

He took a deep breath of what felt like his first actual oxygen in the last two hours. "And I got some answers I didn't have for the take-home practice quiz."

"Sucks what happened to him," Shawn said, and Justin blew out a long exhale.

"I think he's okay now."

"Can you imagine, though?" Shawn shook his head.

Everyone knew who Ethan Andrews was and what had happened to him from the night campus had gone on lockdown, and three students were arrested after jumping him. Ethan had been hospitalized and all classes and activities canceled while campus and municipal police conducted criminal investigations. Crime scene tape had been strung up and students directed away from that part of campus. An entire building was shut down for two weeks. It had been on national news.

"That was some bad shit." Justin rubbed at his study-strained eyes, remembering some of the darker details from the gossip. No one knew the real story, as the university had tried to protect the victim as much as possible. But the aftermath on campus, all the safety and security changes that had happened as a direct result, left little doubt about what had happened to Ethan Andrews in that elevator and then the basement where he'd been found.

"I can't believe he stayed here," Shawn said, glancing at the door. "But I heard he's got a free ride, and the university did everything they could to make it right."

"How do you make something like that right?" Justin asked, not wanting to think about what *might* have happened and the parts he and everyone else knew *did happen* to Ethan a year ago. An assault and battery victim jumped in a three-on-one situation. No one wanted to confirm the unspoken allegations of what else had happened to Ethan in that basement storage room.

"I don't think you can," Shawn said. "Man, you should invite him to the game." He motioned to the coffee table notes and Justin's phone. "You never use your will calls."

"And if something happens to him there?" Justin frowned at Shawn.

"Man, that dude is untouchable now. Nobody is ever going to fuck with him. I feel bad for him, just like everyone else. If anyone was stupid enough to try, they'd get mobbed by the entire student body and the faculty. Hell, I bet the dean would drop-kick them himself."

Justin agreed with Shawn on that point. It was as if the student body had handed down some unwritten rule. If Ethan stayed, he would be safe. Then Justin said, "We'll see."

"Keep up with your phone, man." Shawn laughed as he got up, "What is that, like, number six now?"

Justin admitted, "Only the fourth."

"Thank God you can keep track of a football," Shawn said as he went back through the bathroom passageway.

With Shawn gone, Justin picked up his phone, scrolled to his burning new contact, and stared at the irresistible name.

"Bad idea," he said as he typed out the text. *Fuck yes*, he wanted Ethan Andrews at his game, and *thank you, Shawn*. Just the thought of Ethan in the stands made Justin's heart beat faster and familiar football adrenaline pump through his veins.

Justin: *I never use my will call guest tickets if you want to come to the game.*

Ethan: *Yeah, I've never been to one, thanks.*

Justin: *Show your student ID at the will-call window, and they'll be there. How many? If you want to bring someone.*

Justin had been hesitant about that last question, but it was something he wanted to know, shouldn't want to know, and had to know, all at the same time. Did Ethan have someone? A partner, a…

"Fuck," Justin muttered, unable to even think the word. He was getting way ahead of himself but had already sent the damn message.

Ethan: *No, just the one ticket will be great. Do I have to cheer for you?*

Justin smiled, but his competitive athletic side had his fingers typing before his brain could catch up.

Justin: *Yes. Only me.*

Justin's knee bounced as he stared at the dots in the message window. They vanished and then started over again. *Come on, come on*, he encouraged his phone screen.

Ethan: *Will do.*

He wasn't sure how to take the response, but Ethan was coming to his game. Justin could already feel the hyped-up high he'd be riding for the next forty-eight until kickoff. He called the athletics department office to request the single ticket and asked for one of the better seats closer to the field rather than the student section or general admission. Swinging a single for those would be easier than multiples, and excitement almost overwhelmed him as it was handled.

"All season?" the girl asked.

"Yeah," Justin said, thinking, why not? Hell, if he was this pumped over Ethan coming to his game… Instant superstition struck him, as if Ethan had to be there for every single game.

Justin: *It's taken care of. Your ticket will be there.*

Ethan: *Do I cheer now?*

Justin stretched out on the loveseat couch as best he could and enjoyed Ethan's humorous side for the first time. He rubbed at his cheek and the strange twinging sensation there. Justin realized he'd been smiling the entire time, and it wasn't something he usually did. He tried to think of something else to send, but with the ticket business handled, he drew a blank. He closed his eyes, imagining Saturday, then jerked at the sound of his phone.

Ethan: *Are you taking me up on the quiet study spot? Your dorm is ridiculous.*

Justin: *I think I am.*

Ethan: *You feel sorry for me, don't you?*

Justin: *Nope, just trying to say thanks, and Shawn suggested it.*

Ethan: *Well, if Shawn suggested it, I'll be there.*

Chapter Four

Ethan

ETHAN GRINNED AT his phone screen. It was a nice gesture, the game ticket, and he did get that Justin felt terrible for him. Just like everyone else on campus, but Justin hadn't asked for the gory details. He hadn't dwelled on it or allowed Ethan to either. Hell, he practically refused to look at him. *That* was a different response, and Ethan took it for what it was. Shawn, who did act like everyone else on campus, had suggested it, and Justin agreed. So…Ethan guessed he was going to a football game tomorrow.

No big deal.

Just like any typical college student whose lifeblood was football.

"What do you think I should wear to a football game?" Ethan asked his mom on the phone as he stared into his closet.

"Oh my God, hang on, and let me get your dad. Are you seriously going to a football game?"

"Yeah, a player in my study group gave me a ticket." Ethan pulled out a university hoodie and a clean pair of jeans.

"Hey, son, Mom says you needed some football advice?" His dad sounded amused.

"No, just what to wear…" Ethan sighed reluctantly. "But what to expect?"

"A big crowd. It will be insanely loud. Are you good with that?" His father's concern was unmistakable.

"Yeah, crowds are better for me."

"Dress warm, cover your head, gloves, too, and you should be good. Grab some hot cocoa from the concession, and you'll be just fine. Their team's done pretty well so far this season. Who is the player?"

"Justin Halstead. I don't know what he does on the team."

His father jokingly repeated, "'*What he does*.' Oh, Ethan, what position he plays, and he's a tight end." His father sighed. "A football game, after all this time."

"Yeah, I love how Mom passed the phone to you. Did she throw it?"

"Nearly. You can leave or find security if you feel…"

"I'm good, Dad. I promise. I have a knit cap, hoodie, and winter jacket. There will be a lot of people there. The traffic near the stadium is always bad on game days, so I know it's a big crowd."

There was a long pause, and Ethan waited.

"Study group," his father said, letting the words linger. But Ethan hadn't missed the suspicion in his tone. And the attention to detail, typical of his father.

"Yeah, he left his phone in the library. I found it and returned it to him, and then to thank me, he got me a ticket. He's a lit major, but he's also in my science class. We had freshman composition together last year. I know *who* he is."

"All right, sorry."

"No, it's fine; I appreciate it. Maybe if I'd paid more attention to your advice…"

"Don't," his father stopped him. "Don't do that."

"Yeah, I know."

"You still want to stay?"

"Yes, things are getting better. And hey, I think I made a friend—well, maybe. I'm not sure yet. He's not like those I've had or been making…" Ethan trailed off, unsure how to describe Justin's reaction or attitude about him compared to everyone else.

"Hang on," his dad said, and Ethan could hear his old-school, fat-finger, keyboard-clacking sounds in the background and his mother asking *who that was*.

Ethan cringed at the curiosity in her tone. His dad put the phone on speaker and then relayed what Ethan had said. Ethan shook his head as his father read off Justin Halstead's football stats. When your dad was a high school football coach, this was what happened, and Ethan silently waited, understanding little of it.

"He's looking pretty good this year, hmm, last year too," his dad said, sounding more excited.

"Cute too," his mom said through the speaker, and Ethan groaned.

"Really?" Ethan and his dad said it simultaneously, and they all laughed.

"I think you're good. This kid's probably already got scouts looking at him, so no doubt, he's keeping out of trouble. No red flags on my end," his dad confirmed.

"So, not a psycho killer?" Ethan only half joked.

"I think you're okay. Dress warm; he'll be the one blocking, catching the football, and running it in to score." There was a pause. "Yeah, forget what I just said; just look for number fourteen," his dad corrected and then laughed, loud and long.

It was something none of them had genuinely done in quite a while, and Ethan nodded, surprisingly pleased over this call. This was good. And he was talking football with his dad. Ethan asked a few more questions just for the sake of making his father believe he was actually interested in his beloved sport.

"So, he'll be the one scoring the points," Ethan said. "Oh, or getting tackled."

"Most likely." His dad's tone was still upbeat. "I'm telling you, he's got promising numbers for next year's draft."

"Okay, Dad, that's all the football I can take," Ethan said with a teasing groan.

"Charge your phone, text me, and check in regularly if you can," his dad said—back to the role of the cautious father of a traumatized son.

"I will—love you guys," Ethan said, and they repeated it and ended the call.

It had been a good conversation, and Ethan plugged his phone in and got dressed. Gone were the days of blowing off his parents' advice. *No*, he listened now, after last year.

*

ETHAN WAS AN idiot. Of all the places he'd never been and never imagined himself ever being, but there he sat, his torn single ticket stub still in his hand.

Thanks to one Justin *Fucking* Halstead.

Ethan slipped the stub into his wallet, shoved a bag under his seat, and leaned back in the slightly comfortable stadium seat. He looked behind him and up, noticing the seats above weren't like his. He'd missed the game opening as the girl behind the window had taken forever explaining about picking up his ticket there each time unless he wanted to use the app. He'd argued he only had one ticket, and she politely informed him he had the seat for the rest of the season at a player's request. Then, she handed him a bag full of team swag.

"Season ticket holder perk," she said, then told him to enjoy the game, ending his argument.

That had been unexpected.

Ethan had finally found his seat, suspiciously close to the field. He sidestepped, interrupting nachos, avoiding knees, purses, and cups of beer with several apologies on the way to the only empty seat left in the row. Ethan took in the insanity around him—the painted faces and bodies, the bleeding school pride dripping in red and black—utter chaos and complete fandemonium.

Ethan pulled out his phone, snapped a picture of the madness and the field, and sent them to his dad with a message confirming he hadn't chickened out and had a decent seat. He didn't mention he apparently had season tickets. He wasn't sure what to think about *that*. And it had to be a mistake. Ethan sent another message to his parents to reassure them.

Ethan: *I am good, promise.*

He scanned the players wearing white jerseys with red numbers, tight black pants, and cleats. All of them were so huge. Ethan searched the row of numbers across the players' backs for a one and a four. Then, with no luck, he turned to the field.

And there he was.

Pushing an opponent away and breaking free from the hold, Justin ran down the field.

Whoa, he's fast.

The ball sailed through the air, and Ethan leaned forward and held his breath as Justin caught it mid-run and made a few more strides. Ethan cringed as a beastly player from the other team slammed Justin to the ground. He watched in an almost horrified fascination as Justin's teammate extended a hand and pulled him up, and Justin tossed the ball to the ref like it was nothing.

And they all lined up to do it again.

"Brutal," Ethan exclaimed, and the guy next to him, who looked like someone's father, chuckled.

But Ethan, surprising himself, sat there on the semi-hard-ass seat, completely sucked in by the intrigue of this dangerous game, awestruck by Justin's ability to take hit after hit and just keep going. He'd scored a touchdown before the half, and Ethan had found himself standing and screaming with the madness along with everyone else, consumed by the fandom.

You do have a good seat, his dad messaged back, *And they are winning.* His dad was likely watching the game or at least listening to it.

Ethan glanced down at the cameras on the field. *Watching then.*

Ethan: *I didn't realize how good he is.*

Dad: *There will be parties after the game.*

Ethan: *I think we both know that's not something I'm doing.*

Dad: *Good, enjoy the game. I'd like to take this opportunity to say I told you so. That one day, you might love football.*

Ethan: *But I do love hockey.*

Dad: *Hockey.*

Ethan smiled at his father's attempt at using unhappy emojis and put his phone away for the second half. His dad had been trying for years to get Ethan into football, but Ethan had never had an interest—until now.

Justin scored another touchdown in the second half, and there were two more by other teammates, so they won the game by a significant lead at the end. At one point during the second half, Ethan noticed Justin on the sideline. After talking to his coach, he'd turned and looked up into the stands. Ethan glanced around, wondering which of the people were Justin's parents.

After the game, Ethan boarded the student fan bus provided by the school, then walked back to his dorm, sticking to the well-lit paths and noting the new emergency phone stands with blue lights shining brightly above them. Those had been added after…*everything.* Security guards and cameras were everywhere now, more so than the few there'd been before.

But even those had been enough to keep Ethan from having to testify. He'd been allowed to give a deposition. The security camera footage and testimony of the custodian who had found him had been the saving grace of Ethan never having to go into that courtroom. His parents, on the other hand, had attended court each day, wanting justice for their son.

Ethan swiped his ID card and went inside Lawson. The guard at the desk nodded, and he headed up the stairs to his room. He might not ever get over his avoidance of elevators, but Ethan forced himself not to keep thinking about any of it. He put away the swag, pinned the ticket stub to his corkboard, and sighed.

"Justin Halstead."

He stared at the memento for a moment and then sent a text to his parents, letting them know he was back in his room and home safe and sound.

Ethan changed and got ready for bed. It had been a good night, *a real one*, where he wasn't faking his smile, putting on a show, or forcing his laughter. It had been the first in a long time since he'd allowed himself to let his guard down. Ethan had just closed his eyes and rolled over when his phone went off. The newly designated sound of the home game touchdown crowd he'd recorded while at the game filled his quiet room. He'd assigned it to a specific contact in his phone.

A spark of hope ignited, and it was a devastating thing.

Devastating because while Ethan wasn't clueless, he was an overthinker. He'd seen something in the hard look Justin had given him. He thought about the assignment from their shared class last spring and possibly having a genuine friend who didn't come across as obsessed with another's trauma. One who wouldn't bring it up every five minutes or smile at him while their eyes spoke the truths of their pity. People meant well; they just didn't always realize how much they kept the trauma alive with those good intentions.

Then, there was the other issue. Ethan wondered what Justin's intentions truly were. He was straight, no doubt about it. Ethan had seen Justin Halstead with the same girl several times during the previous fall semester.

He reached for his phone but didn't swipe the screen. Too many conflicting thoughts filtered through his mind. It wasn't that a straight guy couldn't be friends with him, but it wasn't really the norm. Girls, sure, they were like a flock.

Sighing, then rubbing at his eyes with the headache he was giving himself, Ethan swiped the screen.

Justin: *I saw you there. What did you think?*

Ethan bit his lip trying not to grin as he read the message a second time and then typed back.

Ethan: *Just so you know, my dad is a high school football coach. He was pretty pumped and encouraged me to go. I think you have a new fan in him since that was the first football game of my life. It was good, congratulations, but how bad are you hurt?*

Justin: *Wait, holy shit, is your dad Coach John Andrews? That's your dad?*

Ethan: *That's him.*

Justin: *Damn, dude, he's a great HS coach. And you never played?*

"'Dude,'" Ethan said and rolled his eyes.

He guessed he was going there, into the land of despised dude-bro slang and diving headfirst into the pit of very bad, bad ideas. While Ethan knew he should end this conversation, probably stop this…*whatever it was*, he couldn't push the button and lay his phone down. His thumbs went to work, and he sat up a bit straighter in the bed.

Ethan: *"Dude," have you seen me? I played hockey when I was a kid, but no football. Track and cross country, like my mom. I take after her. Let's just say she's the bean pole, and he's "the mountain."*

Justin: *The mountain is your dad. I can't believe it. He's a legend.*

Ethan was about to respond and continue the conversation about his father and football history and why it had made him hate football as a child.

Tell Justin all about his dad's constant traveling and, unfortunately, missing out on many milestones in Ethan's life. His dad loved him fiercely, and Ethan equally loved his father. He'd just grown up directing his anger at the sport that consumed the time he wanted with his hero. Before he could type in all of that, another message popped up.

Justin: *What are you doing?*

Ethan: *Lying in bed and watching TV.*

Ethan reached for his remote, flipped it on, and thumbed through the channels until he stopped on an old movie.

Justin: *What are you watching?*

Ethan: *Half-ass watching Twister for the millionth time.*

Justin: *Dude, that's on repeat, or it's Shawshank.*

Ethan: *Right.*

Justin: *Do you game?*

Ethan: *Not really. Why?*

Justin: *I was going to see if you played online.*

Ethan: *I have the gear. I just never set it all up. You know why.*

Ethan had to be sure to test the waters with that last comment, and he waited to see what Justin would say, to see if their convo took a turn in the typical direction.

Justin: *No shit. What games do you have?*

And Ethan sighed, sat all the way up, got up, and turned on his light. He opened the cabinet door beneath his television and pulled out the box of stuff his parents had bought him. His phone roared like the stadium, and he answered instantly.

"Yeah, yeah, I'm dragging it all out to look and see. My parents got me all of this, and I've never opened any of it."

"Want some help setting it up? Then we can play."

"Sure, you aren't at a party?" Ethan asked.

"I don't party, but I do game," Justin said, and the phone clicked silent.

Ethan looked at his screen and saw Justin had, in fact, abruptly ended the call. Shit, he hadn't meant *right now*.

*

ETHAN ABANDONED THE game box and, in instant panic, ran to his dresser and pulled on a pair of sleep pants and a T-shirt, followed by a minor run-around freak-out session, a toothbrush in his mouth with one hand and cramming his dirty clothes into the hamper with the other. At the same time, he kicked at his shoes, hurling them haphazardly into the closet. Ethan heard a quiet knock.

What the fuck, did he run here?

Ethan visualized Justin as the athlete he was and hastily spit into the sink and rinsed. Unlocking his door and opening it, the coolness of the hallway hit the sheen of sweat he'd worked up in his *holy shit, holy shit* haste.

"I didn't think you meant right this minute," Ethan panted, glaring at Justin.

"You said *game*. Magic words, man, magic words." Justin grinned wide and slapped Ethan on the shoulder hard as he barreled into his suite.

Ethan *umphed* and closed the door. *Jesus.* He rubbed at his shoulder, still feeling the friendly and unfamiliar stinging greeting.

"Um…" Ethan held out his hands, indicating his living space. "This is it."

But Justin was already at the television, pointing down to a gift-wrapped box halfway dragged out of the cabinet and resting angled on the floor.

Ethan sat on the couch and stared at the box. He knew what was inside. The console, the games, and all the equipment, still wrapped in cheerful holiday paper. None of it had been taken out of the original boxes or packaging. It hadn't been a good Christmas, and his parents had bought gifts, all the things Ethan had asked for, before everything had happened.

Before.

Ethan swallowed hard and shook his head. *Nope, not going there.* He looked at the wall where his breathing exercise instructions were taped and followed them, trying desperately to bring himself down from the beginnings of a flashback.

"Hey," Justin whispered.

Ethan could see Justin turn to where Ethan's attention was deadlocked. His eyes ping-ponged back and forth between Ethan's counted exhales and the poster-sized instructions on the wall. Ethan couldn't speak as he worked through it. Such shit timing, but he never could plan for these things. He couldn't prepare for something as insignificant as Christmas wrapping paper and what it could do to him. These attacks just happened when they wanted to, almost always with the worst possible timing.

Justin frowned at the poster momentarily and then turned with almost a glare to Ethan. His eyes seemed to assess, and then he put his hand in front of Ethan's face and snapped his fingers harshly.

Ethan jerked, sucked in a breath that wasn't to a count, and widened his eyes.

"Nope, snap out of that shit," Justin said, and then he turned and ripped the Christmas paper off the box, brutally crushing it before hurling it away and out of Ethan's sight.

Ethan's eyes burned, but he could breathe in gasps, and he blinked at Justin, wanting to know what the hell he'd just done to make that happen.

"Come on; this is a two-man job," Justin said with authority, leaning over and dragging the box in front of the couch. "The faster we get this set up, the quicker I'm ending you. Unless we play two-player as a team. Then I won't kill you."

And Ethan calmed down as he watched Justin slice across the unbroken tape with a key from his keyring and flip open the flaps. Next, Ethan was clutching a factory-packaged bundle of chords and a controller that had been shoved into his hands. He sat dumbstruck, until Justin snapped those fingers again, jerking Ethan into action, yanking him away from Christmas paper images and back to the task at hand.

"And, yes, I am definitely studying here. Holy shit, this is the fucking Zen dorm," Justin announced as he continued to empty the big box. It was all spread out on the coffee table and between them on the couch. Justin leaned back for a moment as he seemed to assess it all, as if in *all* its glory, and then looked at Ethan and grinned.

"Dude."

"Dude," Ethan lamely repeated and mustered a little laugh. *What the fuck was happening?*

"We can play online with this one, those too," Justin said, assessing the games. "But I don't have that one. And you still need a few others. But this one—" He tapped the case. "This is where we'll start."

Justin took over once more, giving directions to Ethan that Ethan followed, strangely going along for this unexpected ride. Together, they set up everything and waited for a system update to finish loading. Justin flopped down on the couch next to him again and indicated the controller in Ethan's hands and the matching headset he now wore, as well as Justin.

"You'll need a player name, and then we'll create your character profile," Justin said.

"Ethan."

"*No*, you don't use your real name. You have to have a screen name. We're killing a few twelve-year-olds along the way. You don't want those little bastards to know your real name. They are vicious," Justin said seriously, then laughed. "We'll also play other teams, older players, players our age. But *those kids…*" Justin shook his head with a grim expression. "You'll see. They are the worst shit-talkers."

"What's yours?"

"Turfrunner14," Justin said and then grinned.

"Crosscountry309," Ethan said. The update had been completed, and he watched as Justin typed it in and set up Ethan's profile.

"Now, pick your character." Justin motioned to his controller.

"You go ahead since you know what you're doing. Do you want some water? Snacks?" Ethan asked as he got up.

"Yeah, but you'll regret this." Justin went to work, creating a ridiculous character for Ethan.

Ethan watched Justin and the screen as he gathered supplies, setting everything down on his coffee table. Justin took a water and glanced at him—for real this time—not with the frenzy of his entrance or the insanity they weren't acknowledging throughout the setup. Justin scanned Ethan's arms. Ethan wondered what Justin would think of the worst of the scars hidden beneath his shirt.

"Permanent?" Justin asked.

Ethan nodded. "But they're getting better; they're fading. I have these scar patches the doctor prescribes. They've helped."

"All right," Justin said, his attention back on the screen. "We'll start from the beginning so you can learn and catch up to where I am. Then, we can switch to online."

"And kill the evil gamer children?"

"Every last one."

And that was how he and Justin spent the next four hours, with Justin teaching him the game and Ethan dying so many times with Justin explaining where he went wrong. It was all so *normal*. Ethan's eyes stung, but he nodded as his fingers got accustomed to the fast buttons and what function each one did.

"So, these are pretty sweet," Justin said, tapping the side of the gaming headset.

"Yeah, you have those, too?"

"Different, but just as good. We should be able to play, no problem." Justin stood, stretched, and groaned.

"How are you even walking?"

"It only hurts when I move," Justin admitted.

"Want to stay over and keep playing?" Ethan motioned to the other bed in his large suite. "I have a spare. They did this room right before they put me in here. My parents have stayed here with me on their visits."

"Hell, yeah." Justin kicked off his shoes and sat back down, grimacing. "But now I'm fixing to kick your ass in this game. You have any Aleve?"

"No doubt. I've got Tylenol."

"That'll work."

It was all so strange, as he and Justin played and ate candy and shit they shouldn't. The snack basket his mom replenished each visit was now completely empty, his trashcan full. He yawned, and Justin contagious-yawned after him.

"All right," Justin agreed without it being said, saving their progress and shutting down the game. "Toothbrush?"

"Yeah, top drawer, but you won't like the color," Ethan said, testing.

"I don't care, as long as it gets the Sour Patch Kids taste out of my mouth." Justin headed into Ethan's bathroom.

Ethan flipped off the lights, turned on the lamp by the spare bed, and then the light by his. He went into the bathroom as Justin came out. The sparkly purple toothbrush now joined his in the cup, just thrown in there with Ethan's like it was nothing. *No big deal.*

He finished up and shut off the light. Justin was already in the other bed, his clothes folded on the desk chair and lamp light out. Ethan crawled into his own and turned off the light, smiling in the dark. It was strange to have a friend, someone to hang out with and who could crash over.

Ethan found himself wanting to thank Justin, but he rolled over, deciding to be cool and not make a big deal out of it, take a page out of Justin's book, it seemed. And with Justin breathing evenly, Ethan closed his eyes.

*

"WAKE UP, ETHAN, wake up," Justin said next to him. His hands were up like he was under arrest.

"What?" Ethan asked, confused.

"You were having a bad dream," Justin said, hands still up and unmoving.

"Why are you holding your hands up like that?" Ethan rubbed his eyes in the light.

"No threat. I am not a threat," Justin said, a little panicky. "I just thought…" He lowered his hands. "It was a bad dream, man."

Ethan nodded. "I'm good. Sorry I woke you up."

Justin shook his head. "No, it's fine; go back to sleep." He clicked off the light for a second time that night and headed back across the room.

"Sorry," Ethan said and pulled up the blankets he'd clearly kicked off as he fought his demons in the night. He could only imagine what Justin had heard.

Chapter Five

Justin

JUSTIN LAY BACK down, his heart thundering in his chest and rage boiling in his veins from what he'd heard and seen of Ethan's nightmare, from the shit taped on his wall for panic attack breathing and PTSD exercises taped to his bathroom mirror, to the panic button on a long cord fastened to his nightstand. The note on the closet mirror reminded Ethan to *Take it one day at a time*. Justin closed his eyes hard, trying not to rehear Ethan's pleas or the things he'd cried out as he thrashed.

He knew the things in Ethan's room must be part of some recovery plan. But to Justin, they felt like constant reminders. In every direction Ethan turned, there was a sign telling him he was fucked up. Justin knew Ethan was, but something about these methods didn't sit well.

How was a person supposed to ever move forward if they were con-stantly being told they would never be okay? If you read a sign each day telling you that you were broken, it would become your mantra. And *yeah*, he'd seen that weekly pill container on the bathroom counter. Each day was stuffed full of pills.

Somehow, Justin found sleep again until Ethan's ringing phone woke him.

*

ETHAN WHISPERED INTO the phone, "Hey, I forgot you guys were com-ing up. Sure, but I have company. Give us a couple of minutes." Ethan ended his call, and Justin rolled over.

"Your folks?" Justin asked.

"Yeah, they're already outside the building. They usually come by on Sundays. They're a bit overprotective."

"You're good, man." Justin yawned and didn't miss how Ethan averted his eyes as Justin pulled on his shirt and jeans. "I want to meet your dad. Are they close?" he asked just as a knock sounded on the door.

Ethan pulled the door open and let his parents in as Justin stood awkwardly by the bed, nerves ramping up at the quick turn of events.

"Sorry, we usually take Ethan to lunch on Sundays," Ethan's mother said, and Justin tried to smooth down his sleep hair, then shrugged as Ethan introduced her.

"Nice to meet you, Mrs. Andrews; I'm Justin Halstead." He reached out a hand to her, then turned to Ethan's father. "Coach," Justin said, hop-ing Ethan heard the respect in his tone.

Ethan's father grinned at the recognition and shook Justin's hand.

"Good to meet you, son; hell of a game last night."

"Oh, I see I have some work to do." Ethan's mom indicated the empty snack basket and overflowing trash can. She looked pleased as she took in the game setup and evidence of fun being had.

"Yeah, Justin came over after the game, and we set it all up, finally," Ethan said.

"And we demolished that snack basket of yours, Mrs. Andrews," Justin said.

"Bethany," she corrected.

But Ethan stayed focused on his father, who glanced at the spare bed and the gaming system, the long-overdue Christmas wrapping paper evident in the trash. He looked at Ethan with the beginnings of a question. Justin wasn't sure what Ethan's father saw, but he nodded, and Justin started for the bathroom.

"You're good?" Coach asked Ethan quietly.

"Yes."

"How about Justin coming with us to lunch? Would that be ok, Ethan?"

"Sure," Ethan said. "I'm sure he'd love to talk football with you. I think he's a fan. Would you like to join us, Justin?"

"I'd love to."

When Justin came out of the bathroom, Ethan went in. Justin headed to the guest bed to finish making it up. "Are you guys staying? Want me to change these?"

"No, honey, this is just a day trip for us," Bethany said, glancing at her husband for confirmation and nodding over some unspoken agreement between them.

"Are you sure about lunch? I wouldn't want to intrude," Justin said.

"Oh, I think he'd be happy for you to join us," Ethan's mother said as she tied the knot in the trash bag and put a replacement in the can.

"All right then," Justin said and tucked in his shirt.

Coach Andrews looked at the closed bathroom door and then at Justin. He lifted a brow.

"I think he is doing okay," Justin said very quietly.

Coach nodded. "You won't mind taking my number, then?"

Justin shook his head and accepted the card Coach handed him. Justin nodded his answer to the unspoken question about Ethan's safety, and they both played it cool as Ethan came out.

"Mom," he scolded and took the full bag, "I'll be right back." Ethan sighed and took out the trash.

"So, he's okay?" Bethany asked her husband. "I told you we were worried for nothing. He messaged you and checked in—just like he promised."

Coach blew out a hard breath but pasted on a smile as Ethan returned.

"Where are we going? Justin, did they twist your arm?" Ethan asked.

"No twisting."

"It's going to be *all football*. I already know it." Ethan put on his coat and hat as his mother winked at him.

Chapter Six

Ethan

ETHAN GROANED FROM the backseat of his dad's Yukon. "So yeah, Justin got the game system set up, and we played the rest of the night. We're also going to play online."

"You have all the parts and pieces you need?" Bethany asked.

"I need a few other games, but yes, right?" Ethan asked Justin.

"Yeah, you're good."

"So, Justin, finishing college or heading for the draft after next year?" Coach asked as he drove.

"Here we go," Ethan lamented, and Justin grinned.

The barbeque place was the perfect choice as they all settled in and ordered heaps of food. And Ethan turned to his mom as the two across from them carried on about *all* that was, is, and ever could be…football.

"Your classes are going okay?" she asked quietly.

Ethan nodded as he chewed. He tilted his head at Justin and wiped his mouth. "We have geology and the lab together. We passed the quiz after studying together."

"And your weekly thing?"

Ethan was glad she didn't press over his therapy appointments in front of Justin. "It's going well." He glanced at Justin, who had looked at him directly three times now over lunch. And, well, wasn't that an improvement. He also seemed…calmer.

"Good," she chirped and then changed the subject. "So, more gaming snacks, and do you have enough winter clothes? I fear it's going to be a bad one."

"I'm good, maybe another hat," he said just to give her something to *mom him* over.

She brightened and had a mission. "I'll make sure you get that."

"Eat, Mom," Ethan finally said, pointing at her to quit worrying over him.

"My mom does the same thing to me," Justin said between bites. "I have more underwear and socks than I'll wear in a lifetime. I still haven't done laundry from the haul after the break. New socks every day."

They all laughed, and his father seemed as if he understood exactly.

"We can't help it," Bethany shamelessly admitted, as moms did.

And the talk went back, thankfully, to football. Justin asked about Ethan's father's time in the NFL, retirement after an injury, and transition into coaching. Ethan gathered from their conversation that Justin's plan was to teach English like his mother and coach when his football career came to an end. Ethan silently reeled. It was all so *normal*. It was strange, even a little uncomfortable.

Ethan wasn't sure how to process what was happening. But after lunch, they dropped Justin off in the parking lot at his dorm, and he thanked them for the meal and gave a cheerful wave as they drove off. That was it. And Ethan watched through the window as his dad drove off, and Justin jogged up to the back door of the football dorm.

"Spill it," Bethany demanded and then giggled as if she'd been holding it in and could finally let it go now that they were alone.

"We gamed all night. He was sore from his game, and I offered for him to just crash. That's all, except we ate way too much junk food. I gave him three aspirins, and we stayed up entirely too late."

"He did take some bad hits in that game," his father said.

"Yeah, and when he stood up to leave, I could see he was in bad shape. I just said, there you go. That's all, Mom. I think he wants to be my friend. I knew him before, you know, from freshman comp class last year."

"He knows," his dad said more than asked.

"*Everyone* knows, and then he was there when I had a nightmare," Ethan admitted. "He woke me up, checked on me, and went back to sleep."

His mother turned in her seat to look at him.

"I'm fine. He woke me up, and he had his hands up like this." Ethan held his hands up how Justin had. "I mean, it was obvious he was sensitive to not touching me during a nightmare. And he was saying, 'I'm not a threat, and you're okay.' Stuff like that. I think you can relax, Mom."

His father nodded. "I agree." He looked at his wife. "Bethany."

She turned around and then began on the forced topics of the game store and supermarket trip they were now taking to restock Ethan's tiny kitchen.

After the supermarket, they dropped his mother off with her grocery bags at his dorm, and Ethan and his dad headed to the game store together.

"You had fun at the game, then?"

"Yeah, rub it in," Ethan offered. "He reserved that seat for me for the rest of the season. Don't tell Mom, but I'm not sure what to think about that. It's a mistake, right?"

His dad chewed on his lip.

"Stop worrying," Ethan said. "I don't think Justin has any bad intentions. We hit it off in class discussions and group work, and then he left his phone in the library, which connected us again. He's a good guy, a good person. I've never heard anything bad about him, and honestly, I'd really like to be friends with him. I just don't know what to think about the ticket thing. The rest feels normal."

"All right." His dad blew out a breath. "I'm worse than your mother, aren't I?"

"Nope, you're still good there."

They stopped and parked outside of the store. "All season?"

"Seems like."

Again, with the eyebrow. "Players on his level get a certain number of comp tickets to give away. For parents, visitors, and friends. Did you sit next to anyone he's associated with?"

"I don't think so. The guy on my left, I think, was a player's parent; he wore a jersey with a different number. And the girl on the other side of me looked like someone's little sister, then what seemed like a mom and a dad after that. That mom was wearing a shirt that said 'My son is number 33.' So those weren't Justin's parents."

Ethan remembered something else. "And they have this app. I logged into it and had to set up a profile, and the tickets are there for the season. My name is assigned to them. So, could that be a clerical error?"

His father gave him a look.

"Fine, but why would he do that?"

Ethan pointed at his father's face before the brow could lift again.

"I'm not sure what I should say here, Ethan. Part of me wonders if there's something more you aren't telling me. The other part of me knows a player like him wouldn't give those away without a reason. I saw where you sat."

"And see, *that*," Ethan agreed, pointing at his father again. "I'm right there, like, right next to the field."

His father thought for a moment. "That isn't a discreet move."

"Right? I was sitting with families and—" Ethan cringed. "—girlfriends."

"Oh boy."

"See my point? What the fuck, Dad?"

"Ethan."

"What the hell."

"What did he say about the season tickets?"

Now Ethan gave his father a look since his father had just given him one.

"Then ask him."

"Yeah, right," Ethan said and rolled his eyes.

"Do you not want to know why he did it?" his father asked, almost knowingly, and then continued before Ethan could answer. "Or...you're afraid to know. *You* like him."

"He's straight, Dad."

They went quiet momentarily, then got out of the truck and stood outside the store as several students passed them.

His dad hummed for a moment. "Is he?" He scratched his chin thoughtfully. "He seemed…well…" He sighed. "…attentive at lunch."

"Attentive."

"When you spoke, he stopped our conversation to listen to you and look at you." His father let that observation hang in the air for far too long.

"Dad."

His father just shrugged and reached for the game store door.

Three new games later, Ethan thanked his father as they left. Back in the car, they headed to Ethan's dorm.

"One more, and I swear." His dad started right where they'd left off outside the store, but Ethan already knew what he wanted to know.

"I don't get that impression, but fine, you saw the same thing I did," Ethan answered.

His dad nodded.

"Even if that was something I was willing to consider—which I haven't at all until possibly this very moment with us talking about it—I'd want to talk to my counselor first," Ethan said. "But I don't see that happening anytime soon. *That's* the last thing on my mind."

His father nodded again, remaining silent and letting Ethan talk.

"Fine. Let's say I was interested in someone. I'd hope it would be someone like him. Someone nice, somebody who doesn't want to know all the gory details and seems to respect I have trauma. I mean, when things come up, he just doesn't make a big deal about it like everyone else. He snapped me out of a flashback like it was just something normal to do. He even threatened to kick my ass when we gamed, and he didn't even flinch. It was just so…"

Ethan paused for several long minutes. "God, I hate this word, but…normal, you know?"

His father remained silent.

"I don't know," Ethan said with a groan, noticing how much slower his father was driving, and then he smiled a little. "Ugh, fine. He's hot. I'm not gonna lie. But I don't get the vibe from him that he's even curious. So it's gotta be a friend thing, all right, and I think I need that more than anything else right now. Okay, that's all of it. Jesus, you should have been some super-secret interrogator with the government." Ethan blew out a long breath and turned to his dad expectantly.

"I think friendship *is* what you need, and you know we support you if it were something more."

"I know. Thanks, Dad. If I'm lucky in anything, it's you guys," Ethan said as they pulled into the parking lot.

*

AFTER HIS PARENTS left, after all his mom's fretting and refilling, Ethan stood in his kitchenette at his refrigerator door and stared at the beer now residing there. This was something new, along with an unopened bottle of Aleve in his bathroom. Ethan sighed, tracking right along with his mother's thoughts and knowing who the intended drinks and pain relief were hopefully for. He glanced at the clock; it was only four in the afternoon. *Nope*, subtlety was not one of his mother's strengths.

He got the hint.

"Fuck it," Ethan announced and grabbed a beer. He could drink one and not worry about his medication. He cracked it, sat down on his couch, and fired up the game console to see if Justin was online.

"What are we doing, Justin Fucking Halstead? I really want to know," Ethan said to the television screen as his eyes scanned and found the character and screenname he'd memorized.

An instant message appeared: *Look who decided to join in.*

Ethan took a drink of his beer, frowned, but downed another shot to get used to the taste. He typed back: *My mother decided my refrigerator needed to house beer now.*

Is that an invitation?

It's already cold.

Ethan felt oddly pleased as Justin's screen name vanished from the list of online players. Ethan wasn't shocked by how quickly there was a knock at his door. And before he knew it, Justin had ordered pizza delivery, was on his third beer, and had his shirt off with an icepack he'd made in Ethan's kitchen taped to his side. Ethan side-eyed as they gamed and, between his numerous deaths, took in the multitude of bruises on Justin's body and their varying stages of colors.

Justin glanced over when Ethan failed to rejoin the next game. "What?"

"The bruises," Ethan said.

Justin shrugged. "It's part of it." But his eyes stayed fixed on Ethan's for longer than they ever had.

"What?" Ethan asked.

"Nothing." Justin directed his attention back to the game. "You're up."

Ethan played. He played and turned off his mind until Justin yawned, and a row of bottles lined his coffee table.

"All right, I'm calling it," Ethan said. "We both have class in the morning."

Justin leaned back, his melted icepack long gone, but somehow, his shirt had never made it back on. Ethan glanced over but then averted his eyes.

"Why did you give me season tickets?"

"Superstition," Justin answered instantly.

"What?"

"We won, didn't we? So now you have to come to all the games. So I'll win."

Ethan didn't respond since he sensed some bullshit in the answer. Those season tickets were arranged before Justin's team had won.

"You'll be there, at least for the home games," Justin said more than asked.

"Sure."

Justin looked sleepy and pleased. "Good. Then it's going to be a winning season." He tried to speak through his next yawn.

"Oh, so I'm like a good luck charm?"

Justin just pointed a finger at him as if that was an answer.

Ethan stood, headed for the bathroom. He said nothing about Justin, next to him, brushing his teeth at the same time, or how they easily alternated at the sink.

It's weird, right? The thought kept running through Ethan's mind. *Maybe he acts like this with everyone?* Ethan frowned at his own reflection at that thought.

"What?" Justin asked as he dried his hands.

"So, are we, like, gaming friends now?"

"Yeah, friends." Justin began to twirl the hand towel between his hands.

"No, I know what that is," Ethan tried to say but yelped as Justin expertly snapped him with the twined towel, laughed, tossed it on the counter, and headed to the bed he'd slept in before.

"Fucker," Ethan said as he shut off the light and rubbed at the welt on his arm.

Justin just laughed again. "You ask too many questions, Ethan."

Or you don't want to answer them. And that was the last thought Ethan had before his alarm for class went off, and he couldn't recall struggling to get to sleep for a change.

*

TWO WEEKS LATER, Ethan smiled as he entered his geology class and saw that Justin had swapped places with his usual seatmate.

"Thank God," Ethan whispered as he unzipped his bag and retrieved his books.

"I figured. You're welcome."

"Yeah, thanks. You ready for this?"

Justin indicated he was. They'd studied together for this test and had hung out regularly in Ethan's room. When they weren't together during Justin's downtime, they played each other online or sent text messages of stupid shit back and forth. Ethan had gone to one more game, with the other being an away game.

Ethan now smiled to himself over bitching about his seatmate to Justin—a girl who was always playing with her hair, texting under the table, and then having the audacity to ask for his notes. He didn't know what Justin had said to her to get her to move, but he was grateful. Seventy minutes later, they left their geology class, unit exam over.

"I feel good about it," Justin said as they walked together.

"Yeah, same," Ethan agreed as Shawn joined them.

"Hey, Ethan," Shawn said. "What are you two doing?"

"Heading to the dining hall; want to join?" Justin asked.

"Yeah," Shawn said, and that was how Ethan found himself sitting next to Justin, squeezed into a big round booth with four football players who ate like they were consuming the food supply of a small nation.

"Jesus, I bet your moms were glad when you left for college," Ethan said jokingly, and they all nodded.

"Man, my mom used to threaten to buy a minivan just to go grocery shopping for me and my brothers," Cliff, one of the guys, said. "I have four brothers."

Ethan acknowledged that idea. "A food van."

Justin laughed, and Shawn did too.

Justin nudged Ethan's plate with an unfinished grilled chicken sandwich and fruit cup closer to him. "Eat up if you want to hang with this crowd."

"Are you working out with us later, Ethan?" Shawn asked.

"Oh, I don't think—" he started, but Justin was already saying *Yes, he was.* And Ethan picked up his sandwich and ate the rest. Apparently, he was going to work out with the Goliaths of the university because *that* was something he usually did. With his plate finally empty, they all worked themselves out of the big booth, put up their trays, and headed to the gym.

Justin leaned in alongside Ethan. "Don't worry. They'll be cool."

"When does cross country start back up?" Shawn asked once they were in the weight room.

"We're already training. Our first meet is next month," Ethan answered as Justin adjusted the weight setting on the pull-down bar.

And that was how it went as they all clanged metal and sweated through a late afternoon workout.

"You coming to the game Saturday?" Cliff asked Ethan as they all grabbed their gear and headed for the locker room.

"Yeah, I'll be there," Ethan said, wiping his face. He grabbed his stuff, then tilted his head to the door as he turned to Justin. "I'm going to shower at home."

"Yeah, I'll catch up with you later." And Justin headed into the locker room with his teammates.

Ethan lagged as he walked home. He tried to stay active, in good shape, and worked out with his cross-country team, but he wasn't a "hit the heavy weights" guy. Of course, maybe if he had been—*before*—he could have better defended himself last year. Ethan tried hard not to constantly think about *shoulda, coulda, woulda's*, as his dad liked to call them. It happened; it was horrible, and he was taking one step at a time on the path to healing.

He saw his therapist regularly, employed the exercises he needed to get through the more challenging times, and took medication, which seemed to be helping. Over the last few weeks, though, the bright spot in his life wasn't speaking with his therapist, where he could let his façade fall away. No, it was spending time with Justin.

Ethan shook his head as he walked. They were so different, such unlikely friends. And even Justin's friends impressed Ethan, or at least the group he typically hung out with. Ethan thought they were all part of the offensive group, line, or whatever it was called. Still, he'd caught a few looks exchanged at lunch and in the weight room. Justin tended to hover—not really hover, but he kept close—and he didn't seem to notice when he did subtle things like pushing Ethan's plate closer or handing him a towel. Justin didn't notice it, but Ethan and Justin's friends did.

That was the thing, though; Ethan had seen Justin hand Shawn an extra water bottle he'd brought for his roommate. He was just like that, thoughtful. That voice in Ethan's head pointed out the obvious: *then why isn't he spending all his spare time with Shawn?* Sometimes, Ethan hated that little voice. But honestly, if he were frank with himself, voice be damned, he liked Justin.

And that was the problem.

Chapter Seven

Justin

JUSTIN TURNED ON the hot water and stepped under the shower. "Thanks for that," he said to Shawn and Cliff as they all lathered up.

"Yeah, man," they both said.

"He's doing good. He looks better," Cliff pointed out.

Justin nodded, recalling how gaunt Ethan had been when he returned to school. He still wasn't back to his old self, but it seemed he was slowly getting there, at least physically. Justin dried off, dressed, and walked back with Shawn to their dorm. Cliff was off to see his girlfriend.

"So," Shawn said, sounding suspicious.

"What?" Justin narrowed his eyes.

"I mean… You know what. It's none of my business," Shawn said.

"Right."

"It's just an odd friendship."

Justin sighed. "He's cool. I like hanging out with him. Don't make a big deal out of it."

"I'm not."

"You are."

"Fine, I am," Shawn said, "but I'm not the only one who's noticed." He held up his hands. "No girlfriend this year. You don't seem interested in Holly anymore. She's been asking about you, and what's the deal? Man, you're always with Ethan."

"It's not like that," Justin said and realized how *like that* it must all look to his friends, to his team, to the girl he'd dated off and on last year and then dropped like an asshole.

"If it was… I'm just saying." Shawn gave Justin a light punch. "It's cool, man."

"It's not, though." Justin shook his head. "Talk about something else, and tell the guys to shut the fuck up. Holly knew she was a regular hookup and didn't complain."

"Fine," Shawn said, retreating.

*

JUSTIN YAWNED AND then glanced at Ethan as he stretched. Though he'd tried hard to talk himself out of it, he was back at Ethan's and crashing there another night. He'd lost count of the number of times he'd stayed over by this point, but it had been after every home game and every Sunday night between when he could get away with it and not violate the weekday curfew. There had already been one very risky Friday night spent at Ethan's as well.

But it was Tuesday, and their dorm monitor had been sick, assigning a player to make the rounds for him. With the promise of a case of beer and covering for him if Justin got busted, he was back at Ethan's with a food delivery for their dinner and another night of intense trash-talking and strategy planning on how they would take out their opponents in their game. They'd been playing these same kids for over a week now, and Justin had to admit, the juvie crew was crushing it.

But Ethan was dying less and less, getting a game mentality of always being on the lookout for hidden supplies, more ammunition, and first aid. Tonight, he'd even gotten to Justin's character in time to save him, and they were back in the fight together. Then, they'd watched some sports high-lights, and Ethan had convinced Justin to eat a bowl of ice cream from the colossal carton his mom had slipped into the freezer for them.

It had been a good night.

Ethan exited the bathroom after his shower and shut off the lights. Justin rolled over and got comfortable but froze as his bed dipped, and Ethan sat down behind him.

Justin rolled back over. "What's wrong?"

"I want to talk to you about something," Ethan said quietly.

"All right. In the dark?"

"Yeah, I don't think I have the nerve to talk to you about it any other way."

"Oh, *that* conversation." Justin sat up, propping himself. He could still see Ethan's form in the ambient light from the small plug-in night-light. Ethan never slept in complete darkness.

Ethan swallowed hard. "*That* conversation, which one is that?

Because there is more than one of those."

"The one you want to have now. Go on," Justin said.

Ethan nodded as if reassuring himself. "I'm glad we're friends. I don't want that to change. But I think it's fair for you to know. I mean, I feel like I need to be honest with you. Justin, I'm sure you already know, but I'm gay, and your friends are starting to notice how much we hang out together. Your friendship is something I don't want to lose, but I feel like you need to know I'm interested in more than friendship if that were ever an option. And we never have to have this conversation again, but friends are honest with each other."

Justin blew out a frustrated breath. "I can't, Ethan."

Ethan nodded. "I know. It's because of football."

"Football," he confirmed.

"But if it wasn't for football?"

Justin was quiet for several long minutes. "Look. I've had a thing for you since freshman year in comp class. But this, our friendship, that's all I can do about it. It doesn't matter how I feel."

"I understand. So will this make it weird between us?"

"No."

"Good." Ethan got up and headed across the room.

Justin lay there in the dark, a million questions racing in his mind, answers he wanted. He knew he didn't want to use Ethan either. And he never would. But damn, it was driving him crazy, especially now with the knowledge that Ethan was interested in more, interested in him too.

Chapter Eight

Ethan

ETHAN'S EYES FLEW open as Justin flipped on the lamp and sat on the side of Ethan's bed. Ethan scooted over, and Justin shifted, leaning against Ethan's thigh, and scrubbed his face with his hands. He lowered them, turned and looked at Ethan, and then down at the floor as he cracked his knuckles one by one.

"This is a bad idea," Justin said quietly.

"But here you are," Ethan whispered, almost too afraid to speak any louder. "And you want to be here, or you wouldn't be. You crossed the room."

Justin nodded slowly and then swallowed hard.

"You should be out celebrating at some party, but instead, you're here with me, week after week," Ethan said slowly.

"Pretty much," Justin said in the same careful cadence. Justin swallowed hard for a second time. "I want to know… What it is… Why is it every time I see you or I'm around you, I'm all…nervous and confused. Excited and"—he lowered his voice—"hard."

Ethan's eyes widened at such an admission, but he already knew what he was about to do. Not only for Justin but for himself. He'd been the prince of restraint throughout the weeks of their strange friendship, but Justin had crossed the room, coming to him. Justin was sitting on his bed, searching for answers.

"I see." Ethan sat up slowly as he spoke as if approaching something that might attack, but he shifted behind Justin and eased his legs to either side of his. "You want to know an answer to the 'Ethan question,'" he whispered as Justin began to breathe harder.

"I don't want to fuck up this thing we have," Justin said.

Ethan couldn't believe he was doing this but slid his hands around the waistband of Justin's boxers and whispered close to Justin's ear, "Is it just me, or in general?"

Justin hadn't tensed at his touch. "Just you." But his chest was heaving as he tracked where Ethan's hand had slid up to his stomach and grazed down the line of trimmed hair, then dipped beneath the waistband of his boxers.

"Fuck." Justin panted as Ethan's hand found him, and his body began to shake against Ethan's chest.

"You want to know what it would feel like between us, between just you and me." Ethan breathed across his ear. Goosebumps sprang across Justin's neck as he shuddered, and Ethan ran his thumb over the surprising slickness already there. Slowly, he wrapped his fingers around Justin's girth and took a solid hold of him.

Justin groaned as his head fell back on Ethan's shoulder. "Yes, but I would never use you, Ethan. You should stop."

"Oh, and don't I already know that about you," Ethan confessed, not stopping. There had been no heat behind those words. "If anything, I feel like I'm taking advantage of you."

"You aren't." It seemed as if Justin could barely get the words out, and he moaned.

Ethan pumped his hand as Justin held on to Ethan's thighs like his death grip on the football.

Ethan had started slowly, but Justin's reactions made it clear this wasn't lasting long.

"There you go," Ethan breathed out, stroking his hand in earnest now. "Let all that shit in your head leave and just get your answer. One time. We do this one time, and we forget it."

Justin panted, "Does this hurt you?"

"No. And you aren't using me. I want this. I want this so much."

Justin's fingers dug into Ethan's thighs as his hips pushed into Ethan's fist, matching the steady attention of Ethan's hand.

"God, that's it; just let yourself go," Ethan panted as he looked down the length of Justin's body, fascinated by what he was doing to him. Ethan reached his other hand around and pushed away the boxer fabric, freeing the restriction. Ethan watched as he worked Justin over for only a moment before returning his mouth to Justin's ear. His free hand moved behind Justin to push down his own waistband and free himself. He licked, teased with a suck, and breathed against Justin's ear as Justin gripped Ethan's thighs even tighter. Ethan would have bruises, but he could care less at the moment.

"Yes," Ethan hissed over Justin's cheek. "Do you feel what I'm doing behind you? It's the same for me."

Justin made a desperate noise. He cursed as his body tensed, and Ethan stroked him through his fast release. He slowed his hand on himself behind Justin. Justin's fingers eased their death grip, and Ethan leaned back across his bed, away from Justin—stretched out flat to finish himself off. Justin turned to him.

"Yeah, you watch me," Ethan groaned as Justin stared. Ethan jerked off, eyes locked on Justin, and streaked his stomach for the only guy he'd hoped might one day be staring at him like that.

Justin sat there, breathing hard, with a matching mess. When they'd both calmed, he stood and headed for the bathroom.

"I can't believe that just happened," Justin said.

"You wanted that to happen."

"Well, *yeah*, but no." Justin returned and tossed Ethan a hand towel. "That's not why I came across the room." He shook his head and laughed. "*Fuck*, I was just hoping to get the nerve up to kiss you."

Ethan's eyes widened, but he couldn't fight a grin and then his own belt of laughter. "Oh, shit," he sputtered. "I fucked that up." He laughed again, "Big time."

Ethan sobered, taking in Justin's look and serious expression. "Then kiss me if that's what you want to know."

Justin just sat there, and it looked as if he was waging an internal war with himself. He was quiet but nodded slightly. "I got your essay in freshman composition."

"And I got yours."

"Yeah. It was dumb—about football."

"Ah, it makes more sense now. So, you got a little peek inside my soul." Ethan hummed, nodding to himself and remembering some of what he'd written in the essay.

"Was it all true?" Justin asked.

"Yes, that was the assignment."

"I made a copy of it."

Ethan smiled, intrigued by the admission. "And?"

Justin shrugged, looking bemused. "I just did. I wanted it to be like what you wrote about."

Ethan stopped, realizing. "Aw, and I spoiled the moment."

"Oh, I wouldn't say that." Justin rubbed the back of his neck uncomfortably and shook his head over what they'd just done. He got serious again. "I would never ask you to keep this hidden. That's why we can't."

"But you want to," Ethan said with a sigh.

"I want to kiss you like that essay," Justin admitted, appearing embarrassed as he scrubbed his face. "That's so selfish."

"You want to kiss me like the essay," Ethan repeated, recalling more now about what he'd written.

"More than anything."

It was a long moment before Ethan spoke again. "Friends," he finally said. "I think that's our only path. I'm still fucked up, and then there's you and football. Of all people, I do understand the complexities there. Trust me, I'm the gay son of a football coach. I get it." Ethan waved a finger between them. "This…is impossible. Look, we know there is something here, but we can't, Justin."

Justin nodded his agreement. "I know. I'm not going to kiss you, Ethan."

"I know."

And that's how they left it. How they were. Two close, if not best, friends, with Ethan going to Justin's football games, Justin showing up for Ethan's cross-country meets, Justin watching Ethan play amateur beer-league hockey, and Ethan dragging Justin home for a quick Thanksgiving break, his mother's home cooking, and more time with Ethan's family.

Chapter Nine

Justin

"I HOPE YOUR parents don't get mad at me," Bethany said as she set the carving knife and meat fork in front of Ethan's dad and took her seat with a guilty smile.

"No, ma'am, they know I have football, and now that we're headed for the playoffs…" Justin said, shrugging. "They've always known this was how it was going to be. We often celebrate things before or after the real holiday because of football."

"Don't I know that," she said and gave her husband a look only the wife of a football coach could.

Coach carved the turkey, and Bethany filled plates with far too much food and passed them back. Justin liked how Bethany and Coach had started to call them *boys*. It was silly, but Justin was fond of Ethan's parents, their acceptance of their son, and their lack of prying with too many questions like his parents might.

"So, boys," Coach started, and Ethan nudged Justin with his elbow. "We need to talk about the Bears' defense."

Bethany huffed but took a bite and chewed.

"They're a tough team," Justin admitted. "We've been watching game tape, and when we get back, I have a feeling we'll be watching more and running some new plays. I've got to work on getting faster."

Coach nodded, his mouth full.

"You're already fast," Ethan said.

"I'm faster in the first half than I am in the second, and they know it," Justin said between mouthfuls of Bethany's feast.

"Run with Ethan," Coach suggested, then asked, "Why'd they decide to switch your position freshman year?"

"I was a backup quarterback and not getting enough playing time, so I jumped on it when they brought up the idea because of my speed. More exposure, rather than sitting on the bench."

"Good move, but you also had some pretty strong stats."

Justin shrugged. "I'll play whatever puts me on the turf."

"That's the spirit," Ethan joked.

"And the grades? Both of you," Bethany interjected.

"Good," Ethan said but thumbed at Justin. "He scored two points higher on our last geology lab test."

"I told you that was going to be a trick question," Justin said, shaking his head at Ethan in disappointment, then looking at Ethan's parents. "I told him."

Coach chuckled. "Our son can be stubborn sometimes."

"And are you going to even be able to have a Christmas?" Bethany asked.

"Not if they get to a bowl game," Ethan said, and then Coach really did crack up.

"My God, I never thought this day would come."

"Stop, Dad," Ethan said, but he was just as happy to be talking football with his father. Justin could see it in both of them.

"We'll see," Justin said, answering Bethany.

They sat, with full bellies and half-eaten pie, on the couches, watching the NFL game. Bethany fussed about how there shouldn't be football on holidays. And Coach gave her grief over being thankful he didn't have to watch back-to-back parades as Ethan began to yawn. Bethany headed to the kitchen, leaving the guys to the big screen.

Justin grabbed one of the pillows next to him and laid it next to his leg on the couch. Ethan needed no convincing as he flopped down, his head next to Justin's thigh.

"I'm in a food coma," he mumbled. "Save me."

"Nah, you're gonna have to sleep it off, man. All those carbs." Justin returned his attention to the game. "Or, it's just the Thanksgiving dose of tryptophan."

"It was the pie," Ethan said as he yawned again. "Gets me every year."

Several minutes later, Justin looked down to check on Ethan, softly snoring, only to find Coach catching him doing it. Justin shrugged, reached to the back of the couch, and pulled down Bethany's folded afghan. He carefully spread it over Ethan so as not to wake him.

"You two have gotten close," Coach said.

"We have."

Coach's fingers thrummed on the arm of his recliner.

"I care about him."

Coach nodded, but the silent question lingered without being spoken. Justin felt compelled.

"We're just friends. It's all we can be. We've discussed it," Justin said quietly.

"So you two are in agreement?"

"Yes. I'll never hurt him, never ask him to hide. That's why."

"Good. If you lose in the playoffs, I hope you'll come home for Christmas. And, Justin, you can call me John."

Justin's throat tightened, and he could only nod.

*

JUSTIN SAT ON Ethan's couch, his laptop on the coffee table next to Ethan's.

"We could take a math class together or this Early American Lit class," Ethan said with a slight groan.

"Why not both?" Justin suggested, scrolling through the spring semester courses as they tried to plan out their classes and get registered.

"All right," Ethan said, and Justin leaned in and selected the same course numbers on his screen as Ethan's.

"Now, what do you want to eat?" Justin grabbed his phone and searched through the menus he'd downloaded last fall of their favorite places to order from. "You haven't had eighteen Crab Rangoons in what?" Justin exaggeratedly looked up at the ceiling. "A week now?"

"Stop. It's not like you don't love your fifteen eggrolls," Ethan shot back.

"So fucking good," Justin said with favorite food appreciation in his tone.

"Yeah, order the usual. I'm taking my shower now before I'm too tired later. You need in the bathroom?"

Justin shook his head and watched as Ethan got up and headed in. He stared at the phone screen button to the restaurant until the water turned on, but he laid his phone down as he stood and adjusted the uncomfortable tightness in his jeans. Ethan did this to him without even trying. Justin had been fighting it off for weeks now, but *damn*, everyone had their breaking point.

With a quick flip over his head, his shirt was off, his jeans hit the floor in a heap with his briefs, and he was already across the room and opening the bathroom door before he could talk himself out of this move. He knew he shouldn't do it. The boundaries had been set and agreed to, but he couldn't shake the feeling of Ethan's hand around him or that nagging desire that *he'd* never gotten the chance to touch Ethan.

The water was loud, and Ethan clearly hadn't heard the door open or had and was ignoring it as Justin slid the shower door open and waited. Ethan turned, his eyes moved down Justin's naked body and lingered on what Justin was making no attempt to hide from him.

"It took you long enough," Ethan said and turned back to the spray.

Justin climbed in, and Ethan maneuvered to swap places.

"What do you mean 'took me long enough'?"

"Two months," Ethan said.

"We have an agreement," Justin reminded Ethan. "I don't want to break the rules."

Ethan looked down again, this time with a suspicious expression.

"I said *I* don't want to break the rules," Justin said, pointing below to the obvious. "*That guy* could give two fucks about the rules. It just wants what it wants." Justin swiped the water from his hair as he stepped closer to reach for the shampoo. He dropped his gaze to Ethan's now-matching problem. "And it seems like someone else has joined the conversation."

"Yeah, I don't think mine gives two fucks right now," Ethan said.

"What if we broke the rules just once more," Justin whispered as he stepped in closer, the shampoo forgotten.

"Just one more time," Ethan agreed as he reached out and took Justin's hand, guided it between them, and used his own hand to control Justin's around Ethan's shaft. "Is this okay?"

"Anything." Justin could barely answer as he felt Ethan's hot skin for the first time. He didn't try to take over, studying how Ethan's fingers controlled his grip—the tightness and motion as he maneuvered Justin's stroking hand.

"Ethan." Justin knew he breathed his name.

"I got you," Ethan whispered back, his free hand wrapping around Justin's length and matching the pace he set with his other hand.

Justin reached his arm over Ethan's shoulder without touching him and planted his hand on the back shower wall behind Ethan for support as he continued to look between them, up at Ethan's face and then back down again.

"It's you," Justin whispered. "Only you make me feel this way. I thought I could… Fuck, slow down, Ethan."

"You thought we could never touch each other again."

Justin could only nod as Ethan deliberately slowed to a torturous pace. His fingers and palm worked around Justin's sensitive head, and Justin shuddered as Ethan's hand slid back down to the base.

"I think we gave it a good effort," Ethan said. "And I've been doing some thinking."

"I can't think right now, Ethan." Justin pushed his hips forward as Ethan pulled, seeking the sensation of driving back into Ethan's hand and imagining what sex with Ethan would feel like if Ethan's hand could undo him like this. Justin watched as Ethan, too, looked between them, observing as he completely controlled this interaction. "Are you okay?"

"Better than okay," Ethan said through a moan. And then he leaned in and rested his forehead against Justin's chest. Justin lay his cheek against the back of Ethan's head and kept his one hand glued to the wall, his other careful not to take over, relishing finally touching Ethan. *Well*, he enjoyed it for a moment; it was over far too quickly for him, and this time, Ethan was just as quick.

Ethan pulled back and smiled, releasing them, and Justin moved again to let Ethan under the water.

"Look at that; the water didn't even get cold."

Justin laughed at his admission. "We're pathetic."

"Pretty much."

*

"FORTY MINUTES," JUSTIN said after finally ordering their food.

"We aren't talking about it?" Ethan seemed to say more than he asked.

Justin lay against the couch with his head back and eyes closed. "You said you'd been thinking. I do want to know that part."

Ethan sighed. "I know most people are pretty proud to be out. But for me, the closet isn't nearly as scary a place or as doomed place to be in."

"I would never…"

"I know that. But what if I don't want to have my life on public display? What if I'm happiest and feel the safest I've ever felt right here with you?"

"We can't live in a bubble, Ethan."

"We can if that's what we want. Where does it say we must live a certain way or by anyone else's labels, agendas, and expectations?" Ethan rested his head on Justin's shoulder. "Don't we determine our own happiness?"

They were quiet for a long time.

"I know you now," Ethan said. "You're holding back and stopping everything because you think you're asking me to hide. I'm not hiding. I'm happier than I've ever been. Who are you to say we can't if it's my choice?"

Justin laughed, jostling Ethan's head.

"What?"

"'Who am I to say'? That was just funny." Justin slid his hand over until he found Ethan's. Ethan held his back, and they stayed like that until Ethan's phone rang, the front desk calling about the food delivery.

Chapter Ten

Ethan

ETHAN HELD JUSTIN'S hug a moment longer, smiled as he stepped back, and watched as Justin left. It was one of those dreaded weeknights when Justin would stay until the last minute, then sprint back to his dorm before his curfew. Ethan's room always felt so empty when Justin couldn't stay over. Ethan looked at his room, the bed where Justin usually slept, and imagined pushing the two beds together, making one large one.

Instant panic came over him, and he fought it off, wondering whether he could handle sleeping next to Justin or what moving the beds together might lead to.

He wasn't ready.

He felt pathetic for a moment, so weak to let this shit keep him from moving forward with his life. Images flashed through his mind, and he lay down on the cold tile floor as he battled his monsters. Just as he was going to let himself break down, the familiar crowd cheered, and Ethan sat up, rubbed his face, and went for his phone.

Justin: *Yes.*

Ethan already knew that answer in his bones, throughout his soul. It still felt good to see it. The confirmation that Justin was *in* this, no matter what careful and cautious path they were on.

Ethan: *See you after practice.*

And they started the spring semester at a snail's pace, still hanging out as friends when out and about on campus, often eating in the dining hall with Justin and his close teammates or doing various things together. Not much had changed behind the closed door of Ethan's room either. They seemed more relaxed and comfortable around each other.

Justin often held Ethan's hand. Ethan played with Justin's hair when they watched a movie on the couch together. They'd gotten uncomfortable and switched around a few times, safely spooning, but things were cautious on the naked front. They hadn't moved past a hands-only approach, and only one other time had they repeated the shower scene.

Justin didn't pressure him or bring it up; Ethan was grateful for that. Every time, he began to doubt how much longer Justin would stick around like this, in a not-going-anywhere relationship of sorts, Ethan's doubts would vanish with one smile as Justin walked through his door—like he was the best thing Justin had seen all day. Or when they'd do dumb normal shit together, like make a shopping run because they both needed laundry detergent or some other necessity—it was just a deep friendship that continued to grow.

With Justin's football season over and Ethan's cross country wrapping up, Justin had come to several of Ethan's meets that weren't too far away. And he blended in at beer league when he could make it. The crowd only half-filled the local rink seats. For the longer track meets or away league games, Justin had used the time to travel home and see his parents. An invite Ethan hadn't gotten yet, but he'd been dragged to dinner when Justin's parents had come to an awards banquet for Justin. They were friendly and seemed like kind people who loved their son, and they'd been welcoming to Ethan as their son's "best friend."

It also seemed that being best friends with a football player meant people suddenly lost interest in your personal drama, and more than once, Ethan handed over some scrap of paper with a name and girl's number to Justin. And Ethan might have taken a ridiculous bit of pride every time Justin wadded them up and threw them in the trash without looking at who they were from or asking anything about them. When Ethan would get insecure, Justin let him vent. He'd say nothing and then just wave a finger between them as if that said it all.

Ethan was home for a weekend with his parents, guiltily bringing his laundry at his mother's command. Justin was doing something with the team—some spring float trip guests weren't invited to.

"I expected much more than this," his mother accused as she looked at Ethan's single basket.

"We've been doing our laundry like adult children should?"

His dad laughed.

"These don't even look dirty, Ethan," she reprimanded and picked up his basket.

He never could get much past her, and he shrugged at his dad, who was still grinning at him.

"The things we do," his dad whispered, winking after his wife.

They were on the back patio, watching the robotic pool cleaner make its Tetris-like journey as it worked over the stairs. They sat with beers in hand and the steady squeak of his dad's chair rocking.

"Justin had his big float trip this weekend," his dad said and left it hanging in the air between them.

"Yeah, the team only. He and I, uh…" Ethan took a drink and searched for the right words. "We're close, you know that. Maybe trying to figure some things out about our friendship. He doesn't seem to be going anywhere."

"And your feelings about him?"

"I'm so screwed, Dad."

John chuckled but drank his beer.

"I mean, I'm not trying to plan out my life here. This is college, how it was supposed to be, trying new things, meeting people. I just…" Ethan blew out a breath. "He doesn't want to ask me to hide this thing. But I'm okay with keeping it quiet, private. It's weird, right? Like I should be the one with the issues, but it's him. He's got this mindset that he's doing something wrong or making me do something wrong when I don't even want what he thinks I want."

"And you've discussed it?"

"A hundred times. He listens to me and then does this thing." Ethan imitated Justin's always answer to relationship talk, the finger motion between them.

"And that means?"

"*You and me, Ethan,*" he said, mocking Justin's voice. "That's it. Like that's enough."

His father hummed. "Isn't it?"

"Isn't it what?

"Enough?"

Ethan looked at his father and slowly nodded.

"Then be happy, Ethan. It's okay to let yourself be happy again."

"You think he really means it?"

"I don't take Justin for a guy who wastes his time."

Ethan laughed. "No, no one could ever accuse him of that."

"Then don't make up different rules for yourself because you're afraid."

Hearing it hurt. It was amazing how well his dad could pinpoint what Ethan couldn't identify for himself.

"I am. That's exactly what it is, Dad."

"It's okay to be scared. It's also okay to believe another person who you've built some trust in."

"I have. Too scared to be happy." Ethan repeated what his dad had ultimately said. "That's pathetic."

"No, it's safe. And there's nothing wrong with that."

They were quiet for a while until the pool bot got hung up in the one spot it always struggled with, and they both laughed as Ethan got up to give it a nudge. When he came back, his dad was still smiling.

"What?"

"It's just nice to see you happy."

"Happy enough to know when to call *stop* on the question session."

His dad tilted his bottle and clanked it with Ethan's. "Fair enough."

*

"HOW DID I let you talk me into this?" Ethan groaned, and Justin looked back at him as he dragged his feet along the intermediate hiking trail. "This is not cross country. This is hell and rocks."

"Hell's not so bad." Justin shook his head at how miserable Ethan was playing at being.

"Who goes on an eight-mile hike for fun?" Ethan muttered but picked up his pace to walk next to Justin.

Their break trip together was unusual, unlike most college students who preferred to hit the beach and party it up during spring break. They were camping in the national forest, visiting a famous cave on a guided tour, hiking this trail, and then spending their last two days at a river cabin rental and doing some trout fishing.

"You said you wanted the pictures," Justin said as he reached for a rock above and checked his footing before hoisting himself higher. "*Wouldn't it be cool if one day we had an entire wall of framed photos of all the adventures we went on together?*" Justin repeated Ethan's words for the hundredth time as he stood and turned, waiting for Ethan to follow him up the few boulders on the elevated path.

"Correction to the original plan," Ethan said, brushing his hands off on his pants. "I want the reward of the picture, the work getting there, not so much."

Justin fished out the camera and skinny tripod while Ethan sat and drank some water and continued to pretend-bitch about hiking. He'd been just as much in on the planning of this trip as Justin.

"Vacations are supposed to be lazy," Ethan stated.

"You're going to get lazy in the tent when we get back." Justin grinned as he set the timer, motioning Ethan to get up and get in the picture. "Smile, try and look like you like me."

Ethan turned to Justin and did as ordered. "You only do this kind of shit for the one person you like." And then he turned his face back to the camera in time for the next click.

"It might be my favorite picture yet. I can't believe that background, that view. And your hair isn't even sweaty."

Ethan sighed and leaned in. "Fine, it's a good picture."

"Better than that thing where you made me stick my head in the hole," Justin reminded him.

Ethan remembered the tourist trap they'd stopped at and the classic farmer with his pitchfork and wife photo op with head holes cut out for tourists to snap pictures there. Like hundreds of others before them, they'd done it and then hit the little shop buying T-shirts, key chains, and another sticker for Ethan to put on Justin's truck. Currently, he was not only saving the North American wolf and the Florida manatees, but it seemed he'd be saving the entire national forest as well.

Ethan held up a sticker with evergreen trees on it with expectant hope in his eyes.

"Whatever." Justin waved a hand and examined some bracelets on a rack. He pulled two off, inspected the intricate leather braiding, and tossed them in Ethan's basket with their other garb. "My truck will end up looking like a Subaru before you're done with it. Do you know how much shit I get from the guys over the manatee one?"

"Oh, he's cute," Ethan said.

"Cliff said it looks like an old gray nut sack," Justin shared.

Ethan burst out laughing, thought about it, then couldn't contain it. Justin smiled and followed him down the next aisle of roadside bullshit. They ate at a diner, cheating with greasy burgers and ice-cold shakes before hitting the road again and leaving the last of civilization behind.

The tent setup was not only entertaining but theatrical. There never seemed to be a dull moment with Justin. They were finally settled in on their large air mattress and looking at the stars through the mosquito screen at the top of the tent.

"Free," Ethan said in a breath.

"It's nice." Justin very carefully rolled to his side, reached over slowly, and took Ethan's hand.

"I know, no sudden moves, or we'll go flying off this thing again." Ethan's voice grew shaky as he continued. "We put too much air in it, I think. Maybe we should let some out so it's not so…"

"It's just holding hands. We've done this a hundred times before, Ethan."

Ethan blew out a long breath and ceased his nervous ramble. He turned his head to the side, his hand already clammy but still holding Justin's. "How did I get so lucky?"

"Oh, that's my line. But slow is good for both of us, and I'm happy with this, happy with you."

"My therapist said it takes some victims years to get to a point where they can have a healthy relationship," Ethan whispered.

"Then it takes years," Justin said simply. "I'm not going anywhere."

*

ETHAN FINISHED PUTTING the photo in the frame. It was of himself and Justin holding their trout, taken by their guide. The frame had the lodge's name engraved on it, and yet another touristy frame now sat on Ethan's new bookshelf. Justin had shown up with the large box, assembled it, then stretched out on the couch and fallen asleep half watching a baseball game.

Ethan quietly moved the overcrowded photo frames from his desk and arranged them on the shelves with his books, along with a football from Justin's bowl game that now lived in Ethan's dorm room.

Ethan remembered fondly how Justin had walked in, tossed him the ball, and said, "That's for you."

Like it was nothing. Just the winning touchdown ball.

Ethan stuck the pencil tip eraser in front of the ball to keep it from rolling off the shelf. Justin's genius solution. Ethan finished and stepped back, taking in the new shelf and its contents.

My God, they were a couple. With all their pictures and adventures to- gether, it couldn't be denied as Ethan studied how close they'd stood to each other, shoulders bumping, seemingly connected at the hip. In one, Jus- tin had an arm slung over Ethan's shoulders, and in another, Ethan had wrapped his hand around Justin's back, and the timer had gone off with a smiling Justin looking directly at Ethan.

Ethan couldn't deny what they were to each other any longer, and he turned to tell Justin his epiphany only to shake his head at his…*boyfriend* asleep on the couch, mouth agape and sprawled out as some team manager argued with an umpire in the background.

"Okay, Justin Halstead," Ethan whispered. "It's yours; just don't break it."

Chapter Eleven

Justin

BEFORE JUSTIN KNEW it, summer was almost upon them, and they'd practically wrapped up their sophomore year.

"What are we doing about summer?" Justin asked as he flopped down on Ethan's couch.

"I'm going home. Dad already told you he expected you there," Ethan said as Justin smirked knowingly.

"I have to be back early for training and spend some time at home with my parents," Justin said.

"Yeah, but you have a month and a half to burn before all that."

"Where would I sleep?"

"In my room. I mean, they totally know. They know the deal, and we can move another bed into my room. No more guest room for you. Not for that long anyway."

"That would be weird," Justin said with a sigh.

"It's no different than what we do here, except Mom will cook for us all summer. And Dad will want to drag you to practice with him if the schedules work out right. What will you tell your parents?"

"That I'm going to stay with you and help your dad out with his team for the summer." Justin shrugged. "It's not a lie."

"Nope," Ethan agreed.

"That's what we're doing, then."

*

"BOYS." BETHANY HUGGED them both and kissed their cheeks as John entered the kitchen and gave his round of hugs and hearty backslaps.

"I'm glad you decided to come. Ethan was worried you wouldn't," he said, and Justin agreed because there was no place he'd rather be—wherever Ethan was.

"You need help with summer practice, right?" Justin asked, and John nodded.

"He just can't get hurt," Ethan reminded them both.

"No, no, I know." John grabbed Ethan's bag. "Come on. I got it set up like you asked."

"Thanks, Dad." Ethan gave Justin a *see?* look over his shoulder.

Sure enough, two beds sat across the room from each other. Ethan pointed at a twin bed next to the window wall.

"That's yours," he said, and Justin groaned as he compared Ethan's queen and then the twin bed.

They unpacked their bags, and John helped until they were situated. Then, the three of them returned to the kitchen, where Bethany was getting dinner ready.

"Put us to work, Mom," Ethan said, and she dished out orders just as she did the food.

Justin sat down after helping, and John seemed to approve of the filled chairs at the dinner table before they all dug in.

"I'll be running even more with you," Justin said between bites. "I can tell already."

John hummed his agreement with a mouthful, and Bethany seemed pleased with the compliments of hungry men and forks scraping plates. Seconds were even more compliments to her.

"All summer," Ethan warned, but then he lit up. "It's gonna make training camp so much fun."

"Now, you boys aren't going to work out, run, and play ball all summer," Bethany said. "Tell me what your other plans are. There has to be some fun in there somewhere."

"Oh, we'll probably take a trip or two to the beach, maybe go fishing." Ethan turned expectantly to his father, who nodded. "The waterpark…" Ethan shrugged. "There'll be plenty to keep us busy."

"And," Justin said, "I did agree to help with some things around here that Ethan mentioned."

Bethany appeared pleased, as did John, to have help with a few large projects he couldn't handle alone.

Ethan and Justin took over dish duty for the summer stay, then joined his parents on the back patio by the pool, where they had a grill and lounge area. John muttered as he filled the pottery chimenea for Bethany, who claimed it helped with bugs, that he thought it was entirely too nice out for a fire.

Justin listened to the two lightheartedly bicker as he and Ethan sat next to each other on an outdoor sofa. Once the kindling was crackling and Bethany was pleased, John reclined in his chair. Bethany got up and came back with cold beers from the outdoor kitchen beer fridge and passed them out.

"See, beer and a fire," she justified, and Coach shook his head at his wife.

He turned his attention to them.

"Here we go," Ethan said.

"I just gotta ask. I mean…" John shrugged. "Do I knock first, or what?"

Justin coughed, feeling *so awkward* despite their few previous exchanges. He shook his head as he pulled his cap brim down and rested his forearms on his thighs.

Ethan waited next to him, being absolutely no help as Justin glanced at him. He just lifted a brow like his father to see if Justin would answer.

"Knock first, if it's no disrespect, sir," Justin finally said, sitting back up and addressing John directly.

Coach nodded once. "All right, then."

"Good," Bethany said.

And that was it as Ethan shot another *see?* at Justin. Ethan's parents were cool like that—not shake the walls down cool, but they wouldn't be pissed about other things happening under their roof. Not that things were happening or going to happen, but Ethan and Justin had fewer boundaries than most. Those lines just seemed to disappear more, one by one.

They changed clothes in front of each other. There was no awkwardness when one needed to take a piss or a shower. They'd showered together, but Ethan frequently bitched about Justin using his towel rather than getting a clean one out of the cabinet. They lounged around in sweatpants or shorts, shirtless. They heckled and grabbed at each other, doing dumb shit. They crossed no additional lines, but there was an easy comfort between them. Ethan had finally seemed to accept it, and so had Justin.

Justin glanced at Ethan again. No, he'd never imagined this for himself, but he also recognized he'd never been happier in his life than when he was with Ethan. He knew Ethan was still dealing with a lot. And Justin had a harrowing reminder each time he realized he'd memorized Ethan's scars. He knew each one. Justin didn't know what had caused them for a fact, but it wasn't difficult to make assumptions about the kinds of marks that marred Ethan's back, his chest, and the different one on the side of his head.

Ethan slid his hand from the top of his thigh to the seat cushion between them, his pinky looping over Justin's absently as he stared off at the pool water rippling in the early summer breeze.

Justin drank some of his beer and relaxed, banishing his dark thoughts as he sat next to Ethan while his father talked about his players and the team's issues, and Bethany enjoyed the low crackle of her unnecessary fire.

Chapter Twelve

Ethan

ETHAN SHOWERED FIRST, and then Justin. They brushed their teeth to-gether at the double sink vanity. Justin flipped the light switch to the bath-room, paused in the doorway, and watched Ethan climb into bed. Justin's eyes narrowed at his ridiculous twin toddler-like bed and then at Ethan's queen-sized.

"Do you think your dad did that intentionally?"

"Yes. Fuck it." Ethan scooted over.

"No, that's not part of our plan," Justin pointed out.

"No one here knows you. It's just for the summer." Ethan braved to say what he'd been thinking for the entire semester, a chance to try to do things the way he imagined Justin wanted. He put it out there as the tension rose and then left Justin. He climbed in with Ethan and sighed the biggest sigh Ethan had ever heard as they rolled to their sides, and Justin slid an arm across Ethan.

"It's hard to turn off and turn back on," Justin said.

"I know. But our deal is for school. We aren't at school."

Justin nodded against the back of his neck, and Ethan closed his eyes. He felt strangely safe. That was his last thought until they woke next to each other, covers kicked off, to a tap on the closed door.

"Breakfast, boys," his dad said through the door and then barked out, "Five minutes!" chuckling as he stomped down the stairs.

"Come on." Ethan groaned and got out of bed.

They got dressed, and Ethan took several pills from his organizer for the day, Justin looking on.

"How much longer do you have to take those," he asked as they headed down the stairs to the kitchen.

"I don't know. My therapist seems to think we could cut back on the dosage, maybe drop one of them altogether."

"What's that?" his dad asked.

"Dropping the dosage on one of my medications and maybe ending one altogether," Ethan repeated. "That's what my doctor said at my last visit. If I was still doing well at my next appointment. So, cutting them back."

"That's good, then," his dad said, and Bethany agreed.

"I scheduled all my sessions online for the summer."

"Well," Bethany said, "What's the plan for today?"

"If the boys don't have something else, I thought we'd head to the hardware store and knock out that flowerbed first. I'd like to get that done, and then you'll have your summer project."

Ethan and Justin agreed with the plan with their mouths full.

They spent two days building a retaining-wall flowerbed in front of the house for Bethany, and John was pleased to have the extra hands and muscle. Ethan and Justin spent their afternoons swimming in the pool and bathing in the sun. They woke up each morning together and tackled another project or two until John said that was everything on his list.

They planned a beach trip the next day and dragged snorkeling equipment out of the garage storage bins to take with them. Bethany loaded them down with a cooler of snacks and another ice chest of drinks, and they were off.

"This is the shit," Justin said, stretched out on a beach towel, glistening in the sun. "We are so living on a beach somewhere someday."

Ethan glanced over at Justin, eyes closed, slathered in glistening sunscreen and nothing but his swim trunks on. Ethan felt the same, but he hadn't missed what Justin had just said.

"Then you better get drafted somewhere on a coast," Ethan said but didn't acknowledge the other part of his statement.

"And the other?" Justin turned his head and opened one eye.

"Live on a beach with you while you play in the NFL, and we try not to get busted, Justin." Ethan shook his head at him.

Justin sighed and turned back to the sun. "There has to be a way. Be my agent, or lawyer, or PA, something."

Ethan sighed. "Because pro ballers have their PA living with them. And when your agent says you have to go to some event and bring a date for a photo op?"

"I wouldn't do that."

"I know. But what? Are we going to live behind some gates and have metal shutters on our windows with the knowledge that *one* photo, one single photo, and it's over? One paparazzi in a bush with a long lens, and then kiss your career goodbye. Coaching is out. That would be no different. Even in high school, there's a fine line to walk. One false accusation from a benched little shit player, and that's over. Unwinnable. I've had endless conversations with my dad and what alternative options to consider."

"And?" Justin turned his head again.

"You could be an agent. That's the only option Dad sees if this—" Ethan waved a finger between them. "—was really a thing."

"An agent," Justin said, turning his face back to the sun and closing his eyes.

"I would never ask you to do that."

Justin just nodded.

"Agents do well. The beach house would still be an option," Ethan said, and at Justin's grin, added, "You're an idiot. Maybe if you *owned* your own agency."

"Ah, an even better idea." Justin hummed and flipped over. "Do my back."

Ethan reached over with the can of oily spray and snorted as if something amused him.

"Funny." Justin shook his head and after a few minutes, added, "Is that how it would go?"

"Either way, both, none. You?"

"I don't know, I'm worried about answering that."

"Let's cross that bridge when we get there," Ethan said. "We aren't even close to the river, much less the bridge."

"No, but we are still on for the beach house, right? Can't you imagine it?"

"Fine, *yes*, it would be cool to live on the beach with you in a badass house, but I'd want a pool," Ethan said, playing along with the daydream.

"Yeah, because sand is cool for about five seconds. And I get it. I like your parents' pool."

"My dad bitches all the time about having to clean it."

Justin said affectionately, "I could see you doing that, bitching with a dip net."

"What do you think I'll be doing? Staying home and cleaning the pool?"

"Yeah." Justin shrugged. "I'll have an agency; you can just clean the pool and build me fires in our chiminea." Justin howled as if it was the funniest thing. "I swear to God, I'm buying you one of those things one day."

"Don't you dare," Ethan said, imagining it.

"What are you going to do?"

"Well, I was thinking about sports reporting," Ethan said. "Get a job with a newspaper or magazine."

"I could see that. What about something in the hockey world?"

"That's a hobby."

"You love it, though," Justin pointed out, not for the first time.

"I do. It's something to think about."

"So, you're the reporter, and I'm the agency owner."

"No, you are the NFL player, and I'm the sports reporter with an exclusive."

"You're thinking about options, then."

"I mean, sure, do I think it's impossible? *Yes*," Ethan said. "Does that mean I don't have hope or am willing to take some risks? I don't know. Your parents are a bigger obstacle for me than the NFL."

"If they knew, it wouldn't be as bad. I need to tell them before I consider going into the draft. And I need to think about changing my major and taking some business classes even though I won't graduate."

"You could finish school and go after."

"We'll see," Justin said. "Or I could play for a year, get my name out there, and then get a job as an agent."

"Two years, and then we consider the agent idea," Ethan countered.

"Then we are free?"

"Then we are free."

"And you'll be there in two years?" Justin asked, eyes locked on him. Ethan sighed. "Looks like."

"Come on. I want to get in the water and snorkel," Justin said with a laugh. "With that 1980s mask and…"

"I know." Ethan groaned but got up.

"Your dad takes care of his stuff," Justin said, carrying the mask to the water. "How does something like this even last that long?"

"You saw the abnormally organized garage," Ethan said, pointing out the ridiculousness of his coach father, and they headed into the surf.

*

THEY SPENT THE evening on the beach strip and boardwalks, buying dumb matching T-shirts, getting their picture taken at an old-time photoshop, and posing as gunslingers. They ate dinner, bought souvenirs, asked people to take photos, and probably had more fun buying Ethan's parents a pottery sundial that matched their chiminea for their backyard than any-thing else.

The clerk at the shop thought they were insane the way they had car-ried on with each other over Ethan's parents arguing about where it would go in the yard for the best readout. How they joked over imagining Bethany asking what time it was and John frowning down, studying the *damned thing*.

Justin put the bubble-wrapped gift in the trunk and returned for the stand. Ethan stood at the tailgate, gripping his side as Justin told him to stop or he'd drop it.

"Best day ever." Justin leaned and pressed his lips to Ethan's once. "Come on; let's head back."

Ethan nodded, touching his lips as he made his way to the passenger side. This was really happening. It was the first time Justin had ever kissed him. Their future felt planned, or at least dreamed about on a beach earlier. But *he kissed him*, something he'd said he wouldn't do.

He didn't know how in the hell they were going to pull it off. Ethan opened the door and climbed in. He blinked several times when the car engine turned back off.

"Fuck—what?" Justin whispered.

"No, it's fine," Ethan said, shaking his head and wiping his face. "I'm good, it's good. Just—" He shook his head again.

The seatbelt unfastened, and strong arms tugged him over. "Just let it out. You don't have to talk."

And Ethan cried harder as he buried his face into Justin's neck and was held like that until it passed, and he got himself together.

"Good?" Justin asked, and Ethan nodded, clipping his seatbelt.

"You know," Justin started in when they were about halfway home, "if you ever wanted me to go to your counselor with you, or maybe I could go see her and understand better how to do things the right way when you deal with stuff, I'd do that."

"I know. I wasn't even sad or angry. I was happy. That's what's so stupid about it," Ethan said as he looked out the window. "I was happy. You kissed me."

"Ok, but that wasn't a happy reaction afterward, and I want to know what I'm supposed to do. Fucking that up isn't an option, Ethan," Justin said calmly. "I don't know what I'm supposed to do."

"Yeah, okay, I'll talk to her about it. But we aren't mentioning that little meltdown to my parents."

"Fine." Justin reached over and squeezed Ethan's thigh. "Good now?"

"Yeah, I'm good."

And he was by the time they got home and lugged their gift inside.

"That was SPF 50." Bethany tsked, glaring at their reddened skin.

"And we used it, Mom," Ethan said, shooing her away. "Look what Justin said we had to buy." Ethan sputtered, trying to tell his dad the story.

"You two." Bethany shook her head but widened her eyes as John unwrapped the top piece, and a gloating Justin carried the sturdy base to the backyard.

*

"IT DOESN'T HAVE to be like the essay," Ethan whispered in the dark.

"No?" Justin asked as Ethan rolled over and faced him. "The first time I kissed you didn't go so well."

"Try it again."

And Justin leaned in and pressed his lips to Ethan's, cautious, careful, then pulled back. "Tell me what to do so you don't panic."

Justin let his body be moved beneath Ethan's touch as he rolled him to his back, and Ethan crawled over him.

"Like this," Ethan said, and Justin nodded as Ethan bent down.

"You are in control here, Ethan," Justin whispered. "Stop, keep going. It's all up to you. That's why it worked out the times before, isn't it? You were in control."

Ethan nodded as Justin slid his hands up to the headboard and gripped them there, clearly giving Ethan the reins and full access. Ethan pressed his lips to Justin's again, and Justin opened his mouth when Ethan encouraged it, letting him set the pace for every move.

Chapter Thirteen

Justin

AND THE KISS was good, *so good* that Justin warred to keep his hands gripped on the round posts and not touch Ethan. It was unlike any kiss he'd ever experienced. His heart banged, his mind raced wildly with *finally, finally*, as Ethan's mouth became an *everything* in Justin's mind.

It was no easy task gluing his hands to the headboard. Not when Ethan's hands were on him, over his chest, his neck, and in his hair as their tongues tangled, both of them breathing hard and kissing even harder.

And he knew.

At that moment, with that one unbelievable never-ending kiss, Justin knew he'd made his decision. No one, nothing had ever compared to being with Ethan and kissing Ethan for the first time.

Justin was a willing goner.

And he was glad he'd made the decision before Ethan's hands pushed down his sleep shorts, and Ethan maneuvered himself lower and eased down his own. Justin held on tightly, trying to be quiet as Ethan stroked one hand over Justin and the other over himself. He'd positioned them both close to each other, straddling him.

"This is good," Ethan whispered. "So good, like this."

Justin could only stare as he rocked his hips up to meet Ethan's rhythm, matching him and biting his lip so as not to make any noise. Only a few other times had he been *this* hard, this turned on, and only with Ethan—the night he'd crossed the room hoping to kiss Ethan, four times now, in the shower, and once on the couch. Justin hadn't pressed for more, and this was so much more.

He'd been attracted to Holly; the sex had been undeniably great between them, but even she hadn't made Justin's body feel electrified. Ethan's single touch, a mere finger, sent gooseflesh and sparks igniting across Justin's skin. A lone breath from Ethan across his neck or chest, and it seemed as if every hair on his body stood at attention for him. If Ethan teased him, removing his touch for a moment, Justin would jerk in reaction, uncontrollably seeking out Ethan's attention. Justin's toes curled and flexed, his muscles tensing and relaxing, his entire body a live wire, the power source, only Ethan.

And as wonderful as it was, it was also slightly humiliating as he whisper-hissed to warn Ethan it was about to be over. But Ethan lost it first, and Justin turned his face into his arm, muffling himself as he followed right behind. What Ethan could do to him with just his hand, he didn't dare let his mind imagine past that to other possibilities. As quick on the draw as he was with Ethan, they might not ever get there.

Justin lay there, breathing hard as Ethan slid off the bed, and Justin released his grip, got up, and followed him. They cleaned up quietly in the bathroom, returned, assuming their sleep positions, and were quiet for a long time. This was it, and Justin wasn't fucking it up again. He'd come so close at the back of the Yukon earlier.

"I'm in love with you, Ethan," Justin whispered. "I think I have been since the night you brought my phone to me. Shit, maybe even before that."

"I am with you, too," Ethan whispered back. "We're going to figure out a way to make this work."

Justin squeezed him and nodded against him. "Deal." Then he asked, "Can I kiss you again?"

"Yes."

"I never want to kiss anyone else, Ethan."

"Are you sure?"

"Positive."

"I'm scared."

"You never have to be afraid again."

Justin waited as Ethan turned over. They kissed, slow and sweet. Ethan drew Justin's hand to Ethan's neck, lingering momentarily before sliding away and giving him permission to touch him. Justin felt the moment Ethan's body relaxed, and Justin scooted closer. Ethan's fingers were in Justin's hair as they made silent promises to each other. Justin pulled away, ending their kiss, and tugged Ethan in tight.

*

"YOU'RE SURE ABOUT this," Ethan said, and Justin nodded, with only his backpack as his carry-on. "And you don't want me to come? Telling your parents is a big deal."

"No, but you have things to handle, too," Justin said, reminding him about his therapist.

"I'll see you when you get back. I'd say good luck, but I'm worried."

"It'll go how it goes," Justin said and only hugged Ethan. Then, he got out of the car at the airport drop-off lane.

Justin thought about what he would tell his parents during his flight, his Uber ride home, and as he walked up the driveway to the front door. His dad came to the door, letting him in.

"I didn't think you were coming home until late July," he said and hugged him.

"Hey, Mom," Justin said and hugged her too. "What were you guys doing?"

"Watching TV in the den. You aren't staying long," she said, taking his only bag.

"Just here for a night," Justin said as his father's frown drew down. No, there wasn't much to hide from his father.

"What is it?" he asked.

"That obvious?" Justin sighed and motioned to the den. "Let's go sit down."

"You're worrying me, Justin," his mother said as they all moved into the room.

"Don't worry. I'm fine. I'm healthy," Justin said as his father powered off the TV and adjusted the lamps before sitting down next to his mom.

Justin shook his head. "I didn't imagine just walking in and doing it like this."

"Take your time," Nathan Halstead said, and Justin didn't miss that he took his mother's hand and held it.

"I still plan on entering the draft, but will only play for one, maybe two years. Enough to get my name out there, make some connections." Justin kept his eyes on the floor and coffee table. "I'm changing my major to business in the fall. Get a year of business classes under my belt so that when I leave school and leave the game, I can either find a job as a sports agent or maybe, eventually, open my own firm. That's the business side of things. The only hypothetical option I've been able to come up with for the other issue, the real issue, I've come home to talk to you both about."

Justin blew a breath, pulled off his cap, and scrubbed his hand through his hair as his eyes burned. "I had this dream, you know, since I was a kid…"

He pinched the bridge of his nose, but there was no stopping the tears. "I love football…" He looked up, and they were both teary-eyed as they nodded. "But I love someone else more and can't have both dreams. I can't have the person I love and play the sport I love because the world is fucked up. So that's the new plan. We wait it out. I play for two years, turn sports agent, and then we can be together." Justin wiped his face.

"I am terrified, telling you this. I know you love me, but I wanted to so if you ever heard it from anyone else, I'd know I did this the right way. I love Ethan—Ethan Andrews, my best friend at school." Justin lifted his gaze to his parents.

"Oh, thank God," Missy Halstead breathed out. She was off the couch and had her arms around him.

"Thank God, what?" Justin hugged her back as his father joined them.

"I thought you were going to say something horrible like you found out something was wrong, cancer or Jesus, I'm a shit for saying it, but that I was going to be a grandmother, and I'm not ready for that title yet." His mother shook her head and kissed his cheek. "We suspected it, honey. We talked about it after we met Ethan."

"Son," his father said, and Justin hugged him back just as hard. "Have you been beating yourself up over this?"

Justin could only nod as his dad hugged him harder.

"You're right, we do love you, we get it, and we aren't going anywhere," his dad said, the glance he gave his wife was one of relief.

"We've been worried about you," Missy said. "But, honey, we did know, well—we thought we knew. You were just so happy around him." She cupped his cheeks in her hands. "You're right. You do not hide it well. We'll think about this plan of yours. Dad?" She turned to Nathan.

He shook his head. "His parents?"

"They know. They're like you two, supportive. We're both really lucky. They've known about him since he was young. I've never, I mean, not until him. It's him; it's not— I don't even know how to explain it, put a label on it."

"And you don't have to," Missy said, and his father agreed.

"No one ever before him?" his dad asked.

Justin shook his head. "I dated girls, you know that. It wasn't until I met him freshman year in a composition class. Then I lost interest in anyone else, and it was just him." He laughed and looked at his mom. "He wrote this essay, and we had to leave our names off, and the instructor, she passed them all out anonymously. And we had to take the essay we were given and write our own analysis, edit it, and provide feedback."

"And you got his," she surmised, wiping her eyes, "And you fell in love with his words first before you knew whose they were."

Justin nodded.

"Oh, my sweet boy." She sighed. "What was it about?"

Justin shifted and retrieved his wallet. He took out the folded papers that had seen better days. It was the essay Ethan had written a few months before he was attacked. He handed it to her. "I carry it with me every day. I copied it. And then I found out who it belonged to."

She opened it and leaned back on the couch next to him, then searched around, and his father, laughing, got her glasses from the other side of the sofa, and handed them to her.

"Don't read it out loud, Mom," Justin said.

He watched as her eyes moved across the page. Justin pointed to the tissue box, and his dad reached over and moved it next to her. They waited for her, the literature teacher, to read it through, as one, then two tissues were plucked up. When she flipped the page, Justin held his breath. He knew what she was reading now. And then his mom lowered the two-page essay, pulled off her glasses, and just cried.

Justin wiped his own eyes and blew out a breath.

"I really hope he's an English major." She sniffed and nodded, passing the essay over to Nathan.

He began to read, and by the time he was finished, Justin felt they probably understood his feelings for someone who could write in a way that never left the reader. His father carefully folded the pages back as they were and handed them to Justin. He got up and headed into the kitchen.

"He needs a minute. Such a tough guy, your father," she whispered. She rested her head on Justin's shoulder, and they listened as the refrigerator door opened and closed and a beer top cracked open, and Justin knew his father would drink that beer in there before he rejoined them.

"All right," Nathan said, finally returning. "We know you can't be out in the NFL, and the media alone—getting found out—" He shook his head. "But you've got such talent, Justin. You've worked so hard. So, we start thinking differently about contracts, and hire a lawyer."

Justin's eyes widened.

"You heard me. We get legal advice, contract law. And we know our options and where we stand going in. There may be some clause or wording, I don't know, some protection for you. We look at teams that have already dealt with this and aren't assholes. Teams that support their players. We do our homework. Or, you go in it honest and upfront, but I think we know where that choice will lead."

Justin was quiet as he absorbed this new option.

His father nodded solemnly.

"I do want to play, but I also don't want to ask Ethan to hide. That's not fair. I mean, he's willing to lay low; we've already been doing that, but still, it draws suspicion from even my own teammates. But *no*, the poster boy for the NFL is not the option I'm going for. I'd rather see what we can find out legally and be honest with management." Justin shook his head. "I'm not telling every team I meet with."

"No," his dad said. "We're getting ahead of ourselves. We research, find out all the options, then sit down and figure out a plan. If none of it works, it's one or two years and the agent plan. Or you go back to school and finish your degree. But if there is any way you could play…"

"And not force Ethan to hide," Justin said adamantly.

"Honey, what does Ethan say?" his mom asked.

"He says it's impossible. His dad's a coach; you know that. He said all it takes is one overeager pap hiding in a bush with a long lens. One picture, and it's over."

His father frowned. "So we need to find out about no unplanned interviews, no unexpected media, and that's going to be a tough sell."

"We've talked this through and just don't see another way. Two years, then we're free. No one cares if their agent is gay."

"Pathetic," Missy muttered. "We are talking about marriage, eventually."

"Oh, yeah, no question," Justin said. "That's a done deal."

Missy *hmm*ed. "Does Ethan know that part of the plan?"

"Of course not, Mom. Come on," Justin chided.

His father smirked, but Justin could see he was already deep in his head, working through scenarios, constructing ideas and then tearing them down.

"We do our homework and figure out where you stand," his father finally said. He stood and stretched. "What time is your flight in the morning?"

"Not until nine."

They stayed up for a while, the three of them talking more about options and Ethan. When Justin was finally able to lie down in his room, he sent Ethan a text telling him it had gone well and that he'd be back tomorrow afternoon. Justin warmed as he tapped out the last three words and hit send.

*

JUSTIN ROLLED HIS eyes as Ethan whooped in the empty stands and Ethan's father's whistle rang out as Justin ran in a touchdown during their scrimmage. Practice with a high school team was insanely demanding, and Justin couldn't believe he'd forgotten the hell that was two-a-days. Granted, he was on the coaching staff for two months, but he ran with the guys, ran drills, and hit the turf right along with them. He'd return to his team even better than he'd left them.

The whistle blew again. Coach Andrews barked out orders to his men, and Justin grabbed his bag and headed to the stands.

"Ready?" he said, but Ethan was already coming down the steps and nodding that he was.

They'd been in this routine for two weeks. Justin sat and swapped his cleats for running shoes while Ethan stretched on the track. Coach picked up Justin's bag as he walked by, yelling at his players to hustle up and quit whining.

"Did he ever coach you as a kid?" Justin asked as Ethan stretched.

"Hell no. I mean, he has his funny things—*five minutes* and *chop-chop*, shit like that—but no, he never yelled at me like a coach. He was just my dad. And when he could make it to my hockey games, he wasn't ever one of those parents trying to coach from the bench."

"My dad definitely coached from the sideline," Justin said over the memory. "He wasn't the worst parent there though."

"Your dad was at every game, every practice?"

Justin knew the direction this was going. "Professional football has its drawbacks, Ethan. It sucks your dad couldn't always be there for hockey. If this happens, I won't always be able to be there either."

"No, I know. Maybe it just sucked more for a kid. I'll have things to keep me busy."

"And you'll get your degree and find a job you love."

"And you'll still come freeze your ass off at the rink?"

"Such tall orders." Justin sighed. "Now we need a beach house with an ice rink close by. Those two don't really go together, you know."

"No, hockey in the south *is* a tall order," Ethan said but gave Justin that damn look.

"Stop."

"Never."

They warmed up for the first mile home. From the high school to Ethan's parents, it was a solid five-mile run, and Ethan stepped up to the challenge as they took on the second mile at a faster pace. Justin admitted to himself this daily run had improved his running and his breathing as he began to train like Ethan, and he'd be better for it come game one. Sure, he was fast, but now, he was faster without feeling like his lungs were on fire or he was a fish out of water.

Bethany waved them to the back as she watered her flower bed. She shot them both with her hose as they headed to the outdoor shower by the pool to rinse off. Justin had dropped eight pounds in the time they'd started training together, but he was solid muscle, even with Bethany's three squares a day. And Ethan was so good, with high spirits and looking healthier than he ever had.

They'd had a first online meeting with his counselor and talked about ways Justin should and shouldn't help when Ethan had a panic attack or needed to feel in control. Justin was reading a book she had recommended about loving someone with trauma. And Coach and Bethany had pulled out a few books and given them to him, ones that had been referred to them about how they could best help their son recover.

Ethan plucked the book from Justin's hand and dropped it to the floor. He reached over and turned off the lamp.

"Okay, I want to try something," he whispered in the dark, tugging Justin over him.

"You sure?" Justin held his weight off him and pressed his lips to Ethan's.

"Yeah, I'll use my hands."

Justin leaned in a little more as Ethan gripped his sides and guided how much weight he could take. Justin kissed him, then stopped when Ethan's fingers tightened. Ethan's hands slid lower to his hips, and Justin eased his weight down until Ethan stopped him so he was touching but without his weight fully on him, and they kissed like that until Ethan began to relax.

Justin brushed against Ethan's neck and kissed him there and then up to his ear. When Ethan pushed down his shorts, Justin lifted to pull his own off. Ethan guided Justin back to where he was comfortable and then urged Justin to thrust with him as Ethan gripped them both.

"Ethan." Justin breathed his name like a prayer. And found his lips again, and they moved together.

"You okay?" Justin asked after, and Ethan nodded.

"I am. She talked to me in our private session about trust. And I realized I do trust you, and I trust you more than I'm willing to let fear consume me," Ethan said quietly. "You've never asked."

Justin swallowed hard. "I don't know that I can handle knowing." Justin held him. "There were rumors, and I want to believe they aren't true, but I looked it up. I know what they were charged with and convicted of. I know how much time they are serving. That's all I think I can handle, Ethan. If you feel like you need to tell me, I will listen. I'm here for you. But I'll never ask you to relive your trauma."

"You've been reading too many books."

Justin nodded, recognizing he'd just quoted a line from one. "It's true. And hey…" He ran his fingers through Ethan's hair. "I like that you were able to show me what you could handle and when to back off. It was clear. I got it. That works for me, but how did you feel about it?"

"Yeah, that worked. She suggested finding ways to use touch to control the situation without always having to be in complete control blah blah blah. But yeah, it's all about trust."

Justin shifted closer to Ethan's ear. "Trust that I want to try something new next time."

"What?" Ethan whispered back.

"Think about that and how we need to approach it, and let's talk about it when you're ready. Now, I have to get my ass up at 5:30, so shush and hands off *all this*."

Ethan laughed, and Justin tugged him closer. "All this."

"It's all yours."

"All mine."

Chapter Fourteen

Ethan

ETHAN WAS HAPPY. As hard as that was to admit. He glanced over at Justin, who didn't exactly fit comfortably in the double innertube as they floated around the lazy river at the water park. Ethan checked their surroundings and waited until the tide pushed them around a bend.

"I love you," he said, testing out the words he hadn't quite said back. He poked Justin's side before pulling his hand back.

"Mmm, I love you more," Justin said, and the corner of his mouth tipped up. Ethan couldn't see his eyes but didn't doubt the look hidden by the dark lenses.

Other than gaming, their few trips together, their days at the beach, and their time in his parents' pool, Ethan got to enjoy seeing Justin's playful side full-time. He was usually so serious, but these rare big-kid moments were a nice reprieve—the times when they were alone and Justin was entirely unguarded. Ethan hoped he could think of more things for them to do together, these rare occasions where Justin let Ethan see *the real* Justin. Like now, as Ethan felt the splash of water hit the back of his neck and hair, Justin tried not to look guilty as his hand trailed behind them in the water.

"You aren't smooth," Ethan muttered, wiping the side of his cheek.

"Let's go do the big water slides after this," Justin challenged.

"You mean you don't want to try and drown me in the wave pool again?"

Justin didn't comment, only the corner of his eye crinkling. Ethan sighed. Yeah, this was happiness, and Justin was a completely different person when he was like this. From what Ethan had observed, when generally in the presence of others, Justin was kind of an asshole at times. He could get extraordinarily moody and irritated quickly. Ethan had seen that side of Justin rear its ugly head on the football field when something seemed unfair or over a penalty. Ethan didn't fear Justin, but Justin took no shit from anyone. It was strangely comforting.

They climbed the stairs to what seemed like the top of the world four times, just to slide down every single one of the interwoven colorful water slides.

"We have to do all four," Justin had said after Ethan complained the third time up.

"Why?"

"Because we finish shit Ethan. If we start it, we finish it."

"Okay then, equating life rules to waterslide rules sounds logical."

Ethan sucked it up and trudged up the endless wooden stairs for the fourth time. It was ridiculous, but Justin hadn't seemed to be talking about waterslides, not really. Ethan was a part of something bigger with Justin, as if they were their own team.

"Twenty-eight dollars," Justin said later, from behind the driver's wheel as Ethan beamed at the most fabulous photo on the planet of the two of them at the water park. They'd taken it on a stop Ethan had begged for next to one of the tourist traps. Ethan held up the newest photo, showing it to Justin.

"Fuck," Justin grumbled and started looking around for a store.

"*You*. You are so good to me," Ethan praised.

"It's more like the shit I'm willing to do for you. I'm buying picture frames and shit, Ethan."

Ethan bit his lip.

"See, that right there. You know exactly what you're doing; don't think I don't know it. You can't get anything past me, Ethan Andrews."

"Well."

"Well, what?" Justin asked.

"Nothing."

There was a growl.

"I mean, you did just kinda throw down the gauntlet there."

"E-than…" Justin warned.

"I love it when you say my name like that—like it's two names. *E* and then *than*." Ethan schooled his expression as Justin pulled into a local store. "Small victories," he pushed.

"Uh-huh."

"I'll show you a victory later."

THE FOLLOWING WEEKS seemed to fly by. Like a billion other people on the planet, Ethan wondered why summers had to be so short.

He counted for Justin as he did push-ups. "Nine thousand, two hundred and thirty-four…"

"E-than," Justin panted.

The front door opened, and Ethan's father came out with three bottles of beer.

"Saved by Dad," Ethan sang and took one. He'd been cleared to drink alcohol but in moderation after his doctor discontinued two of his medications and reduced the dosage on another. Ethan took the worst of them in the morning, so he was okay as long as he didn't drink right after that one.

Justin snatched up his shirt and used it as a towel as he sat on the step between Ethan's legs, then flopped back, still sweaty.

"Do you see the things I have to put up with, Dad?"

His father handed Justin a beer and the two clanked bottles. "I used to do that shit to your mom. Still do, if I'm honest."

Ethan sighed, sensing it was something these personality types never really grew out of. Then, it hit him. "You're flirts, the both of you."

Justin and his dad took a drink, then eyed each other. There were zero forthcoming admissions. But his father had come outside to talk to Justin about his last day working with the high school team. Deciding he'd see what his mom was up to in the kitchen, Ethan nudged sweaty muscular arms off his thighs and headed inside.

Chapter Fifteen

Justin

JUSTIN WAITED UNTIL Ethan was inside and the door was closed. He scooted up to the step next to John, where Ethan had been.

"Could you drive me to the airport tomorrow?" Justin asked, then took a long drink and added, "Without Ethan."

"I can."

John asked nothing about Justin's reasoning as they sat together and drank their beers. Later, after dinner, Ethan and Justin headed to their room. Once in bed, Justin ran his fingers lightly on Ethan's arm, then slid his arm over Ethan's chest and tugged him back against his chest. He felt Ethan's entire body relax against him, something that had recently started happening, and Justin loved that moment every time it happened.

"You know you're safe with me, don't you?"

"I do know that."

Justin whispered against Ethan's neck, "I would burn down the world if anyone ever tried to hurt you again."

"I know that too."

"What else do you know?"

"That you're a badass who loves me."

Justin smiled against the back of Ethan's neck. "Damn straight."

*

THE LAST DAY of practice, Justin signed footballs and jerseys for the kids on the team as they all took pictures. Coach had gone easy on them for this session and even ordered pizza after. Ethan took pictures, too, and then it was done. Justin's time helping out with the team had concluded, and it was time to return to campus to start training after a quick stop with his parents. Ethan would spend the remainder of his summer break at home, and it would be a challenging month for them.

"You focus on not getting injured," Ethan said, "and as soon as they open the dorms, I'll be back."

Justin kissed him in the room they'd shared, and as Justin had asked of him, John drove him to the airport after his goodbyes with Bethany and Ethan.

In the SUV, John looked at Justin. "Go on. Let's do this."

Justin shook his head. "Drive for a minute, and let me get my nerve up."

John nodded and backed out of the driveway.

"I love him," Justin said, and John nodded again as if it was something he already knew. "I want your blessing; I want to ask for your blessing." Justin's heart was pounding so hard. "I'm going to ask him to spend the rest of his life with me someday. I don't know when that will be—before the draft, after the draft, or after I leave the field. But it's going to happen one day, and I want to ask *now* so I don't have to lie and fly back here. Because I'd never get away with it, not with him." Justin had said it all so fast, then exhaled hard.

"You have my blessing. I couldn't be happier," John said. "You know, I had a feeling this was why you asked for this ride alone."

"I suck at hiding my feelings."

"When it comes to my son, yeah, you really do," John said jovially, but he sobered. "You've impressed us with your patience and commitment to his recovery. Thank you."

"We're figuring things out. The counseling sessions together help, and then his private sessions after those seem to have the most impact. The books helped. We're doing good, but this has been a summer away from campus. I'm no fool; I know what he's like there."

"We've tried to get him to change schools, but—" John's knuckles turned white as he gripped the wheel tighter. "—our therapist has discouraged that now."

Justin agreed. "He mentioned a transfer depending on where I end up."

"Really?" John was pleased by the news. "I'm selfish. I want him away from that school. It's not the school itself; it's walking past that building. It's everyone knowing what happened to him. He needs a fresh start."

"I get it," Justin said.

"Does he ever talk about it with you?"

"No, and I don't ask. I know enough."

John was quiet as he drove.

"You'll talk to Bethany for me?" Justin asked. "I couldn't figure out how to get you both away from Ethan without him catching on."

"She can't keep a secret anyway, so a phone call or text before he calls her with any big news would be great."

"Thank you for your blessing. My dad is looking into some options for me with the draft, with other avenues for after I leave the game."

"Ethan talked to us about the agent idea and your desire to not ask him to hide, but honestly, Justin, I'm not sure how to say this without sounding like a horrible father. I feel better with him tucked away and safe, not out and proud."

"I know; I remember where he'd been before it happened, that student group pride meeting. I won't ask him to hide, but he's offered to lay low for two years until I can make a name for myself and make the connections to be an agent. That's the plan, anyway. Time enough for him to transfer and finish school. Maybe I can convince him to get a graduate degree or Ph.D."

"I have no doubt you two will figure it out. You'll find a way. And if the shit hits the fan…" John shrugged. "You both have good support systems."

Justin agreed.

"Got a ring yet?" John teased.

"I'm getting one before he gets back. It's kinda hard to swing that when we're always together. Think long engagement."

"Wise, and give him the time to process that step. Time to keep working through things and more time to recover. He's happy, and I never thought I'd see that again. Some happiness from him."

"I'm happy too. Did you ever read the essay he wrote freshman year?"

"What essay?"

"You should probably find a parking spot for a few minutes."

Twenty minutes later, Justin stood on the arrivals curb and waved as John waved back, red-faced, teary-eyed, still, and utterly overwhelmed by what his son had written. Justin had known the part about his father's love for his mother and his unflinching love for his gay son would hit hard. He didn't feel guilty for letting him read it, allowing him the more personal parts about how Ethan wanted to be loved like that.

Nope, not guilty at all.

And Justin was proud of himself for making the promise to John that he would love Ethan just like that. He would be the man Ethan had described in the essay.

*

JUSTIN SAT AT his parents' dinner table, ready to nail down the plan for the year, and reviewing all the books and articles, laws, and things his father had been researching, along with a recommendation from the attorney and advice from an old college buddy who knew an agent.

"I think you do Pro Day, get graded, and then talk to your coach about the Combine. But honestly, the best choice is ultimately making a good impression and then going free agent. With less media attention, you can also discuss contract options with one team, not twenty."

"And if they invite me?" Justin asked.

"You tell them to talk to you after the draft. You lose your eligibility to play ball if none of this works out, but you still can consider the free agency route. Or you think about college coaching at a liberal school. I think the draft, the publicity, the media, the questions in the interviews… Not a good idea. From what I've learned, they get pretty personal."

Justin nodded, knowing that. "I'll talk to my coach and Ethan's dad and see what they think. But we're basically saying 'fly in under the radar' with an entry-level contract in the beginning, practice hard, play well, earn the contract I want, and try to sneak past the media for as long as possible."

"It's not ideal, but this is the bottom line here, the worst-case scenario. You could declare, go through it all, and not get drafted. More and more players are declaring early; they can only take so many."

Justin knew that too. "I don't mention free agency until later in the game."

"They've got to know what you can do, and no doubt, they already do. You have three high school state championships and a bowl game win. I think this year, you play hard and do no interviews, no college articles, or statements post-game. You start avoiding the media now, so it's not a big change when you go pro. You become the guy who doesn't *ever* talk to the media."

Justin nodded slowly, seeing his father's point.

"You can do it without being a dick, Justin," his father added humorously.

"No, I know. I was just thinking about talking to Coach about it beforehand, letting him know I don't want to do interviews or talk to them. He's the type it would be better to tell first than explain after he's yelled at me for ten minutes."

"Agreed," his dad said. "And look, this is just what I've come up with, from what I've read and from a friend who talked to an agent for me. The contract lawyer isn't much good without an actual contract, but he still gave me some good advice. Talk to your coach in a way where you are just asking questions. Be undecided and play your best year. Keep your head down with Ethan."

Justin groaned but knew his father was right.

"I know," his dad said, "but for this to have a remote possibility of working, this is the gameplan. Or, you forget the NFL, and you graduate, focus on being an agent. You have your degree and a solid plan." He sighed. "You two have a lot to think about."

*

JUSTIN SAT IN his head coach's office, dreading the conversation they were about to have. He'd always gotten along well with Coach, asked very little, was a solid team player, and had never been "called in." He'd never been on probation or been caught violating curfew. He'd only been barked at over a penalty on the sideline a time or two.

"I hear you wanted to see me."

Justin stood and shook Coach's hand. "Yes, thanks for taking the time to talk to me."

"Shoot," Coach said.

"I wanted to ask for a favor, sort of." Justin confessed. He paused at the look on Coach's face but went on. "I don't want to give interviews or talk to the media this year. And I know you'll want to know why, but that's the favor part." Justin shook his head. "I just don't want to, and I'd rather bring it up now than have you be pissed at me later if I refuse. Respectfully, sir."

"And the draft?" Coach leaned back in his chair, looking suspicious.

"Undecided, but I want to do Pro Day, get graded, and see where I am. I hoped to ask you about free agency later, but…" Justin shrugged. "Might as well give you a heads-up on that now. I don't know if I'm willing to go in the draft, but free agency is looking more appealing to me. And a way to avoid the media."

"So, the ultimate goal here is to avoid the media." Coach tapped his pen on the arm of his chair. "And when they ask me the hard questions because you won't answer them?"

"Say 'He doesn't like talking to the media. He just wants to play ball.'"

"Leave the boy alone and let him play ball," Coach mused and chuckled. Then, he let out a long sigh.

"I know, sir," Justin agreed with a matching heavy sigh of his own.

"We'll see; let me think on it, Justin. I can see how we'd get away with it until we end up in a bowl game again, and you're my top-scoring player."

"I need to play hard, make an impression, and lay low this year," Justin said.

"And they'll smell that like blood in the water." He gave Justin a knowing look. "For now, I'm going to agree while I think of an alternative solution."

"Thank you, Coach," Justin said and stood.

"Stop by the front office and cancel your only will-call ticket holder on your way out. Pay cash and buy the tickets at the front office."

"Yes, sir," Justin said, and Coach waved him on.

Justin's face was on fire as he left Coach and headed for the front office to do exactly what he'd advised. His coach totally knew, and Justin nearly lost it. Of course, he knew. That man knew everything about his players.

"Fuck," Justin muttered over the obvious digital trail he'd left. He took a deep breath as he prepared to do some sweet talking with the office moms, the lovely ladies who worked there.

*

ETHAN AGREED ABOUT the tickets, and they both felt like idiots over the record that someone determined enough could dig around and find.

"Not if I don't give out any will calls for the season. And I already paid cash and bought the season tickets for you. It is a different seat though. You'll be on the thirty, not the fifty."

"You're right; he totally knows," Ethan sputtered but then apologized. "God, now I'm super paranoid about every time you've signed in at my dorm."

"Stop," Justin groaned, commiserating over the ridiculousness of it all.

"Well, at least Coach agreed to the media thing. I bet he'll come up with something. I mean, you're like the goodie-two-shoes on the team." Ethan smirked as Justin frowned at him. "A coach's dream and worst nightmare all rolled up in one." He sighed. "So, how was first practice after that?"

"Good, I was not one of the ones puking. All the coaches knew I'd kept it up over the summer break, so I also have that going. None of them are currently pissed off *at me*."

*

THE FIRST COLLEGE journalism student was an easy blow off. Justin just gave her a wave and said he had somewhere to be. The local sports reporter who came to interview Coach and do a story on the team had the assistant coach sending him home early without explanation.

"Go home, Halstead; Coach said to get the hell out of here," he'd said with a shrug. "I'm just the messenger."

And Justin beat feet, grabbing his shit and not bothering to shower until he got home.

And so it went, with Ethan back in the dorm, and Justin scribbling a name illegibly and 1234-ing his student ID number in an even more illegible scratch. One of Ethan's ideas. Justin was back to sleeping over on the weekends, in his dorm during the week, busy with practice, and playing hard.

They'd had no fall classes together since Justin changed his major to business and was taking a slew of those classes. They ordered in, or Ethan went and got meals and brought them back. Sometimes, Justin ate with his teammates and brought Ethan food back, but they were making it work.

Justin studied and kept his head down, hat low as usual. The first game came and went with a win and Ethan in a cash seat nowhere near the players' families and loved ones. Justin avoided the after-game interview when Coach sent him to the locker room just before the fourth quarter ended and after scoring two touchdowns for their lead and the ultimate win with their defense killing it and keeping the lead.

Justin jogged down the tunnel. In the locker room, he stripped out of his sweaty uniform, threw on his sweats, then made a beeline for a maintenance exit where he now parked his truck. Another of Coach's ideas. And despite parking next to the stadium's dumpsters, it had been a good one. Zero media braved the backside of the stadium.

The reporters would go for their on-field interviews and post-game outside the locker rooms. It had worked this time, but Justin feared it wouldn't work all season. People would begin to notice him getting pulled, especially if they were down to the wire and down points.

Justin showered at his dorm and then drove to Ethan's rather than his usual walk over. He parked his truck behind the dorm, closer to the adjoining dorm that shared the same lot. He used his key to enter and found Ethan, grinning, sitting naked in his desk chair.

Chapter Sixteen

Ethan

"WELL, *HELLO*," JUSTIN said, and Ethan squirmed in his seat as Justin's eyes seemed to darken. He dropped his things by the door, then pulled his shirt over his head. "I'm game for whatever this is."

And Ethan laughed as Justin pulled off his jeans and boxers after fighting his way out of his shoes in his rush, stumbling across the room.

"You said you wanted to try this, so I thought the chair might be something I could handle…" Ethan started to explain his big plan but stopped as Justin's knees eagerly hit the floor, and his hands landed on Ethan's thighs, a hungry look in his eyes.

"Yes," Justin said, and Ethan couldn't speak after that, only stared down, hanging on to the arms of the chair, white-knuckling with Justin's mouth on him for the first time. As Justin struggled, Ethan saw the determination in his eyes when he looked up for approval, and experienced Justin figuring things out in record time.

Ethan had never felt anything like the sensation of Justin's mouth, his firm hand holding his thigh. It seemed to anchor Ethan in a new way, keeping him *with him*. Justin's other hand wrapped around his base, working in tandem with his mouth. It was mind-blowing, the sensations almost too intense to handle.

"Justin," Ethan said through a groan, then covered his mouth to keep quiet as Justin got the hang of it, surpassed amateur hour in seconds flat, and sent Ethan on a ride no thirty-nine-dollar desk chair should endure.

Afterward, Justin shared his latest idea. "I want a soundproof beach house," Justin panted while they showered together, and Ethan shushed him as he jerked Justin off. He'd desperately wanted to return the favor, but Ethan was still struggling with that next step.

Being on his knees instantly brought back images he was working hard to move past. He couldn't even dig around in the bottom of his closet for a lost shoe without it all rushing back, consuming him. Then Justin had arrived only to find him curled in the fetal position, protecting his head with his arms from his past. That had been one of their worst days together. Ethan never wanted Justin to find him like that again.

Ethan kissed him, trying to show Justin how much he meant to him. His mind wandered to the memory of Justin showing up that next afternoon with a box containing a shoe rack and a drill, of Justin mounting the tall rack to the inside of the closet door. Justin had fished out every shoe from the floor, paired and hooked them on the stand. He'd lined up Ethan's laundry baskets and a tub of summer clothes across the bottom of the closet and didn't say a word about any of it.

Ethan kissed him harder, holding him tighter as the shower washed away the slickness from his hand and Justin's stomach. Justin's hold, his arms around him, was just as fierce as he kissed Ethan back.

It was good; their intimacy was improving, with Ethan growing more comfortable, beginning to break down some of those high walls he'd built to protect himself. Ethan knew he was healing.

Chapter Seventeen

Justin

JUSTIN'S COACH HELPED him as much as he could, but Justin was currently working on another plan. He had something burning a hole in his pocket, sort of. He at least had a plan for Sunday when he and Ethan stayed in, gaming together. A lazy day for both of them.

"Did you get those Hot Tamales my mom put in here?" Ethan asked as he dug around in the snack basket.

"Nope," Justin said as Ethan fished them out with a victorious *whoop*. Justin started the game, and they played with Ethan's hand in the box every few minutes as he ate his favorite hot candy and battled it out on-screen, defeating the equally warped youths of the gaming world.

Justin grew increasingly nervous each time those fingers went into the box. He thought hard about what he'd practiced saying while trying to focus on the game and not sweating his ass off with that old nervous feeling he always used to have around Ethan.

"What the hell?" Ethan said and paused their play.

This was it.

And Justin set his controller down and slid off the couch onto the floor, facing Ethan. Ethan's eyes widened as he looked at Justin and then at what he held in his fingers.

"This isn't a Hot Tamale, Justin," Ethan whispered.

Justin shook his head. "No, but I promise to buy you Hot Tamales for the rest of our lives." Ethan's mouth fell open as Justin took a breath and Ethan's other hand.

"Ethan Andrews," Justin said.

"Yes," Ethan blurted out. "A million yeses. But, shit, go on."

"Would you do the honor of spending the rest of your life with me?"

"You totally asked my dad, too, didn't you?"

"Yes, I did," Justin said and waited.

"Yes," Ethan finally answered, and Justin took the ring and slid it onto his finger. "Holy shit," Ethan whispered and then was over him on the floor, kissing him. "Married." Ethan breathed the word with cinnamon breath and kissed him again, shaking his head.

"We may need to be engaged for a while until we know the plan," Justin said, getting his words out between Ethan's panting Hot Tamale-flavored mouth on his.

"I know. I don't care. In my Hot Tamales!" Ethan was dumbfounded. "Good one."

"Right?"

"You had to think so long to come up with that. What—did you su-perglue the bottom back or something?"

Justin nodded.

"What were the other options?"

"It was always going to be in the candy."

"I have to call my mom." Ethan kissed him once more and then was off him and dashing for his phone.

Justin lay on the floor on his back, over the moon as Ethan returned and tugged him to get up. He sat on the couch with Ethan sprawled over his lap and his phone to his ear. Justin had sent the text to his dad that morning, and he bit his lip as he listened to Bethany trying to play it cool on speaker and failing miserably.

"Oh, *hi* Ethan. What a lovely surprise," she said.

"Damn it, you totally already know." Ethan groaned.

"Well, *yes*, honey, but go on and tell me, and we'll pretend like I don't," Bethany said as John lost it in the background.

Ethan told his mom and dad exactly how it had happened and then got the scoop on how Justin had asked his dad during the summer. Ethan gaped at him, shocked, unable to believe Justin had the ring for nearly two months, waiting for their official date on the essay to roll around and mark their anniversary.

Ethan cried, passing the phone to Justin. He talked to Ethan's parents for a few more minutes before saying goodbye and then lay down with Ethan so he could process the high and work through his complex feelings and insecurities.

"And I still love you." Justin answered the following question as Ethan cited all the reasons he wasn't good enough, and they went through some of his anxiety exercises together until he finally settled and fell asleep. When Ethan woke from their unexpected nap, he was much better and could only gaze at Justin, then at the ring on his hand, and nod.

"You love me," he whispered, and Justin would confirm it again.

Justin never failed to confirm it, no matter how many times Ethan struggled or doubted.

*

BY MIDSEASON, THEIR winning record brought in the media and the scouts. The assistant coaches told them there were guests on campus and to be on their best behavior. This was it. Justin played with more determination, knowing Ethan was in the stands supporting him as he fought for their future by winning every game and beating his own stats as well as those of other high-ranking players who would also be declaring as early as he was.

At halftime, Coach pulled him aside. "Just be brief, courteous, and professional. I can't get you out of this one. They hit me up before the game and named you specifically."

Justin nodded and headed for Shawn, his suitemate and dreaded defensive tackle. Quarterbacks throughout their division loathed Shawn and his unprecedented sack record.

They were tied at the half, and it was a dogfight as Justin and the other receivers battled to score. It seemed as if they just couldn't get a break; this game was down to the wire, and they were looking at overtime if a miracle didn't happen in the next two minutes. And then, it happened.

The pass was way too high, but Justin went for it and bobbled it with the tips of his fingers, half caught it on the way down with another bobble, and finally got a grip on the ball. Then, he thanked God and Ethan for all that summer running because, with a firm hold on the leather, he took off…and was gone.

The crowd went crazy, and the coaches had to pull everyone back off the field for the field goal. Coach pointed at the trainer, and then Justin was escorted to the locker room as the crowd screamed. Justin knew the field goal was good, and the game was more than won.

"Holy shit," their trainer yelled over the insane win, and then looked at Justin. "What's wrong?"

Justin motioned to the training room. "I have no idea why he sent me down here."

"Did you pull something? Jesus, that was a hell of a run," he said.

"No. Go on back. I'm going to hit the showers before the chaos begins."

He stripped out of his uniform and had finished showering when everyone began to burst through the door. Justin laughed as Shawn hugged him, and then the other guys followed. His shower had been a waste as he embraced his sweaty team and celebrated with them. He showered again, put on his suit slacks, and buttoned up his dress shirt.

"Coach wants to see you."

Justin draped his tie around his neck and tied it as he headed for the office. Coach waved him in, and Justin didn't fail to notice several familiar faces in the room. Big-time familiar.

"Halstead, good game," Coach said. "Son, you almost gave me a heart attack."

"You and me both. For a second there, I didn't think I had it," Justin said as he turned his collar back down and glanced at the other men.

"It was a hell of a catch."

"It wasn't a pretty one," Justin admitted.

The men chuckled but said nothing more.

"That's all. Go on," Coach said.

Justin nodded at him, closed the door behind him, and headed to get his bag.

"Holy shit, dude." Shawn, wild-eyed, stopped him, and they stood together as their center was called in for the same unofficial non-meet-and-greet session.

"Yeah, holy shit," Justin agreed. "Do you know who that was?"

"Who doesn't."

"Man, I gotta get outta here without talking to the media," Justin said, stressing, and Shawn looked like a guy with a bad idea.

"What?" Justin asked.

"Not a fucking word, man. Come on," Shawn said, and Justin followed him.

"Unbelievable." Justin shook his head as he and Shawn sat on the bench in the back of an ambulance as it rolled through the parking lot to Shawn's truck.

"Here." Shawn handed him his keys, and a "give me a minute" wink told Justin what he needed to know about the blonde ambulance driver.

"You're crazy, but I owe you," Justin said before slipping through the side door and into Shawn's truck.

Ethan had the ESPN highlights on and bit his lip as Justin walked in. "I don't even know how you pulled that off," he said and imitated Justin's fingertips barely touching the ball as he had to jump to get it.

"I honestly don't know how I pulled it off either. But I remember being thankful for running cross country with you this summer."

"You smoked them," Ethan praised and set up the clip he'd recorded for Justin to watch when he got home. Ethan already had clothes laid out for Justin, and he changed quickly, sliding on the comfortable sleep pants while Ethan helped out and hung up his suit for him. Justin was exhausted after games, usually injured or at least hurting, and this had become their routine. Ethan taking care of him without question.

Justin sat down in a near daze, and Ethan slid a box of hot take-out delivery food in front of him. He shook three pills out of the pain relief bottle and set them next to a glass of ice water. Ethan unlatched the food lid and stuck a fork in Justin's hand as he could only stare at the TV, seeing for the first time what he had done.

"Eat, and I'll play it again. I've already seen it, like, twelve times. Dad called; Mom said he jumped around the house and yelled so loud the neighbor's dog started barking, and then Mr. Cole came over to make sure everything was okay. Of course, Dad recorded the game, and then he and Mr. Cole were both freaking out, and so that's where we currently are—with the entire neighborhood at my parents' house for the screaming fest. Eat, and I'll play it again for you," Ethan said again, then sighed as the phone rang.

"He just got here," Ethan said after answering it. "He's watching it now, but I think he's in a bit of shock."

Justin's phone rang next.

"That's not how to stay out of the spotlight," his dad said, but Justin could hear the pride in his tone.

Justin sat in awe, phone in hand, taking in the sports photographer's money shot of his insane leap and outstretched fingertip reach for the nearly impossible ball. The bobbles were worthy of held breaths, but they didn't look as bad as Justin had imagined.

"Holy shit, son," his dad kept saying, and Justin could hear the game on in the background.

"They were there tonight, Dad." Justin told him that Coach and two assistants had called him and one other offensive player in for a quick "good game" before dismissing them, all while a well-known scout and assistant coach from a major team sat in the office.

"Here we go." His dad breathed out the warning. "This is happening, Justin."

"I know." Justin stared at Ethan, who flipped his phone around to show him a social media post as the comments continued. The likes were rolling like a slot machine.

"Call me back when you calm down," his dad said. "Call me back when *I* calm down."

"I don't even know what we're going to do," Ethan was saying on his phone. "This is so good and so bad all at the same time, Dad."

Justin nodded as he picked up the remote, hit replay, and watched it again. The bad throw, the impossible catch, the run, and no one coming close to ever stopping him.

"I'll call you back," Ethan said and sat down. He closed the food box and took the fork from Justin, who was still mindlessly holding it. He took the remote, and they watched it once more.

"I'll never pass the character questions, Ethan. I mean, they aren't supposed to ask you about your sexual orientation anymore, but…" Justin just shook his head.

"We breathe," Ethan said calmly, "And then we find our calm and talk through what has triggered us."

Justin nodded and closed his eyes, using one of Ethan's techniques. "They are going to find out, and it's not about me. It's about them trying to get to you. It's about them bringing it all up again and throwing you back into the spotlight and what that would do to you." Justin said the thing that terrified him most out loud, the truth that was causing his anxiety.

"That is a realistic possibility, and I'm stronger now than I was a year and a half ago," Ethan said. "We have strong support systems. You love me, and I love you, and we have a plan. We know this isn't going to be easy. You had a good game, a great moment. We are going to be happy about that, and you are going to eat, and I'm going to turn off the TV and the phones."

Justin nodded. He did feel calmer, and the panic began to ebb as Ethan powered down the outside world, turned on the lamps, and turned off the overhead lights. He climbed back onto the couch and stretched out as Justin ate his dinner.

"I was thinking about renting an apartment off campus for the rest of the year," Ethan said. "We're right at that six-month lease mark. Dad said there are some outside of town that are gated and sort of like town-houses with garages. He found them and brought it up."

"Why didn't we think of that before?"

"Because we are idiots," Ethan said, and Justin could only agree.

"Do it," he said and looked around. "I mean, it would be a quick move."

"We'd need some furniture."

"Done." Justin tossed Ethan his wallet. "Just buy shit we can move again in six months when you transfer and stuff that can survive moving across the country. You aren't living on campus, wherever that is."

"Agreed."

"Come on, sleep," Justin said. "I'm tired and sore. It always hurts less when I'm next to you."

Chapter Eighteen

Justin

SHAWN STANDING AT Ethan's door was not a good sign as Justin hurriedly dressed and headed to the lobby.

"Coach needs you, and your phone is off," Shawn said.

"So he called *you*." Justin sighed.

"I am your suitemate."

"What did he tell you to do exactly?"

"To get you and not fuck around because he said he knew I knew where you were." Shawn shrugged.

"He's moving off campus."

"Good," Shawn said.

"What's it about?" Justin looked down at his sweats and the hoodie he had on.

"He didn't say, just said to bring you to his office. On a Sunday."

"Thank you, Shawn."

"I've got your back, Justin."

*

JUSTIN BLEW OUT a breath, and Coach waved him in, the door open and him waiting.

"You have to do an interview," Coach said. "Seen the paper? No, you haven't because your phone was turned off." He waved a hand. "Here." He tossed the local paper on the desk and tapped it. "Then he tossed down the sports section of a very recognizable newspaper. "And during the *very* game when *they* were here." He sighed and shook his head, then just stared up at the ceiling for a long time as Justin read.

"*Justin.*" Coach said his name with both pride and exasperation. "I'm worried you're going to have to make a choice."

"I won't make the choice you think," Justin said.

"I know, but I had to ask." Coach rubbed at his chin. He seemed both pleased and irritated, things Justin thought most coaches seemed able to possess simultaneously.

"No interview. We have a media person. Surely, they've called you for your two cents."

"I've had three agents call me this morning," his coach said. "Don't answer any unfamiliar numbers."

"I don't even have voicemail."

Coach grumbled, "And next week's game?"

"It's away. If I can get on the charter before everyone else…" Justin said, and his coach seemed to agree with yet another of his aversion tactics.

Coach's phone rang, and he told their media director to come on back.

"Melanie is coming to give us her report. Just sit there and, hell, look happy," Coach said.

Justin understood that meant to keep his mouth shut. Melanie came in with her tablet and notes. Justin waited as she talked about X, Instagram, Facebook, and trending statistics. The clip was playing on ESPN's *SportsCenter* and the NFL Network. They had calls for interviews, and she began running down the list and clicking her pen as she talked about available times.

"He's not giving any interviews; prepare a press release. I'll give you my statement, and you work your magic. Pull any clips from last season and see if there's anything you can give them to keep them at bay," Coach said.

Melanie's mouth fell open as she looked at her boss, then at Justin, and then back to her boss.

He held up one finger, and her unspoken protest died.

"On it," she said and left the office.

Justin reached over, picked up the sports section, and stared at the picture Ethan had shown him and his dad had sent him. He shook his head, imagining he'd be a meme by the afternoon, if not already, as he scanned the blurb about the winning touchdown and his stats. Justin read Coach's statements about where they could find Halstead. "In the library, since he holds the highest GPA on this team and is on the chancellor's list," Coach was quoted as saying.

"I thought the GPA line was a pretty good one," Coach said with a wink.

"It was. Is it true?"

"It actually is, according to Melanie."

Coach pushed a piece of paper at him. "Here, write down that number, and don't turn your phone off again."

Justin wrote Ethan's number on it. Coach folded the paper and stuck it in his wallet.

"We'll see how it plays out. Be careful, Justin," he warned, and Justin assured him he would be with a wave goodbye.

"Hell of a play," Coach called out, and Justin silently agreed as he headed down the tunnel to meet back up with Shawn in the parking lot.

"Well?" Shawn asked as they arrived at Ethan's dorm ten minutes later. Before Justin could answer, Ethan jogged out, passed a duffle bag to him, and then headed for an Uber.

"Back to the football dorm," Justin said finally.

Justin found his keys and turned his phone on. Shawn fake yawned, patting his mouth like a smartass as the notifications began to ding.

"Don't they think people sleep after games?" Justin said at some of the early times from the out-of-state numbers just as Shawn's phone began to ring as well, and he gloated.

They were both on the phone as they entered the dorm and headed upstairs. Agents had gotten ahold of his parents when they shouldn't have. The media was trying to get ahold of him—through his parents. He did enjoy the texts from the high school kids, congratulating him, and the few posted clips of them trying to recreate the photo and the play on his only social media page. Justin thought it was cool as they started getting likes.

He stretched out on his bed and called Ethan. "Are you there yet?"

"Yes, it's sweet," Ethan whispered.

"Why are you whispering?" Justin appreciated the only calm in his chaos.

"Because I'm signing a lease in the office. Call you back in, like, five?" Ethan said, and Justin agreed.

At a knock on his door, Justin called out that it was unlocked.

His team captain and quarterback, who'd thrown the worst Hail Mary of all Hail Marys, opened it and tilted his head inside. "School paper's downstairs."

"Tell them to call the team media office," Justin said and relayed what Coach had said that morning at the ass-crack of dawn.

Tyler ordered, "Take a nap, man."

"Yeah," Justin said as his phone rang again.

"We got it," Ethan said. "I mean, it's in my name. I got it legally, but it's *ours*. I'm going to the furniture store and buying a king-sized bed and nothing else." He sounded so excited about the prospect of an extra-large bed that could more easily hold Justin.

Justin agreed, then further agreed when Ethan told him to nap too. Despite his coach's advice, he turned off his phone, locked his door, and put his earbuds in. He drifted off with the sleep aid of a storm on repeat, the only thing that drowned out the sounds of the dorm.

*

JUSTIN HAD HOPED the madness over the game would have quelled, but his fellow students seemed to change around him as he sat in class on Monday. They morphed into fans. Congratulating him, high-fiving and backslapping. People he'd never spoken to acted as if they knew him, striking up conversations everywhere he went, between classes, and nearly making him late since he didn't want to be rude.

"And this is just a dose of what it would be like," he said to himself as he opened the door to his second class of the day.

When he exited that class, a reporter was waiting for him, clearly having somehow obtained his schedule by nefarious means.

"Justin Halstead," she said as she approached him, her cameraman jogging with his equipment to catch up. "Just a few questions about Saturday's big win and your plans for the future. Will you be declaring for the draft or finishing school?"

He gave her a friendly wave. "I'd love to chat, but I'm late for my next class. Go Warriors." And he hurried off.

He didn't have any other classes, and he was anxious to get to the new apartment and see what Ethan was so excited about. Ethan's father had driven up to help move his things Sunday evening, and Ethan had skipped class to get the rest of it in, using Justin's truck throughout the day. And there it was, in the parking lot. The plan had been for Ethan's dad to drop it off and Ethan to drive the SUV. Justin headed for the truck, swiped the keys from beneath the seat, and rechecked his phone for the address and gate code Ethan had sent him.

"Yeah," Justin said to himself as he drove through the sliding iron-gated entrance. Private, just what they needed. He wound through the complex until he was at the back of it, which faced the woods, to an end unit in a four-plex. Justin pulled around to the wooded side and parked in one of only four spaces behind the building.

Justin looked up at the balcony, where Ethan stood.

"I did so good," Ethan said, clearly thrilled by the place.

Justin threw a two-finger kiss up at him, then found their door on the bottom floor and headed inside. It was empty except for Ethan's things in boxes, Justin's belongings that had migrated to Ethan's dorm over time, and his television. Justin headed up the stairs and paused to appreciate the large bed in the center of the floor and nothing else.

"Don't worry; they're delivering the rest tomorrow," Ethan said, handing Justin his wallet. He tapped his finger on it for a moment. "I can't believe you kept that."

"Snoop. I can't believe how private this place is. God, this is perfect. Do you know a reporter somehow got my schedule and was waiting for me after class today? She literally chased after me."

Ethan sighed. "You poor thing."

"Stop." Justin hugged him, happy to finally be there. "Your dad got back okay?"

"Yep, and I'm out of the dorm. I turned in my form, so this is it. Home sweet home."

"Tell me what all you got." Justin lay on the bed as Ethan walked around the room and pointed to where the dresser and nightstands would go, the half of the closet that was Justin's, and how there were two sinks in the bathroom, just like they liked, and on and on Ethan went.

Justin just lay there contentedly when Ethan ran out of steam and stretched out next to him.

"I'll help pay for the apartment," Justin said.

"I still get my housing allowance, so food, groceries, necessities. The allowance will cover the rent."

"Thanks for moving and doing all the legwork. I wish we could do it all together."

"Someday," Ethan breathed out. "Someday, we can go stand in IKEA like all the other people and argue over flimsy furniture and ask, *What the hell is that?* at the weird shit they call art."

Justin teased him. "Such daydreams of our future, really profound and deep there, Ethan."

"I know. That's what I want," he said honestly.

Justin rolled over and kissed him. "Okay, my IKEA dreamer, I promise one day to take you there and buy you something ridiculous to sit on the back of our toilet."

"Yes," Ethan said, stretching out the word like he'd won something grand. "But it has to be, like, the worst thing in there, agreed?"

Justin *eww*ed and imagined it too. "The worst."

"Like something we never can figure out what it really is," Ethan said with a faraway look in his eyes.

"I'll buy you that thing and kiss you in IKEA." Justin held Ethan's hand, and they were both quiet, relishing such a silly goal.

"Good," Ethan finally said. "You have a curfew."

"Yeah," Justin groaned out reluctantly. "I'll run and get groceries and things you'll need, bring them back, and then head to the dorm. Or do you want to keep the truck and drop me off at campus?"

"No, go and come back." Ethan sighed. "I'll unpack the boxes and hang up the clothes. But next time you come over, bring what you don't need in the dorm." Ethan waved a hand at the empty closet. "I want it to feel like we are living together."

Justin would do it because he wanted that too.

*

JUSTIN FINISHED HIS homework in his room and then went through the books he wouldn't use for class, packing them in the empty boxes he'd brought back from the apartment. He sorted through his closet, culling school and dress clothes he wouldn't need for pre-and-post games. He tossed in a practice football, thinking he and Ethan could play catch in that greenspace behind their new home together for a change.

He carried his things down to the truck after it got dark but before curfew and then joined the guys in the lounge to watch game footage of the team they were playing next.

"Watch out for *that* guy," Cliff said to Justin as he paused the game and replayed footage of the tackle. "He's a bruiser."

Justin nodded, noting the guy's strengths and determination at keeping the offense from progressing.

His week went fairly well. He stopped by the apartment when he could, after class or between practices. John and Bethany had brought Bethany's car up for Ethan to use to and from classes. The away game meant Justin couldn't return to Ethan until much later in the night, nearly morning, but he worked the new key onto his keyring and kissed Ethan goodbye.

*

IT WAS THE game from hell, one of the toughest Justin had ever played. He was bleeding. Several of his teammates were bloodied and grass-stained, bruised from the brutality of college ball and the shared fighting desire to go to the playoffs. At halftime, Justin sat on the bench while the trainer taped his elbow, busted open from a cleat or some other piece of equipment. They'd stitch it up after the game.

Again, the two teams were neck and neck and down to the wire throughout the second half. Home-field advantage was something Justin could truly respect after witnessing the power of the Bulldog's crowd, student body, relentless band, and spirit teams. And while some Warrior fans had made the journey, the decibel level from the home stands was discouraging and deafening. The only hope was to get within field-goal range.

"Just get us there," Coach growled, his irritation rubbing off onto his team as Justin donned his helmet, waved off the trainer, and ran in.

Justin heard the play call, faked, and got open, running a zigzag and trying to break away from the guy practically up his ass.

"Fuck," Justin cursed and pivoted.

A one-handed catch brought the ball in tight as he was slammed to the ground. The tackle and ensuing pile forced the air out of his lungs. Whistles blew, and Justin gripped the ball, curling in on himself as meaty paws and sweaty bodies tried for a last second to take it from him.

Fuck that; it wasn't happening, and he swore he could have popped the damn pigskin for how hard he held it. There was silence as Justin opened his eyes and saw the referee's arm extend to the side. The crowd booed as Justin rolled to his back and tried to suck in a lungful of air. He unsuccessfully gasped as a teammate reached a hand down to him.

"Get up, man."

Justin tried to breathe, but there was no air. Seventy-three threw up an arm, and a time-out was called as the trainers ran out, got him up to sitting, and Justin finally inhaled a ragged, stinging breath.

"Air…knocked" was all Justin could say as he gasped greedily.

"Yeah, we got that. Let's get you off the field." They hefted him up, and he felt drunk as he tried to walk.

Justin sat on the bench with an oxygen mask on his face as he watched the ball sail through the uprights. Coach turned back to look at him and nodded. He'd done it. He'd gotten them close enough, and thank God, this hellish game was over. They were in the playoffs and hopefully bowl-bound again.

"I want a report on him," Coach said.

"Just got the air knocked out of me by that big motherfucker," Justin wheezed.

Coach headed to ward off the media as the trainer checked his vitals, then removed the mask and oxygen.

"Meet me in the med room; we still need to stitch up that arm," he told him, and Justin stood on weak legs.

Shawn came and walked with him, steering him clear of the crowd now on the field and headed to the visitor locker room.

"Brutal game." Justin winced, and neither Shawn nor the rest of the team was much better.

Justin stripped down and hit the showers. His bruised ribs, not a first for him but never fun, showed a red rose color already blooming and a purple patch growing beneath it. He dried off, wrapped a towel around his waist, and gingerly made it to the trainer's med bay.

"I told you that asshole was trouble," Cliff said, shaking his head at the bruise spreading over Justin's ribcage and the bloody wet bandage on his arm.

"You look pretty too," Justin said, too beat up to really shit talk with Cliff. But he and Cliff attempted weakly with each other, Cliff sitting there with blood trailing down from his kneecap onto the floor.

Two more injured players joined their pathetic party, groaning in pain, followed by the trainers and Coach to assess the damages.

"Ribs and forearm," one rattled off over Justin, and then he was on a table, getting stitched up and taped. Nothing was broken, but he'd be in a world of hurt for the next few days.

"Fuck man," Cliff cursed as the gash on the side of his knee was stitched up. "Numb that shit up."

Justin groaned. "Don't make me laugh, please."

"Sorry, yeah, that sucks, but I'm not a damn pin cushion, man," Cliff bitched.

And it was only funny because he *couldn't* laugh, and Cliff was bitching about a tiny needle when he'd just practically killed players from the other team. No doubt they, too, had casualties, mainly from Cliff.

"You know you're *that asshole* on our team." Justin gritted out the words as he gripped his ribs. "When they were watching game film on us, they were pointing at you and saying 'Watch out for that guy, what a bruiser.'"

"Yeah, they were." Cliff scowled even harder at the trainer.

The bus ride home was hell, and Justin answered the numerous texts from Ethan demanding to know if he was okay. Justin dragged himself into the apartment in the early hours, still dark, and then eased into the bed beside Ethan.

"I want to kill that guy," Ethan seethed next to him.

"Just don't say anything funny, I beg you. That hurts worse than anything."

"Okay, I promise to not be funny." Ethan carefully scooted closer and lay his hand softly on Justin's chest. "You just rest. When do you need to be up to take your next dose of pain medication?"

"Four hours. In my bag." He yawned, which hurt too.

"My parents will be here soon. They insisted on coming to help out after Dad watched the game. He said it was a legal hit, but it was a really unnecessary one. He said you'd have to take it easy for a while; you might need help getting around. And I'd feel better with him here to help you."

"Scared you'll drop me?"

"Yes," Ethan admitted.

Chapter Nineteen

Justin

"NURSE RATCHET," JUSTIN groaned as John rewrapped his chest like he was in a body cast.

"Ah, you'll be fine. Thank God for the bye week," Ethan's dad said, and Justin agreed.

Justin held his arm up while he fussed over it, and then Ethan handed over his next round of medication. Justin eased back down and winced, and Ethan's dad was in coach mode. Justin knew there wasn't anything more to do either.

"Thanks, I think. What's Momma Bethany doing?"

"Organizing our kitchen stuff and cooking us enough food for a week." Ethan winked.

"We have kitchen stuff?" Justin bit his lip, turning his head and not looking at Ethan. He knew if he did, he'd crack up, which would hurt.

"I hate this injury," Ethan muttered. "Don't be funny for a week."

John patted his son on the back. "Come on, let's go help Mom and let Justin rest."

By the end of the week and after several missed practices, Justin was moving but nowhere near top form. He ice-bathed and stretched, he jog-walked on the treadmill, and Coach frowned harder each day they got closer to their next game day. By the middle of the second week, Justin was far better and working hard to regain his lost strength. It wasn't too bad, but also wasn't a good time to not be at the top of his game.

Coach's mood dimmed further with an injured quarterback who'd somehow managed to slice open a finger to the bone. With only a third-string freshman quarterback who still had much to learn while their backup QB was still recovering from a broken collarbone earlier in the season, Coach hit them up with some new plays. They were more like trick plays, and Justin subbed as quarterback rather than receiver as Coach rearranged the roster for this one game.

Somehow, by Saturday, the banged-up team had its shit together for their first playoff game. While it was no walk in the park, they still crushed their opponent. And though he was still sore, it had been a wild thrill that had somehow dulled the sharp pain as Justin called plays and passed the ball again.

Now, he only had to wait out the media. Justin frowned in disappointment at Shawn, who had stopped seeing the pretty paramedic. Shawn just shrugged as he sat with him and waited for the all-clear. Coach called Justin in, and Justin told Shawn to go on home.

"Next month, you'll need to declare, then we'll work through Pro Day and the Combine." Coach grew serious. "I don't doubt you'll be invited."

Justin nodded.

"I think you go through the draft. They can't ask you certain questions now, but that doesn't mean they won't. Deal with those how you see fit. You have a good character profile from the team and my input. They may question your lack of social involvement. Go with the grades."

Justin nodded again.

"Then, you can turn them down and go free agency unless you get a deal and can feel out if they would be comfortable with you as a player, support you, even if it's not openly. Here." He handed Justin a short list of teams.

"These are where I think you shoot for—any of the others…" Coach gave him a grim expression.

"Got it, thanks." Justin studied the list. He was relieved, seeing the team he really wanted to play for on it."

"Which one are you looking at?"

"Let's just say I like the beach," Justin answered in a humorous tone as he got up. "You think I can pull it off? Get through the draft?"

"Academics, a business plan, hard worker, valuable player, what you can bring to them. You're a private person, but no one has said anything bad about you, Justin. They know these things. You don't have to convince them. Just talk about how much you love this damn game. The rest…" He sighed. "I don't know what to tell you, and I wish I did. But, yes, I think you can do it."

"Thanks, Coach. And thanks for this list."

Coach waved him off, out of his office.

*

BACK TO HIS regular position, a tough playoff season, followed by another bowl win, and Pro Day was on them before Justin knew it. Ethan and John were somewhere in the stands with the rest of the crowd as Justin and select players from their team all participated in the day's events. He'd met several scouts and representatives but told himself to keep his shit together as the team he wanted approached him next.

"Justin Halstead," the assistant offensive coordinator said as he enthusiastically pumped Justin's hand.

"I love the beach," Justin said as he shook back firmly.

"Glad to hear it! How are you doing after that injury?"

"Great, top shape, just a few bruised ribs and—" Justin held up his arm. "—a little battle scar."

They inspected the several inches of still-pink scar that ran down the back of Justin's forearm to his elbow.

"What do you think about coming down south for a few days?" the assistant asked.

"It would be an honor, and I mean it. I was really looking forward to meeting with you today."

The man seemed pleased as Justin gave him a nod, hopefully confirming he was a solid bet. "That's good to hear. We thought you might be looking for a colder climate," he said, lifting a brow.

"No sir. Sun and turf. I hate the snow." Justin's heart raced as the assistant told him they'd see him again soon and headed off.

He got a water bottle and tracked the assistant as he strode directly to Coach. Justin prayed but believed his coach would confirm his desire to play in Florida. Justin met with two more team representatives, and everyone talked around—as was done at this stage. He met with one other team from the West Coast he'd consider and two teams he'd never want to play for but still maintained his professionalism while offering no hints of interest in them.

When it was over, John picked him up in the SUV, and they stopped to get Bethany and Ethan at the condo for dinner out.

"He so knew. He was smiling, nodding, and shook your hand twice," Ethan babbled and waved his hands next to Justin in the back seat. "My eyes hurt from…" He held his hands up as if holding binoculars to his face hard. "Oh my God, I was just like…" He did it again, and Justin loved how excited Ethan was.

"I think he got the hint," Justin said, and he told Ethan every single word and detail as he eagerly listened.

"I hate the snow." Ethan cracked up and looked at his father, who was just as amused.

"That's one way to say it without saying it."

Justin told them what each team rep had said, including the one on the West Coast. They went over the list again and the one team on it that hadn't met with him or shown an interest. John had a reason—that they didn't need his position after recruiting for it hard in the last draft, and did so with a veteran already on board. So, it wasn't personal; they needed defensive players this round.

They pulled into an upscale steakhouse Ethan's parents were treating them to. It was an overdue celebration for their engagement, the season, the bowl win, and this new leg of their journey—going pro. They were halfway through their meal, Bethany sitting with Ethan on one side of their booth and John and Justin on the other, when a man in a suit stopped by.

"Justin Halstead," the man said and it wasn't a question.

Justin stared at the head coach of Florida's Bay team. John scooted over so Justin could slide out to stand and shake his hand.

"I'm Coach Robert Nellis. I thought that was you. I hear good news that you're coming down south for a few days."

"Yes, sir, I am looking forward to it." Justin hadn't seen this man at the day's events. He wondered why he was even here.

"These are your parents?" Coach Nellis asked as he extended his hand.

"No, sir, this is Coach John Andrews, his wife Bethany, and their son Ethan," Justin said as the freaking head coach shook hands with everyone.

"Justin spent some time with my team over the summer," John said. "The kids loved him, and I think we increased his speed."

Justin agreed. "Definitely."

"You're fast," Coach Nellis said. "I won't keep you." He motioned across the room to a woman Justin guessed was his wife at another table. "We wanted a great steak; we were here in town for a quick meeting. Congratulations on that bowl win, and *what a season*." Coach Nellis said his good-byes and shot Justin a look that spoke volumes. "We'll see you soon."

"Yes, Coach," Justin said and sat back down once he was gone.

John blew out a breath, just as deer-in-the-headlights as a wide-eyed Justin was, and slightly inclined his head.

"Yeah. After he's gone," Justin said under his breath.

Ethan covered his mouth at how Justin's hand was shaking as he held his fork, trying to finish his meal.

They all gave a smiling wave as Coach Nellis and his wife headed out. No sooner than the door closed behind them, Justin and John pulled "an Ethan" and squealed, hugging each other.

"Do I even have to say it?"

Justin shook his head.

"What?" Ethan asked.

"For the Bay's head coach to recognize you, know your name, come over, and know your stats and season—that's huge," John explained quietly to Ethan. "And that he already knows Justin is coming for a visit." John nodded. "You are on his list. Must have been *some* meeting for him to be here."

"And we like him, his team?" Ethan asked.

"That's your beach house, baby," Justin said, and Ethan nodded, understanding.

"That would mean you'll be closer to us," Bethany whispered, and Justin and John nodded.

*

FOUR DAYS LATER, Justin and two other prospects were on a team plane to the Gulf Coast of Florida to spend two days with the Bayhawks, working out and running drills. Everyone called the team "the Bay." They would tour the facilities and meet the coaching staff. Across the country, other athletes were doing the same, all jetting toward their hopeful futures.

"Top pick?" a player next to Justin asked.

"Oh yeah."

"Me too." The guy tilted his head across the aisle. "Second choice for him."

"This is definitely my top pick," Justin answered, and the guy nodded hard. "Justin Halstead." He held out his hand. "Tight end."

"Reece McReedy, center."

You had to love your center, and Justin was happy to be with another offensive player.

McReedy indicated the other player again. "QB."

Justin glanced over at the other guy sitting alone.

They talked football, growing up, and high school games, and Justin reminisced, as did McReedy, as they got to know each other. The QB slept the entire flight.

McReedy seemed just as eager as Justin and the humor between them came easy. "I hope they take us both. I like you, man."

"Same," Justin said. "I hope we fly back together."

They toured the facilities first, were given swag, and then met the coaching staff and team. After the niceties were out of the way, it was to the training facilities for an unofficial battery of tests and a workout session. Training staff came in with clipboards and stopwatches, and Justin, again damn thankful for Ethan and cross-country, killed it on distance and speed on the treadmill. They went through weights and jumps, with a few remarks about the photograph of Justin and the infamous catch.

Their last station for the day was a chat with the staff, not an interview per se, but an interview nonetheless, as Justin shook hands with everyone, nodded at Coach Nellis over in the corner, and took the lone seat across from the coaching staff.

This was it.

Justin's moment of truth. He conversed with them as they slipped in their questions about his family, his willingness to relocate, his plans for after the NFL, and his social media account. The one.

"Who are the kids?" An assistant flipped his phone around, showing the video clip of the kids on John's team reenacting his leap and catch.

Justin knew he looked proud as he answered, "I trained with those guys last summer while I worked on my speed with a high school coach. They were a great group of kids, and I think I learned as much from them as they did from me."

"You got paid for that?" he asked suspiciously.

"No, sir, it was a volunteer thing. Coach Andrews is a good friend of mine. He needed some help over the summer, and I had a need to improve my speed and distance running and better learn to control my breathing."

"Your speed did increase," Coach Richardson said and then rattled off Justin's stats from the year before and this year.

"Distance running really helped me with not sucking for air in the second half of the game. It improved my endurance."

"And you know Coach Andrews how?" another asked.

"I met his son in a freshman composition class. He said his dad was a football coach, and he was a cross-country runner for the university. It all just worked out."

"We don't have much media on you," the offensive coordinator said.

"No, sir, I'm a private person. I study to keep my grades up, and I know it can't be avoided—the media, but I've never been interested in that scene. It's just always been about playing football for me. That's why I'm rarely on social media either."

"Honor student, chancellor's list for the last three years. *Rare*."

"Yes, sir. My mother is a high school English and literature teacher, and my father is an engineer. Slacking in school was a concept..." Justin paused. "Sorry, it wasn't even a possibility. Not with my parents."

"Hardcore, English-teacher mom and engineer dad," he repeated. "Good influences."

"Yes, sir. I'm fortunate," Justin said, and Richardson turned and gave a nod to Nellis.

"Thank you, Justin. We look forward to talking with you more at the Combine," Coach Richardson said and stood. Justin stood and shook all their hands.

He took a step toward the door but stopped as one of the other men asked, "What'd you think about McReedy?"

Justin turned and answered honestly. "I liked him instantly; he was friendly and funny, said this was his first choice, and I told him it was mine. You have to love the center, and I see that in him. I was impressed by his performance in the gym as well."

"And Johnson?" another asked.

"I didn't get an opportunity to get to know him like I did McReedy," Justin said.

And with that done, they indicated for him to leave. Justin exhaled hard and gave McReedy a discreet thumbs-up as they called him in next.

The final day was a practice session with a few team members. Justin did everything he could to work hard and not be starstruck. It was no easy practice; they worked them hard, giving the impression of how difficult it was to make it in the NFL.

Justin showered and dressed for his flight back home. McReedy sat beaming next to him in the locker room.

"On the plane," Justin said, and McReedy understood.

"But you're dying just like me," Justin said, agreeing with what

McReedy couldn't yet say.

They had their final goodbyes with the staff and were in the air. McReedy and Justin sat together again, with the QB on his phone, his headphones in, closer to the front.

"Spill it, man," McReedy said.

"They asked me about you," Justin said, and McReedy looked like he was about to burst with excitement.

"Same; asked me about you and him." McReedy jerked his head at the QB.

And they talked animatedly, sharing what they'd said about the other and the QB.

"Man, you were nicer than me," McReedy said. "I told them straight up. Dude slept on the flight and showed no interest in getting to know us."

"Thanks for the kind words about me."

"Team captain material, right there. Had me feeling less nervous and having a good time; we talked about growing up and loving the game. A good guy, for real, and that you hoped we'd get to fly back together and pick right up where we left off."

Justin and McReedy exchanged numbers and promised to keep in touch no matter how it went. They shook hands and hugged after they debarked, and Justin hoped, on the taxi home, he'd see him again and play on the same team.

Later, Ethan stood in a Florida team T-shirt from the swag bag that was entirely too big for him. He hopped around like an idiot, doing the stupid bird flap thing Bay fans did.

"You really think it went well?" he asked as he hopped onto the bed and straddled Justin. "I want every single detail and thought you had. Go."

And Justin gazed contentedly up at Ethan, now sitting on him, and told his man everything from start to home.

"That one nod, when he turned and gave it to the head coach—that was it, that was him saying I want *him*," Ethan said and then kissed him. "I'm so proud of you." And then Ethan showed him how much he'd missed him as he slinked down Justin's body.

"Are you sure?" Justin panted. Though there was no doubt Ethan was as in, as Justin saw stars and prayed to gods he didn't know the names of while Ethan crossed another milestone on the physical side of their relationship, one Justin knew was a huge hurdle for him.

"I want you to fuck me," Justin whispered after returning the favor, and they both lay there lazy and satiated.

"You do?"

"I do, Ethan."

"I've never."

"Neither have I. Think about it."

"Yeah, I need some time to think about that, but yes," Ethan said, and Justin kissed him.

Chapter Twenty

Ethan

ETHAN MOPED AROUND their apartment. He went to his classes. He called his parents more often than he should have. He stayed an extra hour and a half after league practice to work on his puck-handling skills. Ethan messaged Justin and got replies when Justin had a single spare minute to respond, but Ethan realized in only two days alone what part of his future might look like when Justin was gone. Justin was in Florida again, visiting another team.

"I *am* codependent," Ethan said to their empty apartment.

He and his therapist had discussed it many times once he and Justin's relationship had become serious. She'd cautioned him. He'd argued he didn't take advantage of Justin, and Justin didn't take advantage of him.

Nor did either one of them confuse love with caretaking or personal sacri-
fice with some fucked up sense of loyalty. They both took care of each
other when the other needed it. They were both making sacrifices for *their*
relationship.

He'd gotten irritated with her during their session. So irritated, he'd
requested admission packets to several potential schools in towns where
Justin might get drafted. Justin was always encouraging him not to live in a
bubble, and he found himself annoyed by everyone who looked down on
it. They didn't understand. Ethan wanted a break—a big break. After the
incident, he'd been so determined to bounce right back and not let it ruin
his life.

Back then, everyone encouraged time off, and Ethan had refused,
insisting on returning to school as soon as he was well enough. Now, everyone seemed opposed to him wanting a moment to breathe, to enjoy the
happiness he never imagined finding, and to do everything he could to try
to move past his trauma. It had taken months for Justin to even kiss him.
They were engaged and had only talked about sex once. Ethan was scared,
scarred, and while he'd finally been given a medical all-clear, he still couldn't
even sleep in the dark. He couldn't have penetrative sex with his partner,
whom he loved, and couldn't find a balance between his wants and everyone
else's expectations.

Everyone except Justin.

It was all so frustrating. Ethan grabbed the mailbox key and headed
downstairs. He got the mail, pulled out three more large envelopes, and
headed back upstairs to check out three more potential colleges and compare their journalism programs and requirements. So far, the other four he'd
looked at would all accept the credits on his transcript, and he wouldn't lose

any hours. Ethan only had one more year after this and realized how stupid it would be to not finish.

"And he wants me to get a master's degree," Ethan muttered over Justin's bright idea.

Tricky man. He knew Ethan too well now and just what to say to have him sitting at the table looking at online programs.

"I want you to get a job you love, not one you feel like you *have to have*," Justin had said. "Work part-time, do online school part-time, and get past this burnout, so what if it takes a little longer. Do an internship. I honestly don't care, Ethan. You could stay home and not do shit, and I'd be happy."

Ethan remembered the joke he'd made about being a kept boy. For a moment or two, Justin had gone all "Neanderthal man" on him; they'd gotten naked and, for about fifteen minutes, Justin had shown him just how great that life might have been.

"You are so much more than that," Justin had said afterward. "But it was a fun thought. Plus, eventually, I think you'd get bored." Then, Justin had started laughing.

"What now?"

"If we ever consider role-playing," Justin had thrown out and waggled his eyebrows.

"You're down for the kept-boy scenario." Ethan had laughed too.

Ethan knew Justin was right, but they were facing many changes in their near future. Their only free time, any real time together, would be during Justin's off-seasons, and no job or school lived by the NFL's schedule.

"Thank God he doesn't play hockey." Ethan realized *that* game schedule would have been impossible. He didn't know how couples pulled it off in the NHL.

Ethan opened the next packet, one of the programs in Florida.

"I am *not* codependent," he told the empty room and began reading.

If they got Florida and all the stars aligned, Ethan had narrowed it down to two schools he was seriously considering transferring to. One with an in-person program he liked and the other with an online program he could see himself taking to avoid complete school burnout. It was only a flicker now, but he knew it wouldn't take too many more dull research papers before he recited Smoky the Bear's mantra: *Only YOU can prevent forest fires.*

Ethan's phone beeped, and he read the group message about movie night. Some movie about a megalodon, and Ethan had seen the previews.

"Sharks," Ethan said as he typed back that he'd join them. "Just what I need to be watching before I possibly move to the coast."

Ethan's phone screen lit up on his thigh in the dark theatre with a message from Justin saying he was boarding his flight. Ethan messaged back for him to have a safe flight, and he'd see him soon.

"Who's that?" Lilly whispered.

"Someone I'm seeing," Ethan whispered back.

He wasn't about to tell Lilly all his business; she was far too chatty, and while Ethan liked her, she wasn't someone Ethan viewed as entirely trustworthy.

"Oh. Well, crap," Lilly said. "I was going to see if I could fix you up with another friend of mine."

"Who?"

"Derek. He's cute, yeah?"

Ethan bit back his comment. *Lilly tried.* She really did. Never in a million years would Ethan even hang out with Derek Milner.

"Please tell me you didn't already say something to him," Ethan whisper-hissed.

"Of course I did. You need to get back out there." Lilly directed her attention to the screen and stuffed her mouth full of popcorn.

And Ethan watched as the megalodon on the screen devoured a baby whale in one bite. He envisioned Justin as the shark and Derek Milner as the baby whale. That was about right, how it would go down, and Ethan lost it. He was the only one in the theater, laughing his ass off over the horrific scene.

When Justin got home, Ethan had made the mistake of telling him about his night with Lilly and Fran, how they'd just so happened to run into Derek Milner as they stopped by an ice cream shop where he worked after leaving the theater, and how awkward it had been.

"I had no idea he worked there, or I never would have agreed to get ice cream," Ethan said, chewing on a nail as Justin lost his shit.

"Show me a picture of him," Justin demanded.

"I never knew you were a jealous person," Ethan said as he retrieved his phone from the coffee table.

"Very," Justin said, and that fact didn't seem to bother him one bit.

"I'm afraid you're getting upset over nothing." Ethan searched his social media. "Lilly meant well. She never would have done that if she knew about you. I didn't tell her I was seeing someone until tonight."

Ethan chuckled and held out his phone. "Just scroll."

Justin snatched the phone and seemed to vibrate with anger as he glared at Ethan and then at the screen. Ethan settled back on the couch and silently counted down *three, two, one.*

"Oh."

"'Oh,' he says." Ethan crossed his leg and bounced his foot as Justin continued to scroll through Derek Milner's social media selfies.

Justin cleared his throat and scratched at his neck.

"That one in the striped ice cream uniform," Ethan said. "No, wait, the one in the neon booty shorts at the club. *That's* the one you gotta worry about." Ethan hummed and waited.

"I'm a dick."

"You are."

"You still love me though."

"I do," Ethan sighed.

"I apologize." Justin hung his head and sat beside Ethan on the couch. He handed back the phone.

"I forgive you," Ethan said and patted his leg. "But you don't ever have to be jealous again, all right?"

Justin shuddered. "Not over *that* guy, anyhow."

"*Any* other guy."

Chapter Twenty-One

Justin

JUSTIN LEFT AGAIN for another team visit. This one was on the West Coast, and he came back torn. It was similar in ways to the first trip but different in that they made it very clear they wanted him. They'd even asked if it was between them and Florida, and Justin had confirmed it was.

"It's like they know everything," Justin said. "It makes me wonder if they *do* know about you."

"The West Coast is more liberal. I mean, Florida's pretty conservative. And *that governor.*" Ethan let out a long whistle. He rolled his head to the side. "You *so* want Florida."

"I do. I want to be closer to your parents; my parents are already considering moving down there if I sign. And I like the team. Besides, governors change." Justin paused and then shrugged. "You pick."

"It doesn't work that way. They'll barter over you and trade picks; it comes down to who wants and needs you the most. Dad says Florida needs your position filled; they've struggled with one of theirs getting into legal trouble and another retiring."

Justin nodded, aware of these things. His phone rang, and Ethan went quiet.

"Hey, Coach," Justin said as he sat up. "No, sir, unless you think I should." He paused to listen. "They aren't on your list." And Ethan waited as Justin continued to listen intently. "Can you hang on one second?" Justin turned to Ethan.

"Texas wants me to come," he said with a frown. "Coach thinks I should go but also recognizes the problem there."

Ethan shook his head and mouthed a word Justin understood clearly.

"I'm going to decline unless you advise otherwise. Thank them for me, but I'd rather not waste their resources and the time they could spend on someone who wants their team." Justin listened again and ended with, "Thank you, sir. Yes, Coach."

"Well?" Ethan asked after he hung up.

"He's calling them back, has a few questions, and will call me back."

"Texas," Ethan practically spat. "That is not for us, Justin."

"I mean, they're not *that* bad…" Justin said, bemused by Ethan's rant.

When he talked to Coach again, he also agreed that declining was the right choice.

*

THE COMBINE WAS an experience Justin would never forget, and it was hard being away from Ethan for so long again. With jam-packed days of activities, hard-core interviews, and daily itineraries, Justin was pumped he and McReedy were roomed together.

"It's definitely a message, a sign." McReedy had high-fived him at the door.

Now, they ran the track together, warming up, and Justin was telling McReedy to stop making him laugh as they were both called over to the Florida reps. They chatted for a few minutes before the next drill and qualifications were scheduled to start and waved them on.

"Halstead." The offensive coordinator called him back. "Atlantic or Pacific?"

"Neither Coach, the Gulf of Mexico."

"Good. Go on, then; that's what I needed to know."

"I love how I have to do throwing drills," Justin grunted to himself as he threw the ball downfield and then another, and another, "when I'm a receiver." He guessed Coach must have put him down as both receiver and QB. As he hurled another and was shocked he could still throw as well as he had in the past, he chanted the mantra:

How smooth can you be?

Other than the one game he'd had to step in and help out with, Justin was happy he'd made Ethan play catch with him so much recently. His footwork felt natural, the pocket still his friend, as he'd nailed the targets. He imagined each runner was Ethan, who couldn't catch for shit—he practically had to land it in his hands, or he'd get pissed off and want to pout and quit playing.

Amused by his thoughts, Justin threw the rest of the session with that one vision in his mind. His last throw had been a nice sixty yards, with the receiver making the catch look effortless. There'd even been a few cheers from the spectators in the stands.

Justin moved to the next station, this time, throwing passes to a guy who should have been him at the pylon. After two more rounds of passing drills, Justin went for his break before his next scheduled event and flipped the page of his itinerary over to see where he needed to report to. He had twenty minutes to grab a water bottle and snack, then sat in the roped-off break area.

"Who knew you could throw a ball?" someone said as they walked by, and Justin nodded as he chewed.

He could, but that wasn't his position anymore. In high school, sure, but when he was recruited for college, the option for being a tight end was presented due to this speed and more playing time, and he jumped on it.

"Halstead," someone barked, and Justin looked up, startled, at Florida's assistant coach. "Bring your stuff; I'm walking you to your next session."

Justin gathered his snacks and water, tucked his schedule under his arm, and quickly joined him.

"Eat and walk," the AC said, then spoke on his phone: "Meet us at Section B8."

"So, you can throw," the coach continued after disconnecting. "Don't ask me how we overlooked that, but we weren't the only ones."

"High school quarterback," Justin said between mouthfuls. "Switched to receiver position in college due to my run times and wanting more playing time."

"Oh, we found those stats *now*," the AC said as if amused. "If you had to choose between QB and tight end?"

"TE," Justin answered honestly. "I like to score. I love to run, but I'll play whatever position you want me to." As they walked, he drank his water and finished his apple, then chunked it in the trash.

He'd wiped his hands clean and taken a last gulp of water, when he saw who they were meeting. The head coach stood next to the offensive coordinator and the special teams coach.

"Well, *Halstead*," the OC chuckled and tapped his clipboard. "As much as we want to look at you to fill our receiver position, that was quite a show you put on during the throwing drills."

"Was it?" Justin frowned, glancing at the assistant coach next to him, who nodded.

"We aren't the only ones who noticed," he said again.

"Would you be willing to play QB?" the OC asked.

"I'll be honest, I haven't played that position since high school, and only a few college games."

"And you were state champs three years running. You've been throwing somewhere," he said.

"Yes, sir, with the high school team I trained with over the summer, I threw nearly all the passes while working with the receivers. I filled in during the playoffs when our QB was injured. And I have a friend at college I toss the ball around with almost daily." Justin stepped in closer as people passed and seemed to try to listen in. "But not in a game. Just throwin' the ball, you know."

"But you've been throwing consistently over the summer with the high school kids and then with your buddy?"

Justin laughed. "Yeah, he's a terrible catcher. I have to literally put it into his hands."

"He's up in five; we have to wrap this up," an assistant said.

Justin turned to his hopefully future head coach. "I'll play whatever position you want."

He nodded, and his coordinator looked pleased as he covered his mouth with his clipboard to hide his expression so no other teams would see.

"Come on," the assistant said, gesturing to his next session.

"We'll talk more later."

"Yes, Coach," Justin said and left to check in.

*

"MAN, WHAT A day," McReedy groaned. "I'm not going to lie. I'm fixin' to straight up take my ass in that bathroom and take a hot bath."

"You want my bubbles?" Justin said with a wink.

McReedy lay on his bed and laughed his ass off without moving, and Justin shook as he joined in.

"Fuckin' bubbles, man," McReedy choked out.

They both froze at the knock on the door but were still goners as McReedy shouted for whoever it was to come in.

"We can't move; just come in. My wallet's on the dresser; just take it," he sputtered, and Justin held his side, wiping his eyes.

He stopped immediately and stood when the offensive coordinator entered.

"Something funny?" he asked, grinning at them.

"McReedy," Justin said as he pulled himself together.

"It wouldn't be as funny retellin' it, Coach," McReedy admitted. "But

I was just groanin' about being sore and lowerin' my standards and checkin' out that bathtub in there. Halstead got a pretty good kick out of it." He sighed and shook his head.

"You've got some time?" the OC said to Justin and, at his nod, continued, "Grab your cleats."

McReedy gave him a wink. Justin threw on a shirt and hoodie. He grabbed his gear bag and followed the OC out.

"We're going to… play catch…so to speak," he explained after Justin got in the SUV.

"All right," Justin said. "Secret catch?"

"Exactly. Glad you're tracking."

They arrived at a high school field, and several key people were there, including a handful of players from the Florida team. Justin's eyes widened, and the OC nodded.

"You are going to throw for me like this is the Superbowl and you want that ring, got it?"

"Yes, sir."

"Stretch and warm up," he said.

After stretching, Justin took a lap around the track, taking note of precisely who was there to watch this very illegal tryout.

Justin returned to the fifty-yard line, where a kid stood by the two bins of balls.

He stuck out his hand. "Justin," he said.

"Matt," the kid said and grinned.

"You got me, Matt?" Justin asked, and the kid looked a little uncertain. "You keep 'em comin' all right?"

"You got it," Matt said.

"I'm a little nervous about this. You?"

"Yeah," the kid admitted.

Justin moved to the center of the field, and Matt tossed him a ball. Justin stepped back and threw to a player, eyes on his hands and imagining they were Ethan's again. The next guy took off running, and Matt tossed, and Justin threw. Then, the big boys came in, and Justin had to throw under pressure, to show them how creative he could get inside and outside the pocket. He had to work for some other passes they called out, and then it was distance.

Just how far could he throw?

"You got this," Matt said, arms full of balls as they moved back ten more yards. Then ten more and ten more still. Then, he was short.

"That's about right," Justin said. "That's my distance."

The coach waved everyone else in, and the OC came out to Justin.

"Hang tight out here for a few." The OC jogged back to discuss with the team players.

"Want some help?" Justin asked Matt, and they dragged the bins down to the endzone and started picking up balls together.

"You work for the team? You seem a little young," Justin said as he and Matt had a little game going of throwing the balls into the bin like basketballs.

Matt giggled. "No, I'm in eighth grade. My dad's here, but I'm not supposed to tell you that. He said he was in a pinch for a secret mission and needed my help."

Justin nodded and showed Matt a trick he knew.

Matt caught on quick and began putting the ball in the bin more times than missing afterward. "That really works," he said, but then the whistle blew, and Justin gave him a salute and ran in.

The team players were gone, and it was just the coaching staff. The OC handed Justin a towel and a water bottle, and Justin sat down in a chair across from them.

"Shit, Halstead, you still got it," the head coach said. "I'm torn. You're a damn fine receiver and a hell of a QB. What to do?"

"I'll play either. It doesn't matter, as long as I play ball," Justin said.

"Reservations. And tell me true," the coach said.

Justin went with honesty. "I don't care for the attention the QB position brings. You already know I'm not a fan of the media. I don't mind giving interviews; I hate being chased and hounded. That position brings on unwanted attention for me, but I'll play it just as hard as I would in a receiver position and hope if no one's open, you'll let me run the ball. Or play me as a receiver and backup QB. We had some success when we switched it up and—" Justin grinned. "—when the receiver was suddenly throwing, and we pulled off a few trick plays." He shrugged.

"I've seen that tape now," the OC said and nodded.

"And the West Coast—when they pull you aside tomorrow and offer you their QB spot? Because I've got to be honest, there were some pretty shocked eyes on you today. We weren't the only ones who overlooked you being on the QB lineup."

"My goal has always been Florida. I want to play for a team that supports their players. My coach listed you as the number one team on his list of where he thought I belonged."

"You have that list?"

"Yes, sir." Justin got up, went to his bag, and took out his wallet. He slipped out the folded paper and handed it over.

The OC looked at it and showed his head coach, and they seemed amused in a good way by the list.

"Okay, Halstead," he said, returning the paper to him.

Then, Justin shook hands with everyone. He followed the OC to the parking lot, where he waved to Matt, and Matt yelled out a "good luck" to him.

The coordinator seemed amused. "Made a friend?"

"Yeah, what a cool kid."

Chapter Twenty-Two

Justin

MCREEDY WAS WATCHING the coverage of the Combine and waved him over. "They're talking about you." He turned up the volume.

A commentator panel sat around a table on one of the major sports networks.

"So, this kid, a tight end, shows up at the Combine, somehow ends up on the QB schedule, and runs through the throwing drills. *Yeah, yeah, let's get this over with, moving right along to what I really play,*" the announcer said and laughed. "And his performance and scores blow all the QB candidates out of the water." They were all hamming it up on the show. "I mean, you can see him muttering about it. Watch this footage. It's just great."

"Fuck," Justin grumbled and sat down at the end of McReedy's bed as McReedy flopped back, laughing his ass off.

Sure enough, Justin watched as *he*, on TV, shook his head and said something as he hurled the ball. Then he was moving along like, *yeah, yeah.*

"And look at these stats," the announcer hooted. "High school state champs *three* years, *this guy*. But this next clip is a classic. A college receiver in the QB position throws a Hail Mary. Sit down, people. You'll be seeing this pass for the next week."

"Fuck." Justin knew the exact pass they were about to show.

McReedy sat up as if he hadn't seen this part yet.

"Look at that score, the time on the clock, the crowd, and watch this…" the announcer was saying. Justin threw the longest, highest pass of his career for the playoff win. And the crowd went absolutely insane, right along with the team and the coaches.

Justin nodded, remembering the moment well.

"Damn, dude," McReedy said. "That shit brings tears to my eyes."

"Yeah."

"*Halstead*, the announcer continued. "Write it down. Remember it as Florida and California duke it out for either the next great quarterback or a future hall of famer receiver. Which will it be? I know where I think he'll land and what position we'll see him playing. Tweet us your votes." The X handle for Justin Halstead popped up across the bottom of the screen.

Justin's phone rang.

"I swear to God," Ethan said. "I mean, we are so fucked."

"I know. I told them I'd rather play receiver or tight end, but I think they're going to push for QB," Justin said quietly as he turned Ethan's shrieking volume down and went out onto the balcony.

"Can we still do this?" Ethan asked, also quiet now.

"I think so, or we can try. Go with the original plan, two years, beach house, and you know the rest."

"Okay, have you seen what they're playing on the network? My Dad is just over the moon, worried, torn," Ethan said. "And now I'm pissed you've been playing catch with me. Of all people, Justin. *My God.*"

"Aww, you're the best person to catch with," Justin said as Ethan momentarily freaked out.

"You're okay?" Ethan asked when he calmed down.

"Yeah, another full day tomorrow and then home. I just miss you."

"Don't say it back, but I love you," Ethan said.

He returned the calls to his dad, John, Shawn, his coach, and ignored all the numbers he didn't recognize from other states, knowing they were probably agents or reps of other teams he had no desire to play for.

"If they put you in QB..." McReedy said.

Justin just realized it. "Holy shit, my center, my man."

"Damn straight," McReedy said with pride. "We'd make a good team."

"I agree. Might make this QB thing worth it."

McReedy high-fived him.

*

JUSTIN RAN HIS ass off, sprinted, and vertical jumped. He cleaned up for final interviews; there were three teams left to meet with. He had a feeling they'd be short meetings.

"I appreciate the interest, but my heart is set in the south," Justin said and thanked them, turning down the hint of one ridiculous offer.

And it was the same with the second one. But the *third*—the third one hit him with a new angle.

"We understand you dislike dealing with the media; you avoid it, sneak out of your locker room, and refuse interviews," the assistant coach said. "There are only a few reasons a player like you would avoid the media like the plague." He nodded knowingly, then held his hands up. "Whatever those reasons may be, we can assure you, no hounding, all interviews with approved questions, and no off-script questions. We will protect you."

Justin leaned back in his chair and thought it over as they waited.

"And if you had a player who presented a media issue," he said finally, "how would you deal with that hypothetical situation?"

Two of the assistants leaned in and spoke quietly to each other, then one turned and whispered something into the coach's ear. Justin wasn't sure what had been said, but the coach seemed pleased, as if understanding they were on the same page. "We respect our players' privacy; they're here to play a game and provide sports entertainment, but they would have our support as long as their media issue was not of an illegal nature. Other than that, we are fully committed to our players, and that would be in your contract."

"Thank you. Seriously, thank you for your time. I have a lot to consider."

They all shook his hand, and he made the call when he left. He met Coach Richardson at a burger joint and explained what the other team had offered.

Richardson chewed his food and wiped his mouth. "We can establish there is a media issue that concerns you, and all you're asking is for us to match the promise they made?"

"Yes, sir. I'm all in as I've said, but they knew what to dangle in front of me."

The coach contemplated this for what seemed like a long time. "And the QB spot puts so much more attention on you," he said, indicating he'd come to some conclusion.

"And I have no interest in being in a particular spotlight."

"You've pulled it off for the last three years. We had no clue."

"I just want to keep it that way and play ball."

"In six months, am I going to be dealing with some picture of you in a bathroom at a club?"

"No sir, I don't party or drink; I rarely go out." Justin chewed on his lip for a moment. "I'm in a committed relationship. Just over a year now."

"I see," the coach said, his eyes widening. "We can swing the approved questions and no off-script. We'll work with our media department and promise support. This is why you don't have an agent?"

Justin nodded.

"Yes," the coach finally said. "But we don't bring anyone else in on this, only you and I. And you'll play for me until we reach a point where we know the gig is up. I'm investing far more into you than you giving me two years."

So apparently, they *did know* a few things about him that he hadn't revealed. Justin closed his eyes and blew out a breath.

"Ah, tough sell," the OC said. "You'd have the same problem with them."

Justin prayed briefly Ethan would forgive him for this. He opened his eyes, decision made. "Yes, sir, I accept. If you still want me—knowing what you do. And if you don't, then I'll sign with them. You have an easy out."

"Oh, no. *I want you*, and I don't know shit," he said, reaching across the table.

"Thank you, Coach," Justin said and shook his hand. "I'm yours."

"I've never had a prospect whose coach was so proud of his player as yours. Just thought you should know that. I have a lot of respect for your coach. And if you play for me like you've played for him, I promise to look out for you as he clearly has done for you the last three years."

"Thank you, I will. I love ball, and *yeah*." Justin smiled. "If you're half the coach he is, I'll still give you my all. He's special."

His coordinator nodded. "You want McReedy then?"

"Definitely."

Richardson smiled too. "You two seem to already have a close bond."

"Yeah, great guy," Justin said.

"I'll let you know if anything changes, but I feel like this is a done deal," he said, and Justin agreed, getting a box for his uneaten food.

"Good, then I can tell you. Matt's my son. Thanks for how you treated him."

"You've got a great kid; tell him I said hi."

They parted ways with another handshake, and Justin took his box and grabbed a taxi back to his hotel. He couldn't wait to tell McReedy. His stomach churned over telling Ethan.

Chapter Twenty-Three

Ethan

ETHAN WAS PRETTY proud of himself. When Justin was out of town, he'd started spending more time at the rink. His stick handling had improved. His shot was more accurate, and though he'd always been a good skater, even he had to admit his speed, stops, and transitions had impressed their coach enough to move him up to the second line. Ethan had always been a third-line hobby player, too busy to put in the true time. They'd won a game, and Ethan had scored a goal.

You'd have thought he was competing in the Olympics and not Wednesday night beer league with the way Justin had acted after he scored, yelling like some beast in the stands, pumping his arms, and high-fiving with people he didn't even know. Ethan had tapped the glass with his stick in an *all-for-you baby* celly before skating down the line for team glove bumps.

After the game, Justin held out his hand and wiggled his fingers expectantly. Sighing, Ethan had dragged back to the equipment room, snagged a puck from the bucket, and returned with his man's prize. It was ridiculous. But the puck sat on a shelf next to a bowl game football, Justin's plaque, and Ethan's cross-country trophy.

Justin's visits were finally over, and they tried to relax as much as possible during the countdown to the draft. ESPN and the NFL Network were a constant back and forth as they watched the coverage and listened to the experts weigh in with draft predictions.

"Do you want to go?" Justin asked for the tenth time.

"I don't think I should," Ethan repeated.

They'd already been over the many reasons. Ethan knew it disappointed Justin, but he honestly thought Justin would blow it. He couldn't ignore Ethan, and there was entirely too much press at the draft.

*

ETHAN THOUGHT THE draft would be a bigger deal. He knew it was huge, but he watched with his father in their living room as Justin walked on stage, put on a team hat, and was presented with a jersey.

Ethan pointed at the screen. "He kept his number."

"Sure did," his father said.

Then things moved along at a clipped pace as Justin's five seconds of fame ended, and they waited to see if McReedy got snatched or if Florida could pull it off.

"Think I was wrong for not going?" Ethan asked as he chewed on a nail nervously.

"Nope. He asked, and you told him how you felt about it. He respected your decision and agreed with your reasons."

"I'm not hiding," Ethan said.

"I know. You are protecting the person you love, Ethan."

"Thanks, Dad."

*

"I'M KIND OF sad. I feel like we just moved in," Ethan said, frowning at the boxes.

"I know, but staying with your parents until we find a house and putting all this in storage until then is the best plan," Justin said for the tenth time. "It's a cool apartment; I'll miss it too. And then you'll start your new school, and we'll have a little time to spend at the beach. We'll have to check out the league teams your coach told you about."

Ethan nodded and taped the last box. "I want a dog after we find a house."

"I will get you a dog," Justin agreed at once. "And you get to pick the houses, top three, and then we decide together."

Ethan pointed at the last box expectantly, giving Justin a hopeful look.

Justin laughed. "Oh my God, I've spoiled you." Then, he picked up the heavy box with a roll of his eyes.

Ethan, pleased, followed him out to the parking lot, giving a little whistle at Justin's muscular arms as he loaded the books into the U-Haul.

"Stop. I'm all sweaty," Justin said.

"Hot," Ethan teased.

And then they were on the road. Ethan rode shotgun as Justin drove.

Ethan watched their city disappear in the sideview mirror, then focused on the road ahead.

"It's really happening."

Justin glanced over. "Yeah, babe, our dreams are happening."

"Scary," Ethan said.

"Is this too much change?"

"Absolutely, but I think the all-at-once approach is going to be easier to handle, honestly. I haven't had time to let my brain kick into overdrive. I do think going to my parents as a transition will be good for me."

"We'll take our time and find the perfect house, a house you love and feel safe at."

"I know. Spoiled, remember?" Ethan knew he was a lucky man with a partner who treated him like he was the most important person in the world.

"Well, if we're diving in headfirst…" Justin started, exhibiting a few of his nervous tells as he drove.

"Yes?"

"What if we, uh, I mean… I know we can't do it for real yet, but what if we could do something private, just us, and go ahead and get married?"

"Oh my God, Justin, we're in a U-Haul, and we stink," Ethan said, outraged.

Justin laughed. "I already asked you to marry me. This isn't that; this is just wondering out loud. Couldn't we do something special for now?"

Ethan chewed on a nail, thinking. "Sure, Justin. On top of finding our dream house and an ice rink in sunny Florida, I'll plan our fake wedding." He waited while Justin lost it, then added affectionately, "You really are ridiculous."

"Nah, I really love you, and there are *five* rinks in Tampa."

"Fine," Ethan said, resigned. "I'll look into it."

"That's a yes."

"Yes, it's a yes." And Ethan relaxed, contented, as Justin drove on, wearing an unerasable smile for miles.

"Are there really five?"

"Sure are."

*

A WEEK LATER, after getting temporarily settled with his parents, Ethan clapped gleefully as Justin held up the two giant ferns. "Yes, those are perfect."

It had been their last stop. They'd already been by the party rental place where they picked up the white arbor. His parents' backyard was the setting. Simple, the arbor and two ferns. His mother had already bought enough flowers and candles to decorate with. Justin's parents were coming down for the private ceremony. Surprisingly, his father asked to officiate, and Justin and Ethan had both instantly agreed.

Justin was excited since part of their plan was to lay out all the houses they'd found and see what everyone thought while they were all there. He'd said something about some legal matters he had to handle with his father and Ethan's.

"Okay, after this, I'll drop you off. I need to run an errand," Ethan said.

"Oh, what do you need? I'll take you," Justin said.

"Nope."

"No?"

"I know you aren't used to that word," Ethan said playfully, "but I have a plan that doesn't involve you."

"Ohh," Justin said, stretching out the word. "We really should come up with a code word for those situations."

"I've got one we can say. 'Golf game.'"

"Why?"

"Because never in my life will I ever play golf; well, I'd play Putt-Putt, but real golf? Never. And I've never even heard you mention it, but I have seen you flip past it on the TV."

"'Golf game.' All right, that works," Justin agreed. "So, you have a golf game?"

"Exactly."

Justin frowned.

"What?"

"Well, now I really don't like golf," Justin said with disappointment.

"I'll be gone for, like, an hour," Ethan soothed. "You'll survive."

"I might not."

"Now, who is spoiled?"

Chapter Twenty-Four

Justin

THEY'D FINALLY FOUND *the* house in a gated beach community farther north than they'd imagined but closer to Ethan's parents. Though Justin would have a commute, the house was their dream. The privacy alone ensured they could keep their heads down but still breathe. And the team would provide Justin with a small apartment close to their facilities. He'd stay there, just as he had in the football dorm during practices and game days, then drive back home to Ethan when he could. There just weren't any houses in the Bay that worked for what they needed, and Justin agreed with John. Having Ethan closer to them in case something happened was also better.

The upscale neighborhood had many wealthy retirees with large, well-built houses, which were older than some of the more modern beach homes farther south. It was quiet, safe, and gated, with security walls and 24/7 security guards. Ethan felt good about it and was aware of Justin's relief that Ethan would be ultra-safe there alone. And while there was only one local rink, Ethan liked it, affectionately calling it "retro," letting Justin know it would do.

John had officiated a private, off-the-record ceremony in their back-yard, and Ethan had gotten Justin a ring. They said their vows, everyone cried, and they signed a certificate John found somewhere. None of it legal because that would be too easily discovered. Still, they felt married, and this would do until Justin left the NFL, when they could do it legally.

Justin had also hired a lawyer, written out a will and trust for Ethan with his father's and John's help, and put everything in Ethan's name. He authorized a living will, giving Ethan power of attorney over any decisions should something happen to him. He paid for Ethan's insurance since he couldn't add him to his policy, and they worked through other legal issues as best they could for now. Ethan knew some of it, not all, but Justin wanted to ensure Ethan was taken care of. He worried that telling Ethan all of this would cause anxiety he didn't need. His father and John had promised to make sure *all* his wishes for Ethan were fulfilled, but both hoped they'd never have to keep those promises.

"You never know," Justin had told them both, and they'd witnessed everything without any arguments.

Justin was spending the day with his parents and looked down at the list Ethan had made out for him.

"Two lamps, and we are in the clear," Justin said, and they headed to the new house.

"I think we got off easy," his dad said.

"Ethan knows shopping isn't my favorite pastime."

"They're handling the kitchen and living room, and we've only got the master bedroom and game room," his father confirmed, rubbing his hands together over the game room.

Justin enjoyed the rest of the day with his parents and later, as his and Ethan's parents worked together to help them create a home. He still couldn't get over his signing bonus and the whirlwind of the draft.

"We have a pool and a hot tub," Ethan whispered as they stood next to them.

"And not a single patio chair. You left out a room."

"I got you something," Ethan said.

Justin grinned. "Give it to me."

Ethan pointed to the far corner of the pool deck, just past where it ended and within a few trees and foliage. "See the top of it, just through those palm things?"

"Palm things," Justin repeated. "Wait, is that a chiminea?" Justin busted out laughing.

"It was Dad's idea."

"That's great," Justin said as they walked over to look at it. "We need an outdoor area here and then the chairs for the pool deck. I think I want a grill too."

"I agree. I'm glad I forgot it. It'll give me a project when everyone leaves."

They headed back inside to help their parents and do all they could to get everything settled. With two spare bedrooms, their parents could stay over when they came for visits and football games. Justin's parents were already looking for something in the same area. Coach and Bethany had debated it, but Coach just couldn't leave his team yet. Justin and Ethan both understood that. So, they had a bedroom at Justin and Ethan's house. Bethany planned a short visit for the first week when Justin left. Ethan wanted to learn his way around town and check out the touristy side of things with her.

Justin had worked hard to get everything out of storage and moved into the new house. They no longer had a rented space but now had a mortgage. They still had some boxes needing to be unpacked, but Ethan didn't seem to be in a rush to do everything all at once. Their parents had left to give them time alone before Justin had to go for training.

*

JUSTIN STOOD IN their driveway in front of his open garage and just stared at the empty space. Ethan's new compact barely occupied any room, and Justin had no intention of parking his truck inside. He considered the area, deciding it would be an excellent place for all the toys he planned to buy for himself and Ethan. Kayaks and bikes. Maybe an air hockey table for Ethan's strange obsession with that game. Their meager camping gear currently sat on one of the lonely shelves. There wasn't even a single tool. The Home Depot beat theme song faintly played in Justin's mind, Josh Lucas, beckoning him to fill the space.

Ethan had already designated the room next to the garage as their home gym, so *this* was up for grabs. Justin turned, gazed out at the lush lawn and tropical beds, and realized they had no lawnmower. Justin laughed as he studied the pristine yard with a more suspicious eye.

"Hey there." A man waved from across the street.

Justin waved back.

"I gotta know what's so funny," the man asked, motioning at Justin's lawn.

"I just realized we don't have a lawnmower," he admitted to the guy.

He crossed the street toward Justin. "Most people around here use a service. I think you might just be the youngest person in this neighborhood. I'm Frank Fortner." He stuck out his hand.

"Justin. Nice to meet you," Justin said and shook his hand.

"Welcome to the neighborhood; a nice place you've bought," Frank said. "The last neighbor was a doctor, but he got transferred to a hospital in another state."

Justin knew what was coming, but he and Ethan had decided there wasn't much hiding from neighbors, and they'd just wing it with Justin using Ethan's last name and hoping no one recognized him.

"Fat chance," Ethan had said at the idea.

"Well, I hope we'll be even better neighbors than your last," Justin said. "You like your service?"

"Oh, yeah, they come once weekly and do about six yards in a row on a schedule. I'll bring you their card. They did this lawn for the previous owner, so you really can't go wrong with them. I want to say they did the pool, but don't hold me to that."

Justin said with amusement, "I may use them for the lawn, but I've got a pool guy."

"Getting settled in then?" Frank peeked past Justin to the empty garage and his lone truck parked behind them in the drive.

"Yeah, I was just out here imagining everything I need to buy to fill that beauty up. An empty garage almost feels wrong. It's almost un-

American, ya know?" Justin said, and they moved onto the lawn as Ethan turned into the driveway in his sporty little Infiniti with the worst timing ever. He pulled into the garage and joined them.

Justin flung his arm over Ethan's shoulders. "Ethan, this is our neighbor Frank Fortner. Frank, Ethan."

"Nice to meet you," Ethan said. "Which house?"

"Right across the street," Frank said, studying them, the rings on their fingers, and returning to Justin.

Justin nodded to confirm what Frank was putting together.

"Thank God!" Frank exclaimed as he blew out a breath. He turned and waved wildly at his house, then grinned back at them. "I want to introduce you to my husband."

"No shit," Justin burst out, and they all laughed as Frank's other half came jogging across the street.

"Oh boy, we were sweating it," Frank said. "The last neighbor was a real dick, to be honest."

Justin held out his hand to Frank's husband. "Justin Halstead and Ethan Halstead," he said with pride as they shook Donovan Fortner's hand.

"Oh, man, we'll all joke about this later," Donovan said, standing next to Frank. "Frank's been peeking through the blinds trying to figure out just who our new neighbors were.

"Our parents helped us get settled in," Ethan said. "I bet that was confusing."

"Halstead…" Frank said and turned to Justin.

"See, *I told you*," Ethan started. "It was never going to work. Go on, Frank."

"First-round draft pick Halstead?" Frank said slowly.

"If you could keep that between neighbors, I can't tell you how much I'd appreciate it," Justin said with a frown.

"Oh no…" Frank nodded, then shook his head. "No, I get it. *Jesus.*" Then he covered his mouth and looked at Ethan, then back to Justin, down at Ethan's finger, then Justin's again.

"Exactly," Justin said.

"That's why you're this far north," Frank said, understanding.

"I have no idea what you're talking about," Donovan said.

"Sports." Frank sighed.

"Oh," Donovan said, clearly not a fan, and Ethan snickered.

"Secret's safe with us," Frank said. "My brother-in-law"—Frank thumbed at his husband and winked—"moved in after his divorce."

"The things we do, huh?"

"So, is it just us?" Ethan waggled his finger between the two houses.

"Nope, we got lesbians down at the end there, but the rest—" Frank shrugged. "A few old shits who will bitch if you don't drag your trashcan back in on trash day, but they mostly stay in the AC or are only here for winter."

"We love it here, no problems," Donovan said.

"Good," Ethan said, brightening.

"What are the chances?" Frank seemed pleased to find out he had new neighbors he would like.

"I gotta go; I've got groceries in the car. Sorry," Ethan said.

"Yeah, be there to help in a second." Justin waited until Ethan was out of earshot. "I'll be out of town a lot. Do you guys mind keeping an eye on the place when he's here alone?"

"Yeah, man," Frank and Donovan both said, and they shook hands with Justin once more before heading back across the street, holding hands.

Justin carried the rest of the bags inside.

"They were *so us* in like twenty years," Ethan said as he put things away.

"Yeah, I see that. And by the way, we don't have a lawnmower."

"Are *you* mowing the yard?" Ethan stopped and pointed to himself, shaking his head. "Because I'm responsible for that pool. *That*, husband, is the life you promised. There was never any mention of yard work."

Justin, always so amused by Ethan, responded happily, "No, I was going to see if you'd agree for me to just hire the service that's been doing it. They do Frank and Donovan's and, like, four others on our street."

"Oh," Ethan said, nodding. "Yeah, the service, then."

Justin sensed zero anxiety from Ethan and could tell he was in a good mood. "You want kayaks or bikes?"

"Bikes. That garage bothers you *so bad*. I knew it would."

Justin leaned on the island and looked around their home.

"It's coming together," Ethan said as he moved in beside him.

"Will you be happy here?"

"Yes, and it feels safe. I am more at ease than I have been in a long time."

"Good." Justin kissed his cheek. "Run or swim or catch?"

"Catch," Ethan grumbled. "Because I know that's what you want to do."

Justin smirked and went to grab a ball. Their new backyard was big, with the pool and patio area, a secluded shaded portion with large trees, native tropicals, and a long green space along the side before a retaining wall, gate, and path down to the beach. They were in an inlet but within walking distance of the main beach. Still, they had a beach-front property with the privacy they'd thought would be impossible to find.

Justin threw the ball, and Ethan lobbed it back. He was pleased at how much better Ethan's throw had gotten over the last six months. Justin threw again and imagined setting up some drill nets in the space to make things a little more challenging for Ethan and for more downtime practice for himself. Back and forth they went until Ethan complained his arm would fall off again.

"What kind of dog?" Justin said as he picked up the ball from the lazy wobbling throw Ethan hurled at him. "We'd need a fenced area."

"They make invisible ones. And no, I'm thinking something small, but I want to wait and see how the school plan and your games go first. I don't want to get a pet and be too busy."

"Smart, we'll wait and see," Justin said, pulling off his sweaty shirt.

They swam and cooled off, with Justin teasing about every leaf and a floating bug or two. He pointed at the long dip net on the back wall of the house with amused satisfaction and already knew he was going to enjoy this teasing game with Ethan for years to come.

"You suck," Ethan said, laughing as he climbed over the pool wall into the hot tub.

"Too hot," Justin said as he propped his arms on the wall and stuck his hand in. "Or not? Did you turn it down?"

Ethan nodded, and Justin climbed over as Ethan reached out and turned on the jets. They sat together in their slightly warm hot tub and talked about all they planned to do. Justin relaxed as Ethan talked about flowerpots and outdoor furniture, where he would put everything and some new plans for inside.

When he stopped and looked over, Justin smiled.

"I love you," he said.

"I love you too. So, the color for the living room?"

"Yes," Justin said, agreeing to whatever Ethan wanted. He tugged Ethan over onto his lap, and Ethan leaned back on him. "Keep telling me."

And Ethan relaxed and told him about all his other ideas.

Chapter Twenty-Five

Justin

JUSTIN SAT AT a long table with the other new additions to the team in the media room full of reporters and journalists. The team owner stood at the podium. McReedy sat next to Justin. The owner talked about how pleased he was with the results of this year's draft and his hopes for the season. He turned it over to his head coach, who began the official introductions of his new players, giving stats and brief bios on each one.

Justin had agreed to this press conference because there was no getting around it. The media coordinator told him most of the questions would likely be geared around his QB time.

"So, as you all know, I went looking for a receiver and a quarterback—" Coach Nellis paused as they all laughed. He scratched his head, playing it up. "—and we got a great receiver. Nick Chastain." Coach nodded down at him. He gave a bio on Nick and his stats.

"Then, I needed a center." He gave McReedy's spiel.

"But I hadn't prepared for the quarterback we found," he said into the microphone, then waited as flashes went off and news cameras rolled.

"Justin Halstead surprised us all. I'm sure you've all seen the footage of the Combine, but what you might not have seen, and I admittedly lost a bet and have to show you—" He paused, hamming it up. "—is this clip." He turned to watch it again.

Justin had already seen it, and it was damn funny. The coaching staff at the Combine was looking bored. An assistant pointed out to the gridiron, read off a name from his clipboard, and then they were all suddenly watching the player on the field throwing the ball. Coach's mouth opened, and he dropped his drink when he also pointed, shaking his head. His offensive coordinator hustled down the aisle to get a closer look, and then the six scrambled to get down to the field.

"Yeah, you won't see that reaction often," Coach said as the clip ended. "But we were as shocked as everyone else that day. So, I'll introduce Justin and give you *two* sets of stats." He went through Justin's high school QB stats and then his college TE stats. He spoke briefly, confirming they had no doubts about Justin's ability as QB and the three-year gap out of the position. Coach moved on to the new defensive players, and then it was question time.

Justin got the first one about McReedy and starting a new team with a new QB and a new center. He answered it fine, praising McReedy and saying he was confident they would work well together. The reporters asked each player questions, all pretty standard stuff, nothing stressful. Justin was pleased with the media event as they posed for pictures, and then it wrapped up.

They all had meetings after the press was gone: paperwork with legal, additional contracts, and any insurance changes. The new players would return in the morning for the equipment managers, which would fill the rest of the day as they were loaded down, shown to their locker room, and went through the ID card and security process.

Justin had to be back the next morning for an offensive line and special teams meeting and to get his official playbook. Then, he would return in two weeks to start training.

*

ETHAN HELD HIS hands up to the giant whiteboard and wiggled his fingers at the marker holder he'd also managed to mount to the wall in their shared office while Justin had been gone.

"What have you done?" Justin asked with pride and amusement as he sat on the small couch next to their shared desk.

"We're learning plays. You have to learn that book, and if I seriously want to consider sports reporting, this helps me too. And for more selfish reasons, so I understand what you're doing down there."

"Good idea, then. I have two weeks to memorize these plays like they are my social."

"We are on this," Ethan said, plucking up a marker and glancing over his shoulder.

Justin opened the binder and called out the name of the first play. By the next afternoon, Ethan had a television and VCR/DVD combo set up, and they were studying discs of the plays the OC had sent. Justin had wanted the combo to view older game tapes; somehow, Ethan had found one.

Ethan was great, quizzing Justin and learning along with him. They practiced out on the lawn, Ethan moving into a position he'd learned as Justin called out the plays, walking through them. Then they were back in their little classroom, going through the playbook each day and watching the films until they had it.

Justin practiced in the backyard with his passing nets, and he'd been right that Ethan did enjoy the new challenge. He enjoyed it until Justin snatched the ball and ran into the house with it. Justin stripped down in the bathroom with the shower already on, knowing Ethan would follow him.

"Sneaky," Ethan praised.

"Hopeful," Justin agreed.

"You're on."

And Ethan eagerly lost his clothes, joining Justin.

"I'm first," Justin said, lowering himself to the tile floor.

"Pretend like you don't know what you're doing," Ethan challenged. "You've gotten too good at this, and I'm going to go off like a teenager on prom night."

"You did that when I sucked at this," Justin reminded him.

"Nice choice of words."

Justin laughed, then got serious. He loved doing this to Ethan, loved his reactions, the faces and sounds he made, and how his legs would begin to shake as things intensified—when that constant tension abandoned Ethan's face, and he was just Ethan, *just his*.

Justin pulled his mouth away, and Ethan panted the answer before he could even ask it.

"Yes, I'm yours."

Justin returned his mouth, resuming until Ethan shuddered and gripped his shoulders to stay upright.

"Bedroom," Ethan said as he gasped for breath.

They rinsed and raced to bed, barely drying off and diving in. Ethan was on him, taking him down, his hand eager and exploring. He'd recently begun exploring other regions of Justin's body since Justin had expressed his sexual desire. Justin fumbled into the bedside drawer and tossed the tube down the bed. He loved this, Ethan's slick fingers exploring inside him until he found that place that made Justin beg.

When Ethan paused, Justin looked down to Ethan staring at where his fingers were buried, and then he gazed up at Justin.

"Ethan, you won't hurt me. You would never hurt me."

"I wouldn't."

"You can stop. Or you can try," Justin said quietly.

Ethan swallowed and repeated, "I would never hurt you."

"I want you, all of you, but not until you're ready."

Ethan grabbed the tube, slicked his fingers again, and lay over Justin, kissing him. Justin thrilled at Ethan's fingers returning, first one, then two. With the new pressure of an unfamiliar third, Ethan slowed, stretching Justin's body carefully. Justin relaxed as he adjusted. Ethan shifted, his fingers withdrawing and replaced by hot slick skin pressing in.

Justin shuddered at the wild, unexpected thrill of Ethan breaching him for the first time, but the pressure was intense. The bare heat of Ethan as he pushed past and paused, breathing hard against Justin's chest, was a new milestone. The burn and stretch subsided as Justin willed himself to relax, and Ethan groaned as Justin's body seemed to pull him in more.

Ethan's hips pressed forward, following the pull, and he looked up at Justin, pausing again.

Justin used his hands at Ethan's waist to encourage him deeper, his body stretching as Ethan pressed in further.

"We're almost there," Ethan said through pants of restraint.

"I'm okay, keep going," Justin said, not in pain but figuring out how he felt about this strange and new experience he'd wanted so much, whether he wanted Ethan all the way in or entirely out.

"This is strange," Justin admitted, trying to widen his legs as he sought out something other than discomfort and immense pressure.

Ethan pushed Justin's knee back with his hand and moved in and stilled.

Justin breathed hard, a sheen of sweat blooming. "Okay, I need a second."

Ethan lay quiet, his free hand gripping Justin's shoulder tightly as Justin struggled through acceptance and the resistance within his body. Justin finally eased, and Ethan sucked in a breath, and then Justin moved, a timid rocking as Ethan began to shake.

The strange tension left Justin as Ethan lifted up, and he had a clear line of sight as Ethan's hips slowly withdrew from between his legs. Justin reached down and pulled his other knee up as Ethan's eyes rolled back, and he pushed back in with one careful thrust and disappeared inside Justin completely.

"Okay, yeah, that's better," Justin decided as it became increasingly easier, and Ethan began a steadier push and pull, slick, hot, and gliding as his hips moved. The sight and sensation started turning Justin on—Ethan's hips, his bare skin and tight muscles above him, feeling so much more of him than ever before. Ethan was strong, hard, and soft at the same time, and it was clear how careful Ethan was being with him. Justin had an unfamiliar sense of being owned and loved simultaneously. He found the new dynamic insanely appealing.

"Still okay?" Ethan asked.

"Don't you dare stop. That first part was rough, but this is starting to get better."

Ethan lowered his upper body, only his hips pumping as he rocked in and out carefully as Justin got more accustomed to the sensation of his body being filled, the emptiness, then the fullness again each time Ethan's groin was flush with his.

"Yeah, okay, really starting to feel good," Justin babbled, lifting his hips to seek Ethan's thrusts. "Kiss me."

And Ethan did. A slow, sweet kiss quickly morphed into something more intense as Ethan thrust against that undefinable place, sending shocking jolts through Justin as he gripped Ethan harder and begged him not to stop. Ethan picked up the pace, but Justin could tell he still held back. Ethan was focused and quiet, and Justin prayed that was all that was on his mind as Ethan kissed his chest and touched his skin.

Then, Ethan shocked him.

"You are mine, Justin Fucking Halstead, and I *will be* the man you deserve," Ethan said, and then he lifted Justin's leg over his shoulder, shifted in closer, and lifted Justin's other leg over. Something seemed to release its crippling grip on Ethan as he got lost in making love to Justin. Then, he owned Justin's body as it seemed all the fear left Ethan, and their bodies filled the room with a steady slapping sound. Ethan's hips pounded into him. The hot, slick, pistoning grew faster until Justin vibrated with the electric shock and greedy sensation, demanding Ethan never stop. He felt so connected to Ethan and didn't take for granted what a monumental milestone this was, not only for Justin but more so for Ethan.

Justin panted, stomach streaked, sheets soaked. Heat like he'd never known filled him as Ethan flopped down next to him, his hair sweat-slicked to his forehead and tiny perspiration dots above his lip as he stared at the ceiling for only a second before turning his head to the side and then crushing himself to Justin.

Justin wrapped his arms around Ethan and squeezed him tight. "Thank you," he whispered, "for giving yourself to me, for trusting me."

"I never knew it could be something beautiful. I mean, I knew it was supposed to be like this, but…" Justin felt Ethan swallow against his skin. "…that was my first time making love like that."

And sadly, Justin knew what was coming next as Ethan began to cry.

"Shh," Justin soothed as he stroked Ethan's back.

"They hurt me so bad," Ethan sobbed.

"I know; let it out, baby. Give me your demons, and we'll fight them together."

"It's so unfair—what they took. It should have been yours, my choice. It should have been something beautiful like you, and it shouldn't have ever happened."

"I've got you. No one will ever hurt you again, Ethan."

Justin soothed as Ethan cried through a ragged bout, then slowly subsided. As Ethan sniffled and clung to him, Justin's chest was wet with his tears.

"You are my rock," Justin whispered. "My everything. You are stronger than you even know. This was a big step for you." Justin winced a little. "And for me."

Ethan lifted his head, looking worried. "I hurt you?"

"Not hurt, but that was a first for me. I'm okay. I think a little sore maybe."

"Come on." Ethan roughly wiped his face and tugged at Justin's hand as he got up.

Justin eased out of bed and, feeling not only the absence of Ethan inside him but the ache of the new experience. Ethan led him to their bathroom and filled the large jacuzzi tub they'd never used. Justin handled his business in the bathroom, then climbed in and eased down with Ethan behind him. He leaned back as Ethan quietly washed him, then rubbed his shoulders and arms and massaged his thighs until Justin was mush. Tenderness forgotten, Justin closed his eyes and enjoyed Ethan taking care of him.

"I'm sorry for that breakdown," Ethan whispered.

"Don't you ever apologize. I was prepared for it."

"You were?"

"I met with your therapist when we began trying new things. I wanted to be sure I didn't do something wrong. She said it might be difficult for you if we decided to have penetrative sex. It helped to understand what emotions you might experience and how intimacy could bring back unwanted memories. She warned me not to overreact or take it personally if you got upset."

"I love you," Ethan said, and Justin knew it, but it never lost its effect when Ethan said it first. "I want a do-over."

Justin smiled. "No, but you can do it again. I want everything with you, Ethan—the good, the bad, the difficult. All of it. No do-overs. We just keep making new memories together."

Chapter Twenty-Six

Justin

AND THEN IT was time.

Ethan was good, Bethany had arrived, and they had big plans to-gether. Justin would be back for the weekend and then go again. Justin kept telling himself it was going to all work out. If he had a winning team, that was his best offense against nosey reporters.

He'd already said goodbye to Bethany, then dragged Ethan into the garage and kissed him silly until Ethan's hair was a mess, his lips red, and he looked so damn hot like that; Justin kissed him again.

"When I get home," Justin warned.

Ethan's cheeks matched his lips, but he shot Justin a surprisingly sexy smirk, bit his lip, and seemed on board.

JUSTIN DRESSED IN his practice gear and checked out his jersey. He'd gotten to keep his lucky number, had asked for it before the draft, and was now in the NFL, sporting number fourteen. It'd been his lucky number since peewee league; there was respect for superstition in sports. He headed out with the rest of the team. They were starting the season with him, a brand-new quarterback after their last one had finally retired, and they'd restructured. So, he wasn't the only new face or replaced player.

"We got this. You and me and communication." McReedy waggled a finger between them.

"Hell yeah, we've got this, man, you and me, from start to finish."

"That's right, brotha'."

It was an adjustment getting used to the helmet and technology he wasn't familiar with and hearing the calls in his ear. Justin called out the first play, and they ran it, with him and McReedy getting accustomed to each other and learning what worked between them. A little confusion on the line, but they reran it, and it was one down as they began working their way through the plays in their bible.

Justin dripped sweat, breathing hard as did everyone else, and McReedy, a farm-grown player, gloated as he handed Justin a bottle.

"'I want the beach,'" McReedy mocked. "Gonna get me a beach house, and then I'm gonna sweat my balls off in the Florida sunshine."

Justin grinned.

"Didn't think about all that heat and the sun," McReedy teased.

"I hate the snow and cold. Do you hear me complaining?" Justin said.

"Nah, man. Just, your pores are all cryin'."

And then they drilled and drilled, and Justin was the one who thought *his* arm would fall off. He had work to do; breathing in the sauna-like humid heat was nothing like breathing in the north. The week was hell. Justin told Ethan they were buying an ice machine and turning the hot tub into an ice bath.

And it was 24/7 football; if they weren't on the field, they were viewing tape, meeting with the coaching staff, drilling, running, working out, physicals and medical, and then repeat. Justin loved it and hated it all at the same time. He felt like he was dying and living simultaneously in the Sunshine State.

"It's just pain. It's subjective, you know." McReedy panted and nodded as they did it again and again until they got it right.

"Dude," McReedy groaned.

"I can't even talk to you right now." Justin had his head back on the rim of the tub in freezing-ass water. "Bubbles." It was all he got out, and he quirked his lip at McReedy's weak-ass laugh next to him.

They dragged themselves out to go eat and barely nodded their heads at the veteran players, who gave them amused looks as they passed by.

"Hang in there; it gets easier," said Holcombe, a beast on their defensive line.

Justin managed one nod. Coming from Holcombe, it wasn't all that reassuring. He was the kind of guy who snuck into dark alley dreams and opposing teams' nightmares. Justin stepped up to the counter and got his food. They sat with Chastain, who looked like he could fall asleep sitting up.

"Fuck, I feel like I'm eighty," Justin said as he eased himself into his chair.

"You may have to help me up," Chastain admitted.

"Eat," McReedy said, and they did, but it was mechanical with zero conversation.

Justin drove to his apartment in a daze. He managed to set his alarm clocks, sent Ethan a text, and crashed out hard on his bed. Football for the majority of his life still had not prepared him for this. The alarms went off entirely too soon, and he was at it again for another torture day. His offensive coordinator, Coach Richardson, officially owned his ass and put him through the wringer daily. By Thursday, it was all becoming a blur.

"Halstead, see me after practice," Coach Richardson said at the end of their first Friday on the turf, so Justin made his way to his office after a quick meeting with his quarterback assistant coordinator and the other QBs.

"Close the door," Richardson said. "Brutal, right?"

"I was not prepared," Justin admitted, sitting down.

"You're doing well. I'm pleased. You have a good handle on the playbook, getting adjusted to the helmet and technology. In another week, you'll be better acclimated. You and McReedy are working well together. So, thoughts?"

"Breathing and getting used to the humidity. If that improves, then I'll be fine; that's my only concern."

"It is difficult, coming from a cold, dry climate to a tropical one. Give it time. Hydrate, you know the routine." Richardson handed him a clipboard. "Anyone on that list you want to keep?"

Justin worked his way down the names, realizing it was a cut list. He studied each one carefully and thought about the first full week of practice—who had shown qualities and who was not an asset to the team. Justin looked up.

"Can I write on this?" he asked.

Richardson handed him a pencil and leaned back. "Think out loud."

Justin let out a tired sigh but went down the list, pointing out what he thought about each player and making short notes.

"Scratch, bad attitude, confrontational with other players and staff," Justin said and moved to the next. "Good character, determined, good work ethic but lacks some skills. Keep."

And so it went as Justin crossed off names and circled others, making notes, and then he was done. He returned the board and sat back. Richardson tore the page off, laid it next to the one underneath, and compared them.

"Miller. Convince me," he said.

"I'd give Miller another week if he can get the plays down; he's got real skill. Maybe get someone to work with him on the playbook. Otherwise, I think he could be a keeper."

"Jones," he said next.

"Horrible attitude, phenomenal skill, that's a hard call."

"How would you handle it if you were sitting here?"

"Oh, do I get to be blunt?" Justin asked, unsure.

"Yeah, this stays in here," Coach said, leaning back again.

"If it were me, I'd call him in here and tell him he has a QB who wants to go to the Superbowl with him, and his talent is amazing, but his attitude and mouth are going to damage this team, and that can't happen. I'd lay down the law, tell him to change or leave because I can take Chastain to the Superbowl just fine too."

Richardson nodded. "Hernandez."

"Keep if you can; I'd take Hernandez over Jones because Hernandez will work for it twice as hard and not be an asshole. He has room to grow."

"Those are the only ones we differed on." Richardson stacked the papers. "You all settled into your apartment?"

"Yes. But I'm getting blackout curtains today," Justin said seriously.

"And your other place?"

"Great, couldn't be happier."

"I wanted to know—since you can't put down your emergency contact—do you want to give me that information in case a call ever needs to be made?"

"Yes, thank you." Justin wrote down Ethan's name, their address, and his phone number. Justin looked up at his coach. "Can I trust you?"

"Yes," Coach Richardson said.

"This is everything to me."

"And it will not leave my possession or be shared with anyone."

Justin passed the paper across the desk. Coach glanced down at the information and nodded. Then he locked it in his drawer.

"I'm going to think a little longer on Hernandez and Miller. I'm cutting the rest we agreed on today. Go tell Jones I want to see him," Richardson said.

"Yes, sir." Justin headed out to find Jones.

"Fuck," Jones said, and Justin stopped him.

"Be respectful; listen to him. Leave your attitude at the door, man." Justin said and went on a search for Miller.

"Hey, Justin," Miller said sadly. "Coach wants to see me? I figured."

"No, man, I wanted to talk to you about the playbook." Justin sat beside him.

"Oh, uh, ok."

"Let's take a look at yours, see where we're getting our lines crossed."

Justin went over the plays, remembering Miller bumbling with Justin's play call, asking where he'd gotten confused.

Miller was adjusting to playing the other side, and Justin asked if he thought switching back to the right side would make it easier until he got the plays down and could master either side. Miller nodded.

"This is the one I completely blew," Miller said.

"I'm shit tired, but you want to run through it?" Justin asked. "We can walk it."

"Yeah," Miller said, and they headed out to the nearly empty field with the playbook. Justin and Miller went through the moves until Miller worked through it on the right and nodded that he was getting it. Then they moved to the left and started again.

"Halstead, Miller, go home," Coach Richardson called out.

Miller shook Justin's hand and thanked him. He hustled off the field as Justin grabbed his bag and helmet to follow.

"And?" Richardson asked.

"He's a stronger right-side player; he needs to learn the plays there first and then move him over to the left," Justin said, and Richardson nodded.

"Jones?" Justin braved to ask as they walked out together.

"He's got one week to prove himself, or I'm cutting him. Be careful driving home. Three hours…" Richardson whistled.

"I know." Justin shrugged.

"See you Monday," Richardson said and headed to his car.

Justin had just reached his truck and was stretching for the long drive. He looked back as the Mustang pulled up and the window rolled down.

"Thanks," Jones said.

"For?" Justin turned, leaning on the window frame.

"Telling Coach to give me a shot and not cut me yet."

"Lose the attitude on the field, and I'll keep fighting for you."

"Thanks, see you Monday."

Justin yawned and climbed into his truck.

Chapter Twenty-Seven

Ethan

WATCHING JUSTIN DRIVE away was sobering and scary, like an open invitation for all of Ethan's insecurities and fears to flood back in. His mom was here, and for that, he was grateful. But at the same time, Ethan didn't want to call it a need to grow up, as much as he wanted to continue on his path of healing and make real progress in this new place and life. While he often got frustrated with his counselor, after a few days of thinking about her suggestions, he'd begin to see things in a clearer light.

She'd won the codependency argument. Ethan had found a group online that ran together three days a week. He had a meeting scheduled with the coach of the local beer league, though they didn't call it that here—the "adult league"—and he'd have to try out for the team as expected. The coach had agreed to a meeting and the possibility of making Ethan an alternate since the team had already had tryouts for their current season. So that was on the schedule, along with a plan to meet up with the running group after his mom left.

Ethan pressed the garage door button and waited as it closed. Inside, he found his mom in the kitchen, sorting through the pod options at the coffee maker.

"You and Dad need to get one of those," Ethan said.

"Maybe for our anniversary," she agreed. "Are you okay?"

"Yeah, *no*. It's going to be hard with him gone. But I'm determined to find things that interest me like my therapist said."

"What does Justin think?"

"You know him; it's whatever I want." Ethan turned the coffee carousel and plucked out the pod he wanted. "But the therapist is always bitching at me about my happiness and not being dependent on Justin."

"Well, listen to her, talk to Justin, and make the decisions that are best for you. There's no ticking clock, Ethan."

"Thanks, Mom," Ethan said as she reached over and ran a hand over his hair.

"You need a haircut."

"*Mom*."

"Fine, so what's your plan?"

"I'm looking into a few things. I just want to get the house in order and finish the painting." Ethan sighed. "I want to rest."

"You haven't really done that."

"No, but I also see her point. I could see myself holing up here and never getting out very easily, and I know that isn't healthy. I didn't do that before, and I'm not sure why I'm doing it now. So, hockey, a running group, this house, maybe write a few freelance articles and send them off, see what happens."

"And school? You are so close to finishing your degree, honey." She took her cup and headed for the counter.

Ethan popped his pod in and retrieved his mug from the cabinet. He leaned against the counter as the machine brewed. "I am going to finish. I just want to slow down for a minute, you know?"

"I do."

"She said I need to make my own friends," Ethan muttered, glancing out at the pool.

"You don't have to only make friends at school or at a job. You could meet new people if you did some volunteer work until you make some decisions. You used to enjoy that and made friends doing that in high school."

"I did. I haven't thought about that in a long time." Ethan took his mug and sat beside his mom at what he and Justin called their breakfast bar.

"Surely, there's something to save in Florida," she teased.

Ethan nodded. "There *has* to be. I want a dog, so maybe I'll look and see if there's an animal shelter nearby."

"You'll end up with more than one if you do that," she chided sweetly.

"I totally would, wouldn't I?"

She smiled knowingly, and together, they drank their morning coffee quietly. It was something he appreciated about his mother, her calmness. Growing up, his mother was always there for him. Every single ass-early-six a.m. hockey practice, every cross-country meet. If Ethan mentioned an interest in something, she packed them up in the car, and Ethan would find himself at a museum or at a state park learning about some endangered animal. She'd even taken him to a few concerts over the years, when she wasn't a fan of the music.

"You're doing some pretty heavy thinking over there," she said. "What do you think about us finding a grocery store you like and figuring out where your bank is. Then, let's explore all the local spots you might want to check out. I did see a cute little bookstore on my way here. Let's look at what's going on around town. There must be a website with local events and venues."

Ethan retrieved his tablet, resumed his morning coffee, and scrolled. "Migratory bird garden tour, there's the Cedar Key lighthouse, and there's a sidewalk arts festival we could do." He glanced at her, knowing it would pique her interest as it had his own.

"Yes!"

Ethan grinned. He polished off the rest of his coffee and went to get dressed. Spending the day with his mom doing the things they used to do together before he left for college seemed like a great way to ensure he got out of the house and did something fun. Plus, spending time with her was always a win.

"This is pretty fancy," she said from the passenger seat of his new car.

"It has way too many buttons, but Justin said it had a good safety rating, all the airbags a car could possibly have," Ethan explained as he backed out of the garage. "He wanted to buy me this huge SUV that looked like a tank, Mom."

"That's sweet, but I'm glad he went with this. It's more *you*."

"He did good. You should have seen him when he drove it home trying to surprise me; he could barely fit in it."

His mom laughed as she scooted the seat up closer. "I'm guessing he was in this seat last?"

"Yeah. GPS me, and let's find the bank first."

They spent the morning at the bank branch he'd use, then stopped by two local grocery stores and one merchandise store. They'd decided on the grocer closest to the house since it had the better produce section. His mom pointed out an oil change shop, and Ethan did a double take.

"What?"

"You honestly think he's going to let me take my car in for an oil change? God, he really is overprotective, isn't he?"

"A bit, but between you and me, I think it's nice. I see how you fuss over him though."

Ethan knew he did and couldn't find fault in the way they took care of each other. He pulled into a parking space along the street, and he and his mom eagerly assessed the sidewalks filled with artists and vendors. They looked at each other with giddy excitement, then raced each other to get out of the car.

"Oh my God, *Mom*, do you smell it?" Ethan said and inhaled deeply.

"Funnel cakes. We're doomed from the start."

"We so are."

Ethan sent Justin funny pictures throughout the day, knowing he wouldn't get them until much later. He and his mom had a great day. He only bought a few things, and they'd had more fun spending time together than anything else.

As she took an afternoon nap, Ethan was back to flipping through the two college packets and still debating what he wanted to do. Part of him wanted to retreat and stick with the safe online program he could do from home. The other part of him wanted to finish his last year in person and then seriously consider graduate school.

"I'm still scared." Ethan knew this about himself and hated how it controlled his life. He picked up his tablet, an idea striking him that he'd considered before but had put off because he'd been too weak throughout his recovery.

I'm not weak anymore.

He found two places offering what he needed. One had a group class, and the other also offered personal training. Ethan chewed on his bottom lip and tried to imagine what a self-defense class would look like, how it could help him with the kind of situation he wanted to ensure never happened to him again. He dialed the number for the private trainer, expecting to leave a message.

"Danny's," a girl said.

"Hi. I'm calling about the personal trainer for the self-defense lessons."

"Danny does those personally. Hang on. He's just finishing up with a client."

Ethan waited as hold music played, and then a gruff voice came on the line.

"This is Danny. Reagan said you were interested in self-defense training?"

"Yeah, I've never taken a class or anything, so I'm not sure what the process is," Ethan said, already feeling the anxiety creeping in.

"Well, the first session is free. You come in, and we chat a bit about what you want to accomplish and what your goals are, and then we practice a few methods. You can see if that's something you'd like to continue, or if you aren't ready, take some time to think about it. Zero commitment and no pressure. If you'd be interested in that, I have a slot at four, and we do offer a group class at six. Some clients do one or the other, some do both."

Ethan glanced at the clock. It was three, and the place was literally down the street.

"Okay, I can come in at four," he said and gave his name and phone number.

"See you in a few." And Danny ended the call.

Ethan swallowed, but the thought that he could walk away if it was too much got him up and heading for the bedroom to change into gym clothes. He left a note on the counter for his mom explaining he was going to the gym and would either be back in an hour or around seven, depending on if he stayed for a group class at six. Then, Ethan headed out, taking a brave first step he prayed wouldn't backfire on him.

*

DANNY'S DIDN'T LOOK like any gym Ethan had seen before, but he noted the Safe Space sticker on the door and several other advocacy indicators. It seemed he was in the right place so far, so he pushed the button on the door and waited.

"Hi, I'm Ethan Andrews." The door buzzer sounded, and Ethan entered.

"Hi, Ethan, I'm Reagan. Danny's expecting you." She pointed to an office at the back. "Just head on in. You'll have a consultation first. And here, he said you might also be interested in the group class tonight. Here's the schedule and phone tree for that class. They've only met once, so you haven't missed too much. Or, you can wait for the next session to start the first Tuesday of next month."

"Thanks." Ethan took the flyer. He followed her directions and headed to the office, a wall of windows, where a big dude sat behind a desk. Ethan was waved in as the man stood.

"You must be Ethan. I'm Danny Harkness. This is my place, have a seat. We can leave the door open or closed. It's up to you."

"Yeah, Ethan. Closed, I guess."

"Go ahead." Danny sat back down, not offering to shake Ethan's hand, which Ethan thought was odd, but he closed the door and took a seat.

"Let's dive right in," Danny said. "Ethan, what brings you to me?"

"I need self-defense classes or private instruction so I can defend myself?" Ethan said and knew it was so lame.

Danny nodded as if *everyone* before him had said this exact thing, and Ethan laughed once and then sighed.

"I'm a sexual assault and battery victim." And *there*. He'd said it. So succinctly and for the first time. Ethan swallowed hard.

"First time saying it?"

"Yeah."

"Feel like you want to get up and run out of here?"

"Yeah," Ethan said, throat tight.

"Don't." Danny rotated his chair and pointed to a photograph of a young girl, probably in her teens, on the wall. "My sister. She's why I do this. She was seventeen and was sexually assaulted at a party. At nineteen, my sister killed herself. We missed all the warning signs. So, I'd like to show you a few things, give you a tour around the facility, and see if we're a good fit for you and what you're hoping to learn."

"I don't ever want it to happen again," Ethan said robotically as he stared at the girl's photograph. "I'm tired of being scared to live."

"Tell me about your support system," Danny said.

"The best anyone could possibly have." Ethan looked at Danny now. "Great parents, a loving husband."

"Your attacker?"

"There were three. All of them are in prison. It happened…almost two years ago now." Ethan glanced at the photo again, doing the math and realizing the timeframe and what point he was at in his life, how crippling it could be and had been for the last two years even though he was happier than he'd ever been. *It* was still there. "I'm sorry about your sister."

"Thank you. Are you in counseling?" Danny asked.

"Regularly, and I take medication daily for depression and anxiety, PTSD episodes, flashbacks. But I've made a lot of progress in a short time. I kept busy with school, and now, I'm out of school because I relocated and…" Ethan stalled out.

"And it's all starting to catch up with you," Danny finished for him.

Ethan nodded.

"Do you have any injuries that would prevent you from this kind of training?"

"No, I'm pretty active. I run cross country and play amateur hockey. I'm cleared by my medical doctor for sports. That happened last year."

"Good. It seems like we might be a good fit for you, then. I do need to tell you we pride ourselves on being a safe space. We have a no-locked-doors policy, and our facility is under surveillance." Danny pointed to the corner at the camera and the windows indicating the gym area beyond. "We also have a no explanation policy. If you need to leave a session at any time, no one will ask you why or what's wrong with you. You just leave, and we ask that you also respect this code should someone from your group leave. And when they return, we ask no questions. We just dive back in with our training. This isn't therapy. It's self-defense. How does that sound?"

"Good, honestly. I *don't* want to talk about it."

"And neither do they. Is there anything else about you I need to know?"

Ethan nodded.

Danny waited.

"I have…scars. A lot of…scars. They cut me when I fought back."

They were quiet for a moment, and Ethan blinked a few times, then looked at Danny.

"What you're wearing is fine. Ready for the tour?"

"Sure," Ethan said, surprised by how to the point Danny was and appreciating that he didn't dwell or want to dig deeper.

Danny showed him the workout equipment, pretty standard gym stuff, and Ethan noticed the lack of mirrors, something most gyms had plenty of. He was shown a large group room with a thick spring floor, and the last room was smaller. It had the same style floor but was used for private instruction. Every room had windows and doorknobs with no locks, just as Danny had described. He followed Danny to the locker room.

"As with any gym locker room, there are no cameras in here." He pointed to a red button on the wall. "But there is a panic button. Back here, we have a sauna." Danny opened the door and indicated a red button there as well. Ethan followed him out to the private instruction room, and Danny asked him to stretch out as he also did.

"Today, we'll just focus on single attacker methods of defense, some tactics to buy time, get away, and stunning techniques. Sound good?"

"Yeah. Are there any men in the group class, or are they all women?"

"There are two males and six females. You are welcome to check it out tonight, and if you don't like it, you can leave or not return to the group. They got the same speech you did. All right, the first move I'll teach you is breaking a hold. I'll explain all the steps first."

Ethan listened and then agreed for Danny to put him in a hold. It was strange and uncomfortable, but Danny walked him through the steps with clear directions, and Ethan followed them, breaking the hold, stepping back, and then running across the room. They repeated it, and each time, Danny made it more challenging until Ethan was breathing hard, sweaty, and surprisingly gaining some confidence, wanting to master the skill.

"Good," Danny said. "You aren't going to hurt me. This isn't about hurt. This is about getting away."

"All right," Ethan said. "I'm ready. *For real* this time."

Danny didn't play, and Ethan respected it. The hold was tight, nearly suffocating, and instantly anxiety-producing.

"Don't panic. Breathe, remember the steps," Danny coached.

Ethan broke the hold, stumbled, and fell on the floor.

"Get up and run," Danny barked.

Ethan did and touched the wall, chills across his entire body as he leaned over, gasping for air.

"Again?"

Ethan nodded, pulled himself together, and crossed the room.

"Good," Danny said, and then his big arms were around Ethan again. This time, Ethan didn't panic when the grip tightened.

"Good work, Ethan. Do you want to stay for group?"

"Sure," Ethan said as Danny handed him a towel and water bottle. "What do I need to do to get signed up for both?"

"Just talk to Reagan. There are some forms to fill out. We have support day once a month."

"What's that?"

"The only time we allow guests to come." Danny pointed to a small three-row bleacher. "Your parents and your spouse are welcome to come on support day, but no other time. We want everyone to feel comfortable here, so we don't allow spectators except on support day."

"*No*, that's good," Ethan said. "I wouldn't want people watching until I learned more."

Danny nodded. "We encourage you to invite them when you're ready, and attendance on support day isn't mandatory if you aren't ready."

"Thank you," Ethan said and dumbly stuck out his hand.

Danny chuckled, and then, Ethan was staring at the ceiling, flat on his back.

"*Never* shake hands, Ethan. You give up your strong hand. You wouldn't hand over a gun or knife; don't hand over your *only* weapon to anyone."

"Point taken," Ethan said and pushed himself up.

"It's a hard habit to break," Danny said, extending his hand to help Ethan up.

"No fucking way," Ethan said through a laugh and got up on his own.

Danny grinned. "Good, you're a quick learner."

"How many people fail that one?" Ethan asked.

"Most of them."

Chapter Twenty-Eight

Ethan

THE GROUP CLASS wasn't at all what Ethan expected. He'd filled out the forms with Reagan to set up his schedule and payment. He knew without asking that Justin would support this decision of his. He had one private session with Danny on Tuesdays before group and group met on Tuesday, Wednesday, and Thursday of each week for one month before the start of a new session. After completing the first group, there were options for an intermediate and an advanced group to continue the training. Ethan felt good about this, and he appreciated that it genuinely felt like a safe space without only claiming to be.

A kid, around thirteen or fourteen, was buzzed in and stopped at the desk next to Ethan. He looked at Ethan, and Ethan naturally looked back, not failing to notice the fading yellowish-green bruise under the kid's eye.

"Markus," he said and handed Reagan his cell phone.

"Ethan." Ethan glanced down at his own cell phone on the counter and then at Markus again.

"You have to give it to her for class," Markus said. "I don't have keys, but the grown-ups give her those too."

"Well, thanks for letting me know." Ethan handed over his phone, keys, and completed forms.

"Markus, you want to show Ethan what to do since he wasn't in the first class?" Reagan said.

"Sure. We just have to stretch."

"All right," Ethan agreed, though he'd already stretched since they still had about twenty minutes before class began.

"I like your shirt. Warriors. That's cool."

"Thanks," Ethan said, following the kid. "What does yours say?"

"Drama club. It's from my school. But it says *Thespian*."

"Yeah, this one is from my old school too."

They sat down on the spring floor, and Ethan copied the stretches Markus did.

"You have to stretch on your own before class," Markus said. "You are supposed to get here fifteen minutes early so you can stretch."

The door opened, and several people came in.

"That's Kelly, Linda, and Micha. This is Ethan," Markus announced.

Ethan gave a wave as the others joined them, everyone getting busy with their tasks and offering simple hellos. When the last four joined them, it was pretty much the same: a brief introduction by Markus, and everyone stretched. There wasn't a lot of chitchat. No one wore fashionable gym clothes; it was down-to-business T-shirts, sweats, shorts, and tennis shoes. Ethan got it; everyone was here for the same reason as him, and he could admit he didn't feel intimidated or embarrassed.

Danny came in, briefly greeted everyone, and said, "Leave any jewelry with Reagan. We don't want any accidental injuries."

Ethan slipped off his ring and headed back to Reagan, along with Linda, who had forgotten to remove her earrings. They handed them over and returned to line up for the session at Danny's direction. Another coach, Jessie, a female instructor, would co-teach the class.

"Jessie is cool," Markus whispered next to Ethan. "Don't worry."

Ethan fought a grin. The kid was a cool little dude, trying to help him out. "Thanks, man."

"I got your back."

"Same," Ethan whispered, and they nodded at each other with a solemn agreement.

*

ETHAN PARKED HIS car in the garage and mustered enough strength to open the door and drag his ass inside. His mom, *my God, he loved her*, was cooking dinner and chuckled at the sight of him.

"Feed me, I'm dying."

"Tell me all about it," she said, scrunching her nose. "After you shower."

A few minutes later, Ethan returned, not much better but clean, and sat at the plate she had ready. Her question couldn't be put off for long, but Ethan greedily ate a few bites and then told her.

"I started a self-defense class today."

"Really?"

"It kicked my ass."

"I see that. Are you going back?"

"*Oh yeah*, tomorrow *and* Thursday," Ethan said, and then he had to stop talking so he could eat more.

"Hmm, maybe it is a good thing Justin isn't here right now," his mom said, lifting a brow.

Ethan only chewed, cheeks full, and shook his head. Justin would be ready to kill someone if he saw Ethan in this state and didn't know why.

"I'll have to give him a heads-up about it," Ethan said between forkfuls.

"I'm proud of you. Eat, and tell me the rest after."

He did, and then he told her everything as they loaded the dishwasher.

"I think I want to go back to in-person school. I just learn better that way. So, I thought I'd take this class while I have time off, and that way, I'll be in the right headspace to go back and finish up."

"You and Dad talked about it before."

"I wasn't ready then. I am now."

"Can I tell him?"

"Yeah." Ethan told her about support day and wanting them to be there.

"We'll be there. Now, we didn't finish talking about this hair situation."

"I'm letting it grow out a little bit. I've never done that, so…" Ethan shrugged.

"Fine."

ETHAN WENT TO his group classes for the next two evenings. During the daytime, his mom helped him with things around the house. They ran errands, tried a few restaurants, found a few take-out places Ethan could use if he didn't want to cook for one, and handled getting his new Florida driver's license. By Thursday evening, she was ready to head back home and help with the Booster club for his dad's team, and Ethan was practically bouncing all day Friday, waiting for Justin to finally come home. He couldn't wait to tell him everything.

Chapter Twenty-Nine

Justin

"OH MY GOD, I love you so much," Justin groaned as Ethan massaged his neck and shoulders, rubbing in muscle cream and massaging *everything* that hurt, which was everything. "Name anything you want that I can afford, and I swear I'll go buy it for you tomorrow if you promise to do this every Friday night when I get home."

Ethan laughed. "Okay, I want this super expensive rug for the living room I talked myself out of. I want this organizer thing for the laundry room that requires assembly, so I talked myself out of that. And I want two flowerpots for the pool deck, but I can't lift them, and neither could you, so it's a delivery thing, and I didn't want to do that while I was home alone. So that's more of I need you to be the big boss man when they bring them."

"And," Justin groaned, "right there, feel that knot? Break it down so I can understand what you want, Ethan. My brain barely works right now. Take it down to…around the third-grade level."

"I got you, baby. Let's see, the pricy rug, the organizer you'd have to assemble, the big-ass pots, hmm, that was really it."

"How was the week with your mom? Sorry, I wasn't up for much phone time."

"No, I know. I get the crash and burn. It was great. We did so many things. I do have some big news. But first, I finished the painting in the living room."

"It looks good; I saw it when I came in," Justin mumbled. "I like the blue swatch in the kitchen too."

"See, I'm not sure about that one. Look at it in the sunlight tomorrow; give it a day. Roll over, let me do the front."

Justin rolled with a groan. "So it looks different in the sun?"

"Yeah, at night with the house lights on, I love it, but then it looks two shades lighter in the daytime. It's so strange."

"What if we got two shades darker of the same color and added a little more light in the kitchen? Then you'd have the color you wanted in the daytime. I like the color now."

"Yeah, we'll see," Ethan said. "I'm not rushing to get everything done. I'm just taking it one project at a time."

"You've got a whole lifetime to get this house how you want it." Justin yawned so big his jaw cracked. "Stop avoiding; what's the big news?"

"Hear me out," Ethan warned.

"Oh boy," Justin groaned.

"So, I signed up for this self-defense class. It's three days a week and one private lesson. I really like the group, and I'm already learning a lot. It's *really* hard though."

Justin was quiet, and Ethan rubbed sore muscles, avoiding a few bruised places.

"What do you think?"

"I think I'm really proud of you, Ethan. What do you mean 'it's really hard'?" Justin pulled his arm away and put both behind his head, his full attention on Ethan.

"Well. We practice getting out of holds. How to not panic and be able to react, to think straight in scary situations."

Justin lifted a brow and then narrowed both at him. Ethan held up a finger.

"I never want it to happen to me again. You wouldn't be happy about some of the methods. They are somewhat realistic. For example, a choke hold or a pinning down hold. And we are learning how to get out of those situations to run. There is a second class that teaches fighting back, but I wanted to talk to you about it first. This class's focus is more on getting away and getting help. It's for beginners."

"Who's pinning you down?" Justin said, and Ethan seemed prepared for his reaction.

"My instructor. Her name is Jessie. My other instructor is Danny. They both perform the holds; they co-teach. And at the end of the month, I want you to come to support day and see what I've learned."

Justin's entire body relaxed, and he lifted his foot and nudged Ethan's hand with it.

"Foot or calf?"

"Calf, and the front of my thigh."

Ethan repositioned and waited, then returned to work on sore muscles and knots.

"All right," Justin said, "but I want you to take the second class too. Do you have to finish the first, or how does that work?"

"I have to finish the first class. So you agree?"

"Yes. What date is the day I can come?"

"Saturday, the first, at six," Ethan answered.

"I'll be there. What else?"

And Ethan told him about Markus, his buddy, and Micha, and all the ladies. He explained everything, about the safety of the gym and all the safe-space protocols, and Justin listened to every word, not interrupting once. By the time he was done, Justin had relaxed and felt more on board with Ethan's plan.

"Who fucked with Markus?"

"I just told you; we aren't allowed to discuss or ask about each other's trauma. Why? Going to go rough up some middle school kids?"

"The thought crossed my mind," Justin said, and Ethan kissed him.

"You can't, but I love that about you, that you want to. Sleep, tough guy," Ethan said but kept working Justin's sore muscles until he lost the battle, fighting to stay awake to spend time with Ethan.

*

JUSTIN SLEPT IN late and felt better as he made his way into the kitchen. He smiled at the covered plate and loaded coffee pod and cup beneath, ready to go. Justin pushed the lever down and looked around. Ethan was outside cleaning the pool. They still had no pool furniture, but Justin decided to go with Ethan's one project-at-a-time concept, to go at his man's pace.

He'd noticed a new miniature painting in the bathroom, one Ethan had sent him a picture of with a text message about finding it at some art fair and how cute it was. Justin poured himself a glass of water as he watched Ethan scoop leaves out and dump them into a trashcan.

He looked up and waved, then lay the pole down and came inside.

"Yeah, you're up," Ethan said and hugged him.

"Thank you so much for healing me." Justin kissed his forehead. "Now feed me and then put me to work."

"I'll heat up your plate. I was worried you'd be up super early."

Justin sat at the barstool, and Ethan brought his coffee to him. "I see what you mean." He nodded at the swatch of paint.

"So weird, right?" Ethan took his plate from the overhead oven and brought it over. He sat beside him, chin in hand, staring at the blue spot.

"You'll work it out," Justin said and took a sip, seeing a few other minor changes—another night-light plugged in and a small plant by the window. *Little things* and that was something Justin loved about Ethan.

"Okay, I want to hear all about it, every detail," Ethan said. "How are you and your center? Is the super nice guy still there? You know I'm rooting for him to make it. Who got cut? How's the apartment?"

Justin smiled as he chewed.

Ethan was Justin's world, but it was a nice feeling to be someone else's. Justin told him all about it, about everyone and everything. He reassured Ethan that Miller had made it through the first cuts. They talked about how hard it was for him to breathe and get used to the humidity.

After his late breakfast, Justin took Ethan to purchase and arrange delivery for the pots. Then, Justin took him to a nursery because he wanted plants. Ethan loved Justin's hat, pulled low, his sunglasses, and his chore clothes. There was one good thing about the past mask debacle as Justin wore one of those too. They held hands as they walked the grounds of the large nursery together, with Ethan adding things to the cart, picking out plants and several large palms for his pots. He would make Justin choose between something when he couldn't decide, and they'd move on.

"Look," Justin said, stopping. "I want that."

Ethan stood next to him, sighing like the weight of the world was on him. "Where would we put it?"

"Right at the end of the pool deck," Justin said. "*Ethan*, I want this."

"We'll think about it." Ethan snapped a picture of the fishpond and waterfall feature with his phone. He shook his head and snapped a photo of Justin squatting down and looking at all the fish. Justin pointed at the koi, and Ethan nodded.

"Yeah, I see them," he said.

"Come on. I never ask for anything."

Ethan just laughed and laughed over that as he dragged Justin away. With all the plants wrapped and loaded in the back of the truck, they headed home, which included a stop as Justin ran in and got them cones for the drive back.

"That's where my classes are," Ethan said, pointing at a building.

"Damn, that's, like, right down the street."

"Yeah, can you believe it?" Ethan said and licked his cone.

"It doesn't look like a gym."

"Nope, it's not supposed to, and I like that about it. You only know it's there and what they do if you're a member. I had to do an interview and everything. Even *you* couldn't get in."

"*Good*, that makes me feel better," Justin admitted, happy to know no one could just walk in the place. It made him like the idea even more.

*

AFTER UNLOADING AND hauling the monster plants to the back, Ethan sent him to the hardware store with a list of his jobs for the weekend. These included all the more difficult jobs, but Justin liked this, being helpful, and Ethan needing him with things. Maybe it was a strange dynamic, but Justin felt a sense of pride as he shopped for items on the list to complete Ethan's few chores for him. He wanted a security light put up and the old doorbell replaced with the camera kind.

Justin was on board with that as he picked out the system. The house had an alarm, but Justin added a few other items to the cart and spent time in the outdoor lighting area. Then, Justin shook his head as he lifted bags of dirt and mulch, loading them on the flat cart. It was a hell of a workout as he finished up in the parking lot.

"You know, it's like three workouts in one day," Justin said when he finished moving all the bags.

"I know; I'm so lucky you're a badass," Ethan said, his new garden gloves on as he planted the new pots at the end of pool deck. The huge concrete urns now had palms and tropical plants in them.

"I like those red and green ones." Justin stretched out on the concrete pool deck, listening to Ethan tell him what kind they were.

Ethan looked over at him and frowned. "You're right; we do need patio furniture soon."

"Actually, this feels good on my back. You want to come to the apartment this week? I mean, all I do is sleep my ass off and get right back up and go again, but you know…" Justin sighed as Ethan shook his head.

"Right," Justin said. "You're right." He sighed again and rolled over, then pushed himself up.

"What happened to the break?" Ethan frowned at him.

"I forgot something I bought for you in the truck, and I want a smoothie. You want one?"

"What is it?"

"A surprise," Justin said with a laugh and headed inside. Ethan had made blender containers full of iced smoothies, and Justin pulled one from the freezer and gave it a whirl. He poured two, then headed out, to set them by the pool. He then grabbed the shopping bags and box out of his truck and set it all down. Stretching out again, he let the heat from the pool deck seep into his back.

Ethan pulled off his gloves, took a sip, and peeked into the first bag. "Aw, those are cute." And on it went for each thing that Justin had bought, thinking of Ethan. One of the boxes included wood for the chiminea, which was ridiculous, but Justin had bought the box because it would make Ethan happy.

"They do make the patio look better," Justin agreed, eyeing Ethan's monster pots after they were all planted. He then got up and finished with the lights at the ends of the house and the doorbell.

They cleaned up, Ethan ordered pizzas, and Justin's big reward followed—they gamed. Justin decided to at least take his system down to the apartment so they could play online when he got to a point he didn't feel like face-planting the bed the second he got home.

"I'd like that."

Justin shared more about Jones, Miller, and Hernandez as he and Ethan moved as a two-man soldier team, shooting enemies and finding more ammo and lives on screen. Ethan laughed his ass off every time they won. It was *almost* perfect, and Justin blinked a few times at their life together.

"Don't," Ethan elbowed him, "I can feel what you're thinking."

"What."

"I wouldn't even want that kind of life anyway. I'm good. I feel good and loved and safe, and I don't want what you think I do."

"No, I know, me neither. But if you wanted to come to the apartment, I'd want you to feel like you could, not like you can't."

"I know, but we have a plan, and that's what we are sticking to," Ethan said, and Justin leaned in and kissed him.

Chapter Thirty

Justin

AVOIDING THE PARTY lifestyle had never been a challenge for Justin, not in high school or college, and now it was no different in the NFL. After a few no's, people stopped asking, and he was glad. They pretty much already knew he wasn't ever going to go. But McReedy was another story.

"You want to hang out this weekend?" McReedy asked.

Justin frowned. "I go out of town when we're off. It would have to be during the week."

"*Every* weekend?"

"Religiously. Weekends aren't an option. It'll be the same when our schedule changes, so it has to be while I'm here. But yes, let's do something," Justin agreed. "I need help finding a grill."

McReedy nodded. "Yeah, man, we'll go tomorrow after practice."

"Sounds good." Justin looked around the room as he tied his shoes, at which lockers were now empty and what faces were missing. He nodded at Hernandez and Miller. And then they were on the field for their second week of hell.

"You lied," Justin said as they passed by a still just as scary Holcombe and the other veteran players.

Holcombe barked out a laugh. "I swear it does; next week, you'll see."

On his way home, Justin stopped and got the things he needed for his apartment and the groceries he needed for the week. With his blackout curtains, all hung up at last, now, whenever someone parked, their headlights could go blind someone else. Justin decided he could survive a week at a time in the place. And it was nice, just not his home.

At last, he was hooked up and playing online with Ethan. He had his headset on, and they were playing against another team as he waited for his dinner to cook in the oven. Ethan asked him about a new game coming out that Justin wanted to play too. He told Ethan he'd get the online version for them and whooped as they destroyed the other team together.

"Still killin' twelve-year-olds in the NFL," Ethan chortled.

Justin had paused their play to eat, and they'd switched over to a phone call. Ethan told him about his day, all the things he was doing and accomplishing. Then Justin told Ethan about his day. He guessed Holcombe was right because it had been getting a little easier. He was in bed early but wasn't walking in the door and going straight cheek to pillow. And Justin realized that the suffocating feeling had faded somewhat. It was still there, just not as bad. Then, he told Ethan not to freak out if he had some things delivered and that he loved him.

Tuesday's practice was brutal, but Justin climbed in with McReedy, and they headed out to eat and then find Justin a grill. They had a good time at a small place, hoping not to get noticed. Justin knew that wouldn't last forever, but he'd enjoy it until it was over.

"So, Coach called me in and talked to me about some stuff," McReedy said.

Justin nodded and chewed as McReedy went on.

"He said the media would probably hit me up at some point," he said, indicating Justin. "Said you weren't a big media fan, so expect some backlash over that when the season starts. He wanted to make sure I understood we don't talk about you to the media. I told him, yeah, sure thing. But I wanted you to know what he said, what I said." And he waved a finger between them. "Trust and shit."

"I don't do the media. And I keep to myself," Justin admitted. "This is the first restaurant I've eaten at since moving here."

"No shit? How do you eat then?"

"I cook." Justin said it as if that's what you were supposed to do, and McReedy had himself a good chuckle.

"I guess that's why the grill makes sense," he carried on. "But back to the other." He gave Justin a severe look.

Justin shrugged. "Tell them to ask me or the media director."

"You seem way more chill about it than Coach."

"It's in my contract."

"No shit?"

"I hate the media, man. I used to sneak out early just to avoid them in college. This one chick got my schedule and was waiting for me when I came out of class. That's crazy. I'm not living like that with people following me around and yelling at me all the time. I just play ball and try to stay off their radar."

"It's cool, man, I won't ever say nothin'," McReedy said.

"Thanks."

"So you thinkin' gas or charcoal?"

Justin ate as McReedy told him everything he thought he knew about grills.

"Damn boy, that's a grill," McReedy said as they looked at the display for an outdoor kitchen grill. "You got room for that? I thought you lived in some apartments?"

"Yeah, I do. But that's just during the week. I have a real home I go to on the weekends. This is for there."

"Ah, a family man," McReedy said. "I get it. I say propane, especially if you plan on grilling a bunch of fish and chicken. Easier to maintain the right temperatures."

"Yeah, I think so too." Justin snapped a picture and sent it in a text.

Ethan: *OMG, Justin, do not buy a grill.*

"Well crap," Justin said.

"Got shot down by the honey?"

"You could say that." Justin sent another text telling Ethan he wouldn't. "I have a feeling I just fucked up a surprise."

McReedy laughed. "When's your birthday?"

And Justin joined him because he nearly forgot. "Yeah, no grill. Damn, I almost forgot my birthday is coming up."

"That's what happens when you're dog-tired, man; you can forget your own birthday. Just make sure you don't forget no one else's."

McReedy and Justin looked up and thought about it for a second.

"Nope, I'm good." Justin nodded.

"Well, what now? If you can't get a grill."

"I need to look at bikes and kayaks," Justin said, and McReedy whooped.

*

"SO, I GOT a boat in the mail today," Ethan said and then busted out.

"You like it?" Justin asked as he smiled wide.

"I do. Is this part of your 'fill the great American garage' plan?" Ethan teased.

"No, this is the 'think of things we can go do together in the off-season' plan," Justin said. "Damn. Hang on, that's Coach calling me."

"Hey, Coach," Justin said after switching to the other call. He listened as his coach told him about a request from a sports magazine to do an article about him.

Justin sighed. "Look, after I win a game, I'll do it, but I'm not interested until I have something to talk about. Tell them it's superstition."

Coach agreed, but Justin knew it would only get worse.

"Do you have to call me every time?" he asked. "I mean, I feel bad telling you no."

"No, this was just a big one management hoped you'd do; they've handled all the other ones."

"I will, but after a win." Justin repeated.

"Understandable." And he was gone.

"All right, sorry," Justin said, continuing with Ethan. "It was about a magazine interview I'm not doing. But I did agree to it after a win so as not to jinx myself."

"No lie," Ethan said. "Get me a sticker for my boat."

"What do you want? And I love how you call it a boat."

"I want a WAG bumper sticker to slap on my boat." Ethan laughed so hard and could barely say it as Justin started cracking up. "You have to…" Ethan tried to suck in air, and Justin was dying over it too.

"All right." Justin wiped his face. "I got you. It's happening."

*

JUSTIN WAS HAPPY at practice, finally starting to get a rhythm with the plays and the pace. He and McReedy clicked, had good communication, and read each other well. McReedy also protected his ass, so he and his offensive line were vital. They drilled snap counts and sacks, with the defense putting the pressure on a little more each day. Justin wrote on the whiteboard in the locker room as a joke:

Days Without Sacks: 0

And he just left it up there like that. He paused in front of the board a few days later when someone erased the zero and changed it to a one. Justin took some pride in the fact that someone had made it a goal and taken notice. No one erased it, either, and nothing else had been written on the board since he'd put it up there. So naturally, it eventually became the Sack Board, and Justin never imagined what a big deal it would become.

He met with Coach Richardson again on Friday. And again, Coach handed him the clipboard.

"This is it, the final ones. You get to keep six on that list. The rest go."

"Does everyone come in here and do this, or just you and I?" Justin asked as he scanned the names.

"Six, six," he mumbled, then circled three: Miller, Hernandez, and Jones. Then added three more who, out of all the rest, had shown the most improvement and had the better attitudes. They were fighting for their spots, and Justin felt good to pick out those names. He put a star by two others he liked but understood there was a cutoff. He handed the clipboard back over.

"Just you," Richardson answered finally. "Keep the circles, and what are the stars?"

"I like those two also but understand there is a line, a cutoff. If one of the others doesn't work out, I gave you my choices for alternates."

"Jones has done well this week. Think he can keep it up?"

"I think we'll have moments when we have to remind him, but I think we keep him."

"Final cuts will be today."

"Yes, Coach," Justin said grimly.

"Tell Bart to get in here," Richardson said, comparing Justin's sheet with his own.

Justin went out to find the assistant OC. He relayed the message and then headed out for some drills.

McReedy lifted a brow. "Cuts?"

Justin confirmed quietly.

"Damn," McReedy said. "Today?"

Justin nodded. "Jones!" he yelled and motioned for the other player to get ready. Justin cracked his neck and stretched his arm. He got loosened up and then turned to McReedy. Justin needed to burn off some steam, and they were going to run Jones like a fast filly on derby day.

McReedy got it. "I'm with you."

And that's what they did. While Bart came out and called names one at a time, McReedy snapped to Justin, and Justin threw to Jones. Running Jones over and over and over until the last cut name was called. And Jones kept his shit together and drilled the whole time, dreading and waiting for his name.

"That's it," Bart called out. "Cuts are over."

And Jones shook his head, ran in, and hugged Justin.

Justin hugged him back. "I have big plans, Jones. You are a part of them, so don't let me down, man."

"Never, thank you," Jones said.

Miller stood there, mouth open, as Bart left. He locked eyes with Justin. "Holy shit," Miller said.

Justin slapped him on the back. "Congratulations."

Then, they got busy again, and the practice moved on. Their team was complete, roster-filled, and *this* would be Justin's new football family.

Three hours later, Justin arrived home only to find Ethan pacing nervously in the driveway.

"Miller made it," Justin said, not dragging it out, and Ethan pumped a fist, doing a little dance.

"I was so worried," Ethan said, taking Justin's bag from his shoulder. "But I also *knew* you wouldn't let him get cut. Thanks for helping him."

"Anything for you, but you do realize it wasn't up to me, and Miller is talented all on his own."

"Oh, I know, but you helped him. Now, time for your reward."

Justin liked the sound of that. It had definitely been worth all the days he'd spent after practice with Miller until he knew that playbook forwards, backwards, and probably dreamed left position plays in his sleep. He had no idea why Ethan had grown so concerned over a guy he'd probably never even meet, but that was Ethan—who was also currently nursing a baby bird he'd practically ripped out of the neighbor's cat's mouth back to health in their garage.

Ethan had sent pictures all week with status updates. He included shots of the new high-powered water gun he'd purchased, adding video clips of his ongoing war with the villain cat next door. Currently, it was Ethan with eight direct hits to Jingles and zero more birds.

Chapter Thirty-One

Justin

THE PRACTICE INTENSITY settled a little after final cuts, and Holcombe had been right. It was *weed out the weak*, and Justin acknowledged him as they walked in to eat. He got it now, and Holcombe nodded back. The board changed from two to three and then back to zero once the defense realized someone was keeping up with sacks, and Justin found himself looking at the blue sky and whistles being blown and pissed-off coaches shouting as Justin lay there grinning.

McReedy cursed and started yelling, and everything went to shit on the offensive line as Holcombe, from their defensive line, looked down at Justin and extended his hand.

"You want up, or do you want to lie there for another second and let them work their shit out?"

"Let's let them work it out. Good hit, man," Justin said.

"Want me to do it again?"

"Yeah, I do. Until they stop you from doing it. Sound good?" Justin reached up and took Holcombe's hand.

"Days. Since. Sacked. Zero, assholes," Holcombe barked, and the offensive line stopped squawking at one another and lined back up with a new target in their sights.

"I love this game!" Justin yelled out and called the play.

The next day, the whiteboard was missing; it now sat out on the field set up in a chair. Coach Richardson let it go, letting it all play out as Justin's back hit the ground again and again. Holcombe pointed to the sign every single time and called them all assholes for being unable to protect their QB. And on it went. Holcombe would back off, and they'd think they had it, and then Justin would hit the ground, and it would start all over again.

"Got big plans this weekend?" Holcombe asked as they walked out to the parking lot together.

"Yeah, it's my birthday on Monday, so celebrate this weekend with my family," Justin said.

"Same plan next week?" he asked.

"Until they get it," Justin said, and Holcombe grinned wickedly as only a twisted defenseman could.

Coach Richardson, standing by his SUV, nodded at Justin, letting him know he was on board with whatever they were up to.

Justin was happy to not feel like a complete shitshow as he drove home. Yeah, he was sore. He had a few new bruises and aches, but it was nothing like the first week.

"I'm on my way," Justin told Ethan on speaker as he drove.

Ethan sighed, long and exaggeratedly. "I guess I'll see you when you get here, then."

"Love you." Justin knew Ethan was so incapable of keeping a secret or playing it cool. Justin had no idea what he was walking into, but he suspected it was something.

He'd so called it as he had to park on the street at his own house due to all the familiar cars parked in the driveway. He shook his head at the balloon on the closed garage door with an arrow pointing to the backyard.

"Here we go," Justin said, so happy to be home. When he got closer, he heard Ethan laughing, trying to shush everyone, and then counting down.

"Surprise," their parents cheered, and Ethan was beaming as Justin widened his eyes and held his arms open.

"Holy…" Justin took it all in, then hugged Ethan, his mom and dad, and John and Bethany. "Look at that." He checked out all the pool patio furniture and the outdoor grill area. And then he turned to the end of the pool deck. "You didn't."

"You love it," Ethan said, beaming.

"I love *you*. I *like* all this. How did you do all this?"

"Oh, I had help."

Justin nodded, seeing John and his father's handiwork in the planning and tool skills that had been put to use.

Justin couldn't stop staring at the fishpond and waterfall, and then Ethan dragged him over to see the outdoor grill area with a new covered roof, rivaling John's setup.

"Thank you, everyone," Justin said, and then they all started in, telling him everything they'd done and how they pulled it all off.

Frank and Donovan came around the corner, and Ethan waved them over. He took the gift they brought and added it to the table. Justin was pleased Ethan had invited them.

John manned the grill while Bethany and Missy finished setting up a buffet line inside. Justin admired the blue kitchen, two shades darker, and winked at Ethan. He would cheat with the cake and appreciated everything they'd done for him.

Then, they all wanted to hear about the team.

Justin told them the latest about what he and Holcombe had going, and they got a kick out of it. Ethan, not so much, but he nodded, understanding the point. Justin and John talked about the cuts as they all ate. Justin shared his hopes for Jones and how it was going with McReedy, and then he discussed with John about how involved he was with Richardson, calling him in each week and his uncertainty over what to think about their meetings.

John thought Richardson was preparing him for a more significant role, possibly an assistant captain. Currently, Holcombe was the team captain, and *he* was a force to be reckoned with. He was also a veteran who had been with the team for a long time. It made more sense that he and Holcombe had bonded from the beginning now that John's perspective clarified it.

Ethan told him all about the new pond and waterfall and each fish's suggested names. It didn't surprise Justin as he produced a list: Finn and Finley, Spots, Coy, and Sunny. Ethan had hired the nursery to come out and replicate the setup. He showed Justin how much fish food to give them. He explained every water plant, and Justin asked if Finn and Finley were a couple. *Of course*, they were, and Justin kissed Ethan's temple, loving him even more, if that was possible.

Justin ate and enjoyed time with his family. His parents had found a condo and decided to keep their house and use the condo when they spent time in Florida. His mom wasn't ready to retire yet, but summer and breaks would be spent there.

It was a good evening. Justin opened his gifts, exclaiming over the electric blower Frank and Donovan had gifted them.

Ethan pointed a warning finger at him. "If you blow one leaf into that pool…"

"Never," Justin lied.

Ethan had given him a new game and some small things he'd mentioned wanting. The chiminea had been moved, and Bethany nodded her approval as the unneeded little fire sticks burned inside.

They were staying the weekend, and Ethan was pleased. It would not be long before the calm ended, and the storm and chaos began again. They spent the next day with their parents on the main beach, and Justin enjoyed watching Ethan look for shells along the shore. There weren't as many on their specific beach, but he managed a few and had a little collection going in the house.

"He's happy," John said, standing next to him, and Justin nodded. "Healthy again."

And he *was*.

Ethan's medications were down to the lowest level they'd ever been; he only took two a day now, and his therapy sessions had been scaled back to once a month. Justin couldn't recall the date of Ethan's last panic attack, but it had been a while.

Financially, Ethan was set for life and would never have to work if he didn't want to. Between Justin's income, the settlement he'd received from the university's insurance company, and the court-ordered restitution the convicted had to pay, financial security would not be a worry. Still, Justin discussed investments and retirement plans with John.

They talked about options, and then John moved on to the media and mentioned a story he'd seen about the lack of coverage on the new quarterback. People were getting curious, and fans were worrying on social media platforms.

"I've agreed to a big interview with a magazine the team wants me to do after our first win. They wanted to do it during training camp, but I asked them to wait until I had something to discuss. And when I could actually move my arms and legs and have the energy to talk."

John listened as he studied the surrounding beach area. "Still feel this is safe enough?"

"Until the season starts. And with everything in his name, my name isn't on a single piece of mail or delivery. All the credit and debit cards are in his name, the cell phones, all of it. You can't get through the gate here without a code or being on a visitor log, and that's a fee I don't mind paying each month. If there's even a hint of a problem, I'll hire personal security for him."

Justin sighed. "I've had a few neighbors recognize me at the apartment complex, so if anyone leaks, it will keep it closer to the Bay."

"I find myself wondering if we've covered it all," John said, worried.

"Me too, all the time. I feel this constant pressure that if I make one slip…" Justin said, sighing. He stood when Ethan waved him to the shore and pointed down at the sand. "Let's see what he's found."

"Don't touch it," Ethan said, his hand gripping Justin's forearm. "What is it?"

"Sea shit," Justin said and he held in his laughter, trying to be serious.

"*So* scientific. Gross, right?"

"Yeah, did it move?" Justin asked, and then he reached over and grabbed at Ethan, who yelled, laughed, hit him, and rubbed at his goose-bump arms.

"Oh my God, you didn't do that!" Ethan shook his head.

"Now boys, what's the fuss all about?" Bethany asked as she and Missy walked over.

Ethan pointed to the thing on the beach, and Justin was still silently carrying on, holding his sides, as John and Nathan joined them to inspect the blob.

"That's a sea pickle," Nathan said, and then the jokes just kept coming. Justin was in tears, waving them all away from himself, and made a beeline heading back to their umbrella as he tried to catch his breath.

Ethan flopped down on his beach chair and sighed. "That hurt."

"I know," Justin said, "Don't start it up again."

"No, I'm not. My side hurts too bad. And now I don't want to go back in the water because I have a new fear I didn't even know I had—defunct sex toys of the sea."

"Stop."

"Right."

"And don't start with googling and sending me links to sea pickles," Justin said wryly.

"Fun killer."

*

TODAY WAS THE day. Justin's mom and dad had headed home early. Ethan had felt awkward about them possibly coming to support day, and Justin understood that. John and Bethany were nervous but put on happy faces. Bethany drank far too many cups of coffee, and Justin noticed how her hand shook slightly when she put her mug in the sink. Ethan and John were outside, putting together a pool cleaner and trying to figure out how to program it to run automatically. They had clearly run into a few problems along the way, with Ethan reading the directions out loud and John shaking his head.

"He's completed the four-week program," Justin said, standing at the closed glass patio door and observing the shitshow outside. "I'm really proud of him but also nervous about today."

Bethany joined him at the door. "You know, this may sound stupid, but I've often thought of trauma like an octopus. It has these arms that reach out and latch on to everyone who loves the person it happens to, and we all feel the squeeze, but it's almost like a secondary trauma. This feeling, the burden that we couldn't stop it, couldn't save him when he needed us the most…I hate that I couldn't protect him." Bethany sniffed.

"Jesus, woman." Justin put his arm around her.

"I know, I'm sorry."

"We're going to go and be there for him today. But we have to be strong for him. And I don't think it's stupid. I wish I could kill all three of those guys. Prison isn't enough; restitution is a joke. So, we'll do this, no matter how hard it is to watch and remember he's been at this for four weeks now, taking back control of his life. It was *his* decision, all on his own."

She sniffed again and nodded against his shirt.

"And if it all goes down the shitter today, we'll go buy a punching bag for the garage and take turns."

Bethany stepped back. "He said he wants to do the next class."

"I think he should if that's what he wants. What did John say?"

"He agrees he should continue with all the sessions but wasn't happy about the sticking around and fighting aspect."

"I'd rather him have every skill available and just pray he never needs to use a single one," Justin said. "Looks like they figured out the problem with the pool vac." He faked a smile as Ethan gave a thumbs-up, and Justin gave him a silent applause through the glass door in return. He turned to her. "Game faces, Bethany."

"Game faces," she agreed.

*

JUSTIN PULLED DOWN the brim of his ballcap and put on the COVID mask before walking into Danny's. Inside, Justin handed over his cell phone and keys to the receptionist after John and Bethany had done so. The girl pointed to a small set of bleachers where only a few people sat. They took their seats and could see Ethan, along with several others, seated on the floor in an adjoining room, listening as a man and woman spoke to them.

"That must be Jessie and Danny," Justin said, then lowered his voice and whispered, "That's Markus, next to Ethan."

John nodded, and Bethany remained transfixed on her son. A few more family members joined in on the bleachers, and the receptionist walked over to address them.

"We have some guidelines we'd like to ask you to follow. There is no applause. We ask for silent support. For some of our clients, having you here is a tough ask. It's a big step, and we are proud of their progress. The maneuvers you will see can be upsetting for some support members, and if you feel you need to leave, just come to the front desk, and I'll assist you." She focused on every single person there; her seriousness could not be mistaken.

John glanced at Bethany, and she clenched her jaw and nodded. He turned to Justin, and he nodded too, but the tension was building. It was getting a little hard for Justin to breathe behind the mask he was wearing. John inhaled and blew out a breath. He reached over and took Bethany's hand and then took Justin's. They were united and ready. Justin turned to the other supporters around them, and they appeared just as nervous.

The room to the door opened, and the group filed out, followed by the two instructors. The presentation started with the first female taken to the ground. A man twice her size pinned her down. Using her feet and leg strength, she pushed the man off, rolled, and was on her feet, sprinting to the far wall and touching a small blue circle. The same or a similar pinning tactic was used on each student. When it was Ethan's turn, Justin used his free hand to pull the mask away from his mouth, and John's grip tightened.

Ethan looked so small compared to Danny, who took him down like a ragdoll. But Ethan was quick, breaking an arm hold around his neck, using his body and legs to free himself. When his hand slapped the blue circle, Justin realized how hard he was breathing and tried to get himself under control as John squeezed his hand harder.

The first scenario had to be the worst, Justin told himself.

And as hard as it was to see Ethan go through it, Markus was almost too much to handle. Jessie had him pinned and gave him no easy out, no breaks for being a kid, and Bethany had silent tears. John's eyes glistened, and there was absolutely *zero oxygen in this fucking place*. Justin watched as Ethan focused so hard on Markus, his fists clenched at his sides as he silently supported his friend.

Markus used the back of his head, a simulated head-butt maneuver no one else had done, then broke the hold, kicked Jessie off him, and scrambled up to race to the wall. Justin felt like a netted fish, sucking for air, and only breathed a little easier when he caught the covert wink Ethan shot Markus and the slight nod Markus returned.

Support. Justin could see it happening. He reminded himself of his own job here as a man behind them silently got up and walked to the desk. The receptionist showed him to a back room, out of sight. Clearly, it was the lose-your-shit room, and Justin hoped like hell he wouldn't have to take a trip there.

The students continued through their rounds, each hold seeming harder than the last, each one painting images in Justin's mind of what had truly happened to Ethan. He felt sick, and it broke his heart each time Ethan worked through and employed the skills he'd learned to keep himself safe. It ripped open the denial Justin had clung to; *yes*, he knew it had happened, but seeing a near replay like this made it so horribly real.

Justin had to let go of John's hand to get the blood flowing back in his own. His free hand still held the mask away from his mouth so he could breathe, and sweat rolled down his spine beneath his T-shirt to gather dampness there and under his arms from the stress.

Red plastic weapons appeared next, and a middle-aged woman took on a knife coming at her in a robbery scenario. His mother and Bethany needed to do this course, Justin decided. He nudged John with his knee. John nodded a slow, silent agreement and swallowed hard. The woman on the floor could have easily been Missy or Bethany.

When there was a short intermission for the students to have a water break and towel off, Justin followed the support group to a refreshment area. He passed the table of cold drinks and headed straight for the receptionist.

"Where's the room?"

She pointed behind her. "Behind the partition. You have ten minutes."

Justin made a beeline around the partition and went through a door. He sat in a chair, ripped off his mask, and put his head between his knees as he gulped for air. He needed two seconds to lose his shit, and then he could handle it again. His hat hit the floor, and he scrubbed his hands through his hair. He didn't fight the tears. Getting them out was better than holding them in for a second longer.

A cup of water was placed in his hand, and Justin leaned back and downed it. He expected to see the receptionist, but the man who had left earlier sat back down across from him and frowned.

"Thanks," Justin said.

He nodded.

Justin crushed the little cone cup in his hand, wiped his face with his shirt tail, and picked up his hat from the floor. He looped the mask back over his ears and stood. Closing his eyes, Justin found his calm. He gave the man a nod, dropped his cup in the trash, and left the room. The last of the supporters were heading back to the bleachers. Justin fell in behind them and retook his seat. John didn't look at him, and Justin could appreciate that as he pulled his hat brim lower, hoping Ethan wouldn't see his red eyes as he steadied himself for the second half.

WHEN IT WAS over, Justin did feel proud of Ethan; he had clearly learned a lot in the four weeks he'd been training. Ethan had to be the bravest person he'd ever known, but the experience had also been far more challenging for Justin than imagined.

Ethan had explained he would come home after the family members had left the gym. So Justin was now home with Bethany and John, who seemed just as shell-shocked as Justin, all of them silent for some time.

"Honey, why don't you go shower and change," Bethany said. "I'm going to start dinner. I'm sure he'll be hungry when he gets home. And I need something to do with myself."

Justin agreed. He reeked like panic, and his shirt was wet. "Give me five, and I'll help." He headed to their bathroom. It had been such a high and low birthday weekend, with one of the best days of his life followed by one of the worst. Justin dried off and changed, then threw his sweaty clothes into the washing machine and started it.

He joined Bethany in the kitchen. John handed him a beer and headed out to the pool deck to sit for a while.

"Mind making the salad?" Bethany asked. She'd already piled everything on the counter for him with a ready knife and cutting board.

"Sure." Justin swallowed down half his beer and got to work.

When the garage door warned them Ethan was home, Justin tapped on the glass patio door, and John came inside, face splotchy but dry. They all seemed to have a silent understanding as Ethan came in.

"Hey," he said and blew out a breath. "Come on." His voice cracked, and he waved them in.

Justin dropped the knife, Bethany left the water running at the sink, and John was a goner as they all embraced one another. Any idea of strength was lost as they cried, and Ethan was the rock.

"I am okay," he said. "I am not weak. And I love you. I know it was hard." And for a long time, they just stood there, falling apart and getting glued back together, as families do. After their moment, Ethan announced he needed to shower and eat.

Justin watched him go down the hallway before returning to the task he'd abandoned. John pulled the large lasagna from the oven for Bethany. She had the bread baking as Justin finished the salad. He took the large bowl to the dining room table. In the pantry, he pulled down two bottles of wine and the ridiculous decanters Ethan had wanted, then had those on the table filled and "breathing," as Ethan called it.

Justin poured two highballs of Scotch, set one down in front of John's plate, and then his own. Ethan joined them, his slightly longer hair damp and curling. Justin liked his longer hair. Ethan took his seat next to Justin at the round table, another of Ethan's decisions, where everyone was equal. Although he very much respected the patriarchy of his own family, it hadn't been what he wanted for their home, that old-school classic head-of-the-table rectangular dining table.

Justin poured Ethan a glass of wine. Bethany began cutting the lasagna, and they passed plates. John passed the salad bowl around.

"Will the next support day be on the twenty-ninth or the fifth?" Justin asked.

"The twenty-ninth, if I decide to take the next session," Ethan said. "I wanted to discuss it with you first."

"If you want to continue, I think you should. I'm not wild about the fighting aspect of it, but at the same time, I recognize you can't predict every situation, so you need the plays," Justin said, tapping the side of his head. "Even if you never use them, you know them."

"I think so too. Dad?"

"Yes, and after seeing that lady and the instructor with the knife…" John glanced at Bethany. "I think you and Missy should take the class this summer."

"Good call," Ethan said, turning to his mom, "Mom?"

"I think you should continue with the sessions, Ethan. I am very proud of you."

"I'm going to move forward with the group, then."

"Good. And Markus?" John asked.

"Oh, yeah, he's going to do them all too."

"Do you want to have a get-together or something for your group?" Justin asked. "I mean, we have this house, the pool, the beach, the grill. We have security."

Ethan paused in raising his wineglass as if considering the logistics of a party.

"You could do a brunch if you didn't want to do an evening thing," Bethany said.

"Markus has school, and several students have daytime jobs. No, I think a weekend afternoon party or a dinner party might be nice." Ethan looked at Justin as another thought seemed to cross his mind.

"I don't have to be here, or I can be. You trust them," Justin said.

"I do," Ethan said. "I'm going to think about it."

*

LATER, ETHAN FLOPPED down onto the bed and poked Justin with his finger.

"What?"

"I know you're upset."

"You think? I could barely breathe, Ethan. I want to support you, but that fucked me up. I want you to know how to protect yourself, and I've been lying here thinking there has to be another way. It's almost revictimizing, you know? Seeing that guy on top of you like that…"

"Murderous," Ethan said quietly. "I know. I saw you."

"Exactly. I was ready to kill someone."

Justin blew out a breath as Ethan scrambled over and plastered himself to Justin—an arm over his chest and his leg over his thighs, squeezing him hard. His head was buried against Justin's neck.

"I love you, Ethan, but fuck."

A hand moved and patted his shoulder.

"Yeah, yeah, I'll be fine because *I'm* the one we have to worry about. You know, I could just hire a security person for you."

"I have a bodyguard."

Justin laughed. "Don't make me lose it, I'm all… *Hell*, I don't know what I am. Pissed off, hurt, sad, selfish."

Ethan shifted over him, still holding on, and Justin slid his arms around Ethan. They adjusted, and Justin threw his leg over Ethan's, wrapping them up.

"I have some errands to run with your dad in the morning, then I want to play catch on the beach with you."

"What errands?" Ethan mumbled, yawning.

"We agreed we're going to buy a taser for the house if you are okay with that? If you're going to be here alone, it's just one more layer of protection. And I'm squashing the little dog idea. I want something that bites."

"Little dogs bite."

"No, I want something that rips off an arm, not an ankle biter, babe."

"You're overreacting because you're upset."

"Yeah, I am, but I don't care."

Chapter Thirty-Two

Ethan

ETHAN SIGHED AS he put the taser in the nightstand drawer. There was also a small personal taser he was supposed to keep charged and carry in his car. He had agreed to all this. A bright orange screaming panic alarm device now lived on Ethan's keychain, not to mention the various cans of pepper spray Justin had put in the house and insisted he carry with him. To say his man had gone slightly overboard at whatever place he and his dad had found was an understatement.

It was love—fucked up—but love all the same. And if Ethan were honest, he should have looked into these kinds of personal protection devices himself long ago. If he'd had a single one of them… He wasn't going there but couldn't deny it might have been a game changer. So, he'd do what

Justin and his father asked. He would heed their advice on this, though he had objected to the firearm suggestion. And he'd made them get the key-chains for everyone. He felt good about those. They were ear-piercing, and he was more comfortable with carrying that and the thought of using it.

Ethan tied his running shoes, clipped the personal alarm onto his shorts, and headed for the beach. Justin had just left, heading back to the Bay for another week, and Ethan needed a good hard run. On the brighter side, Justin had returned from his errand with a business card for a dog trainer and had already emailed the guy about a dog for Ethan. Justin's plan was to get a dog that could run with him. A working dog trained in personal protection.

Ethan had a feeling he'd end up with a security guard before Justin was done. During the games, Ethan would agree. Those would be complete insanity and overwhelming for him. Ethan had to remind himself exactly who he'd married.

"Such a caveman."

But he thought about what precautions any other starting NFL QB would take for their spouse and family, and Ethan understood it. It wasn't like Justin wouldn't be streaming on every *Monday Night Football* outlet in only a few months. He would be front page news with a big-time secret—*him*. And likely, there'd be fanatical fans. Ethan had no doubts about that. The world had no idea *who* was about to hit them, but this—Ethan did know. Justin was unlike anyone else, bottom line.

Ethan wasn't unaware of the dangers of the world anymore. He would never be a victim again. Shaking off the overwhelming thoughts, Ethan set the house alarm, locked the back door, and headed for the beach. He loved the feeling of tennis shoe tread on wet white sand, the smell of

the Gulf on a good day, and the faint taste of sea breeze on his lips. The
waves were lazy today, and the kayakers were out in full force.

Old Florida, they called it.

Ethan nodded at the snowbirds with their oversized sunglasses and
wide-brimmed hats as he took to the sidewalk from the beach, hit the
boardwalk through town, and would make his way back to the less-popu-
lated beach where he could really pick up some speed. He loved this route,
and it was usually on the leg by the old docks that he'd find shells when he
stopped for a break before his return run back home.

Every time Justin came home, Ethan would find him at the fireplace
mantel at some point, picking up the shells and looking at them, comment-
ing on the collection Ethan had started. It made him feel good how interested someone could be in the dumb shit you delighted in. They were shells;
the Shell Shoppe had them by the thousands. But they weren't the same,
not when Ethan had found a "unicorn horn," as Justin had claimed, though
it would have had to have been the tiniest unicorn since the shell was like
an inch long.

Ethan smiled as he ran. Never in his life had he imagined Justin. *Sometimes*, he did feel imagined, as if Ethan had just dreamed him up. Ethan
didn't know what he'd ever done to deserve someone like him, thinking
about the mail he'd recently opened. Discovering that his spouse had not
only taken out a ridiculous life insurance policy on himself for Ethan but
also had a lawyer on retainer for any and all future parole hearings had ce-
mented the faith Ethan had in Justin. He was *in* this.

The good, the bad, and the ugly. Justin had taken the phone when
that damn automated alert call had come, announcing one of *them* was being transferred to another prison. He'd called victim services and ensured

the orders of protection were still in place. He didn't care if they were in prison *now*. Eventually, they would get out. Ethan did well just to get through a day at a time, while Justin played a much longer game—their future.

Ethan stopped, breathing hard, and picked up the banded tulip shell. He checked to make sure it wasn't inhabited and secured it in his zippered shorts pocket. This was a great find, and he strolled along the beach, picking up a few cockle shells in one piece before turning and heading back home. He would have a good six miles in for the day, and from the way the backs of his calves and ankles were beginning to itch, he needed to get back and wash the sand off.

*

ETHAN COMPLETED THE registration packet and sealed it. He put it in the mailbox and raised the red flag. He wouldn't start full-time and in-person until next fall but wanted to go ahead and get accepted, with the option of enrolling in an online class or two while he took this year for himself. Still, he felt solid about his plan.

Ethan stopped in the driveway and glared at the neighbor's cat stretched out, flicking his tail in challenge.

"Jingles, go home."

Ethan shooed the cat, yelling, "Wait till you see the dog we're getting. He's going to eat you in one gulp."

A throat cleared.

"Oh, *hi*, Ms. Cleary," Ethan said, "just yelling at Jingles…*again*."

She flipped him off, and Ethan bowed.

"Always a pleasure."

Chapter Thirty-Three

Justin

JUSTIN DROVE THE three hours back Sunday afternoon, arriving in the dark. He climbed the stairs to his apartment, took one look, turned, and went back down the stairs. He called security and waited in his truck and called Coach Richardson.

"Sorry to bother you so late, Coach," Justin said.

"Not a problem. I'm actually at work and was just finishing up. Is something wrong?"

"I got home, and two girls are waiting at my front door. They look like strippers."

"You called security?"

"Yes, they just pulled up."

"Keep me on the line," Richardson said, and Justin heard keys jingling in the background.

Justin got out and told the officer that two females were at his door that he didn't know, and they didn't belong there.

"My coach is on the line," Justin told him.

The officer spoke with Richardson, and Justin waited as he talked with him, and another police car pulled up behind the first.

"Yes, sir, we'll give you the report number when you get here," the first officer said and handed Justin his phone back. "Mind waiting in your truck? He'll call you back."

"Yeah, and thank you for getting here so quick."

Justin watched as two skimpily dressed women were escorted down his stairs in handcuffs and driven away. He waited until another unit arrived, and then the two officers went back upstairs and were there for a long time.

Justin's phone rang, and he answered. "I'm on my way; just sit tight."

He waited as a man was brought down in cuffs. When a van arrived and people with crime scene equipment went up the stairs, Justin really got freaked out. His finger hovered over Ethan's name, but he didn't want him to worry, and he'd already be asleep. He waited, wondering what in the hell had happened until a few minutes later, Coach Richardson's SUV pulled up next to his truck, and he got out.

"Coach, I'm really sorry," Justin said. "I'm not sure what's happening. They told me to wait, and that's what I've done."

Coach Richardson leaned against Justin's truck next to him and pinched the bridge of his nose. "We'll need to move you after this. What all did you have in the apartment?"

"Next to nothing, other than a TV and a gaming system, my clothes, some gear. Nothing personal, no paperwork or anything. I'm pretty paranoid about personal information."

Coach seemed to understand that, and they continued to wait. Finally, he got on his phone and arranged a hotel room for Justin for the rest of the week until they could find a more secure place for him.

Justin glanced at his watch. "It's my birthday."

Coach shook his head and seemed just as disgusted with the situation. They both turned as the crime scene people returned with tripods and professional cameras, and the two officers followed them down.

"Let's see, but I don't like the looks of this," Coach said.

"They gained access to the vacant apartment next door," the officer said. "The male had a camera set up, and they damaged the apartment and drilled a hole through the wall. The females have already given statements they were paid to make a film with you. Since there's forced entry, and this guy's got a history of fraud and illegal distribution…"

An unfamiliar rage grew in Justin as the words blurred together, and he stared at his coach in horror at what they had tried to do.

"We're pressing charges against all parties," Coach Richardson said, equally pissed. "Can he get his things?"

"Yes," the officer said, and Richardson motioned for Justin to go on.

Justin packed his shit, and Coach came in with the officer, who agreed to stand by while they got everything.

"There isn't much," Justin said, and Coach helped as Justin zipped duffels full of his gear. "I'll return for the rest, just taking my clothes and gear now."

Coach carried two bags down, and the officer helped as Justin, still in a state of fury and shock, locked up.

"Shit," Richardson cursed, peering out past the security gate.

Justin turned also and closed his eyes as a media van parked outside was already rolling tape. Justin changed his direction, went to the passenger side of his truck, and loaded his bags. He crawled through, and Richardson and the officer piled in the rest.

"I'll escort you guys out," the officer said. Richardson agreed, gave him his card, and asked if they needed to go down to the station or if their legal team could respond. The officer confirmed they had all they needed for now. A detective would contact the team's legal department since the apartments were team property, and Coach Richardson told Justin to follow him.

Justin called Ethan, putting him on speaker as he drove. He waited as Ethan got up, searched the station's website on his tablet and watched their live coverage. Justin could faintly hear it in the background.

"It's on the news now," Ethan said, upset and worried. "They're saying your apartment was broken into and team property was stolen."

"That's not what happened, but good, someone's doing damage control," Justin muttered, rubbing his face. "Is this how it's going to be?"

"I don't know. Hey, Dad's calling. Call you back," Ethan said.

Coach pulled into a downtown high-rise, and Justin parked behind him. A man in a suit was waiting for them as a porter rushed forward to collect Justin's bags. Coach shook hands with the man, who gave Justin a nod. They followed him into the lobby, past the desk, and up an elevator ride. He swiped a key card, and they headed inside the suite. The porter unloaded Justin's bags, and he was given the key cards as the manager assured Coach that security was aware of their guest and protocols were in place with access to the floor only by Justin's key card. He'd need to use it on the elevator and the door. If he needed anything, just pick up the phone. And then he left them.

"What the hell?" Justin said.

"This stuff happens. It's not *you*." Coach stressed the word, and Justin got his meaning. "It's the position. The guy was likely trying to make a film or get something on video and blackmail a new, vulnerable player for money to keep him from releasing it. Justin, we deal with it every year. Pregnancy accusations…" Coach roughed a hand through his hair in frustration. "Nine months for those to clear, and when the DNA comes back negative, it's all just been a big nightmare and media storm."

"This is why," Justin said and pointed to himself.

"I get it. All right, I have things to handle with legal. Get some sleep. Practice in the morning, and I'll let you know what we work out about your living arrangements. You'll be here this week, and I'd strongly advise room service."

"Thank you, Coach."

*

ETHAN WAS UPSET, and Justin told him everything he knew as he watched the news. It was the same story on all stations now. The new QB's home had been burglarized. Once he finally got Ethan calmed down, Justin forced himself to get some sleep.

The next morning in the locker room, Justin dressed out and headed over to Holcombe. "Not today, man; rough night, but we'll get back on it tomorrow."

"I saw. You good?"

"Yeah," Justin said. "Thanks, man."

They had a relatively easy practice through half the day, and then they called Justin out for meetings for the rest of it while his backup took over. Justin sat in the head coach's office with numerous staff he hadn't yet met and what he assumed were attorneys. Coach Richardson came in with a detective, and he went through what they knew, what had been released in their press statement, the status of the suspects being charged, and the list of charges. A restraining order had been issued to all three. Justin was given copies of those, as were the team attorneys. Then the detective was gone, a discussion over where Justin should live ensued.

The team had several properties, but Justin said he'd make arrangements if they could find him a realtor.

"I'll just buy something gated and not in an apartment," Justin said, leaning back in the chair.

"I think that's best," Coach Richardson said. "You and the team will have security during all games and events."

"Media?" Coach Nellis asked.

"We've released the press statement reflecting what the police department put out and added a team statement about our players' safety and security," one of the media directors said.

"Legal?" Coach Nellis asked.

Justin listened as they gave their reports and recommendations, and then Justin and the head of security, Stan, were scheduled to meet with a realtor at two.

"No practice tomorrow. Get situated and keep me posted," Coach Richardson said, and Justin headed out with Stan.

"Stan—gated, cameras, alarms," Coach Nellis said, and Stan nodded.

Justin and Stan looked through the listings in the real estate manager's office. He was handling this case personally, and Justin appreciated it. He'd found several properties that met Stan's strict requirements, and they finally settled on a small modern house on a canal. It was gated with a guard shack and 24/7 security. Several other high-profile residents lived on the canal, and all residents had to sign NDAs to even make an offer. Stan agreed with this. So, it was between the canal house and only one condo he approved of.

"Will they take cash with an immediate occupancy?" the realtor asked on the phone. And he nodded to Justin.

It was more than he wanted to fork over, but he realized as Stan scowled at him that this needed to be done. Justin was thankful they'd gone the mortgage route with their real house and he'd not blown through his bank account balance. Still, this was going to sting a bit. Justin flipped through the pictures again and finally agreed.

"I'll have a contract faxed over in five," the realtor said, and then he went to work.

Justin messaged Ethan while they waited to give him an update. It all happened so fast as he and Stan drove to the new house, and his staff arrived with the rest of Justin's things from his apartment. He was grateful to not return to the old apartment and thanked them as they brought in his meager furniture and the few boxes they'd packed for him.

Stan went through the house, testing the security system, resetting everything, and ensuring all the cameras were functioning. He spent time outside, checking the exterior and walking the small inlet with five other houses, and returned feeling good about the location.

"Park in the garage. You're the last house, so no media can gain access through the gate or from the walls. He pointed out to the canal. That's your only weak point."

Justin glanced through the glass door out at the canal and understood. An eager pap on a boat had a clear line of sight. He'd be living in a one-sided fishbowl here. He gazed around the empty space at his one chair and television, his coffee table and game system. Upstairs only had a frame bed, a quick-assemble nightstand, lamp, and two alarm clocks. It seemed nothing like a home.

"Need help getting some furniture?" Stan asked.

"Thanks, but no, it's just me." Justin shrugged, and Stan nodded.

"If you need a keyholder—" Stan said and gave Justin his card. "If anything happens, no matter what time it is, you call me."

"Thanks for today; you really helped," Justin said, scrubbing his hair.

He shook Stan's hand and his staff's, who'd done everything, and then Justin found himself alone in a big empty house that felt more like a holding cell. He headed upstairs to call Ethan and then try to take a nap.

"The cavalry is coming," Ethan said. "Well, me, Mom, and your dad. Missy and John have to work, but we are coming down to make it at least livable. And with them there with me, it won't look like anything."

"Yeah, sounds good," Justin said, admitting, "I need you."

Chapter Thirty-Four

Justin

JUSTIN SLEPT DURING the time it took them to drive down, and then he was up with the call from security, letting him know his visitors had arrived and were through the gate. Justin went downstairs, hit the garage door button, waited until they pulled in, and closed it. After hugs and greetings, they got down to business. His dad was livid, not quite as pissed as Ethan, but Bethany made a good point that Ethan could stay there, and not a soul would know. That seemed to settle him some.

"It is like Fort Knox," his father agreed. "And all NDAs." He whistled.

"Clearly, I'm not the only one who doesn't want their business out there," Justin said.

"Well, it's not *home*, but it will have a good resale value," Ethan said as he looked around. "Too fancy, too modern."

Justin agreed it was not their style at all, but the almost complete privacy of Canal Pointe was appealing. You couldn't even see a neighbor for all the trees and landscaping, the long drives, and houses set back off the one-way in and one-way out cul-de-sac.

"I think I could stay here some," Ethan said, perking Justin up.

"Thank God, this sucks," Justin hated being away from Ethan a week at a time and only having barely two days with him. "But this isn't going to be our real home. I love our house. And we have to be aware of the water-side. It isn't secure."

"I agree, but you can't drive six hours a day," Ethan said, and he was right. "Okay, Mom—food and kitchen. Nathan, you, and me—necessities. Justin, unpack your clothes and get everything else set up." Ethan tossed his keys to his mom and held his hand out for Justin's keys.

Justin was hanging his clothes and folding them when his phone rang, and Coach Richardson called.

"Hey, Coach. Yeah, I was just settling in. Sure, come by. I'll unlock the door and let security know. Just come on in."

Justin glanced at his watch, feeling he'd have enough time since everyone had just left. Justin called security to let them know Coach Richardson was approved, and Justin made quick work of his closet. He looked around. The security guys had done him right; everything was plugged in and set. He headed downstairs, unlocked the front door for Coach, and straightened his pathetic chair and table. It was utterly depressing.

Justin went to the back door and unlocked it, heard the alarm tone sound, and walked out on the deck area. He sighed, sat down on the steps, and looked at the empty dock, out at the water, trying to fight his emotions and keep himself in check.

Coach Richardson sat next to him and squeezed his shoulder. "You all right?"

"Not really," Justin admitted.

"It's a nice house; that empty feeling sucks."

"Yep," Justin said and turned at the sound of McReedy's loud voice.

"Are we having a move-in birthday party or what?" McReedy boomed, and Justin's eyes widened at his teammates, who all smiled back at him.

"Fuck." Justin shook his head, and it was a pointless battle as Coach laughed and tugged him up. They were amazing, all of them, and they'd brought beer, lots of beer. McReedy handed him a cold one as a monstrous-sized sheet cake slid onto the counter, followed by a stack of paper plates, utensils, and napkins. And they brought in more shit. Justin shook his head as Holcombe and another defenseman hauled in a new couch. Miller rolled out a rug, and Jones and Hitchins took down his shit TV and put up a new one.

Justin headed out the front door to help and grabbed what was handed to him from the back of a rental truck.

"How in the world did you guys pull this off?" he asked as everyone was doing something.

"It was easy with an entire administrative staff put to task," Coach Richardson said. "And Coach Nellis—he wanted things to be right, so the team picked up the tab for this."

Justin stared as Bethany peeked her head in the garage door, holding grocery bags and taking in the scene. He went to help, and two more teammates headed out to bring the rest in.

Justin sent a text to Ethan to be calm and tell his dad, and then he was back to helping. Bethany cut the cake and lined up plates with large squares for everyone. Justin's dad and Ethan arrived, and they hauled in their purchases. Justin knew Ethan was overwhelmed and trying not to freak out as he shook hands and met people he'd heard of but didn't know.

Justin kept his eye on Ethan, and when he finally met Miller, he felt slightly better at Miller's natural friendliness with Ethan. Completely unaware, Miller shook hands and chatted it up with his biggest supporter. Justin's dad and Bethany met everyone as "Mom and Dad," and no one pried or asked any further questions about their family dynamics.

McReedy hid a bit lip behind his beer and lifted a brow at Justin. Other than that, no one seemed the wiser except Coach Richardson, who shook Ethan's hand and darted his eyes down for only a moment at Ethan's ring finger. He later glanced at Justin and nodded.

Yep, that's who you'll be calling if shit goes sideways.

"Stop." Justin shook his head. "This is a fucking nightmare," he said to McReedy with a pained expression.

"You are shitting your pants right now."

"You think?"

"They don't have a clue."

"Thank fuck," Justin said.

McReedy slowly shook his head. "No, they don't. You've got that shit locked down tight, brother."

Justin sure hoped so, and he shook hands with one of the assistants who'd come to drop off his contracts for the house. She said she'd be back in touch when things quieted down.

"But we're talking later," McReedy said.

"That's fair. Trust and shit," Justin said, repeating McReedy's mantra.

Justin took in Ethan, tall and thin, with his typical backward ball cap, vintage band T-shirt, skinny jeans, and red Chucks. He was so fucking cute, dimple-cheeked and shy, but doing his best as he listened to something Coach was saying to him. Justin almost couldn't take his eyes off him. But he turned to McReedy and got serious.

"Want to meet him?"

"I do," McReedy said, and Justin saw no judgment in his eyes. McReedy gave him a reassuring nod, and Justin crossed the room with him at his side. They waited for Coach to move on, and both stepped in.

"Ethan, I want you to meet Reese McCreedy," Justin said.

Ethan stared at the monstrous man, who grinned back at him. "*You are the center.*"

"That's right. I keep this guy safe," McReedy said.

Ethan slipped his left hand into his jeans pocket as they small-talked. Justin hated seeing Ethan do it, or that he insisted Justin not wear his ring except at home. Justin eventually dragged McReedy away to help with the last of the surprise birthday move-in.

Justin felt better as he looked around a house that didn't feel quite so impersonal. For a quick throw-together in a pinch, whoever had been on shopping duty had done well.

Ethan and Nathan played it cool and slipped out, texting Justin to let them know when everyone left since Ethan was feeling overwhelmed. Bethany also slipped out, and then it was just him and his team, who all decided cake and beer did not mix.

*

JUSTIN HUGGED ETHAN and apologized repeatedly. He'd had no idea his team would do something like that. Ethan was fine though; Nathan had done dad-duty and talked him down after the ambush they'd walked into.

"Your coach knows, Justin," Ethan said, panicked. His hair was a mess as if he'd run his fingers through it a hundred times in the car.

"He does. I had to trust one person so that if something happened— if I got seriously injured—he'd know who to call, and he'd know who matters."

"Oh," Ethan said.

"Oh, and McReedy knows, but he said no one else has a clue. I'm cringing, telling you they think you're my brother."

Ethan laughed. "We look nothing alike."

"I don't know. They also thought Bethany was my mom and married to my dad." Justin rolled his eyes. "They see what they want to, and it worked out fine. You gotta remember, none of them want people in their business either."

"Well, holy shit, look at all this stuff."

"Yeah, you get to rearrange it and make it not look like a hotel lobby though."

"Yeah, but there's some good stuff to work with." Ethan was visibly relaxing as he began to take in everything. "I want to see the back."

"No, you aren't allowed to see that."

"I'm not allowed?"

"Nope. I already know what will happen."

"What?"

"You'll want a boat," Justin teased.

"I have my WAG boat." Ethan's eyes widened. "Oh my God, Justin, we could get a real boat and name it *The WAG*."

Justin could only agree. "Come on. I'll be broke after you see the neighbors' boats."

*

THE NEXT MORNING, Justin kissed a sleeping Ethan on the side of his forehead. He then locked up the house and headed for the practice field earlier than usual to meet with McReedy. He hadn't wanted to waste any time with this, putting off this talk or risking losing McReedy's trust. Justin felt slightly guilty for not telling McReedy before, but all he could do was hope he would understand. Justin parked his truck and got his equipment bag out of the back. McReedy's truck was already there.

"Let's take the track," McReedy said as a greeting, and Justin fell in, dreading jogging and talking simultaneously. But McReedy walked instead, and Justin started talking.

"I'm sorry for not telling you, but I hope you understand my reasons. I don't tell anyone. Coach is aware, but that's because I need him to know who to call if I get seriously injured. He's also in on it because I had to be honest with him about some things I needed in my contract. Ethan is why I don't do the media. I have to protect him."

"How'd he get that scar on his face?" McReedy asked and touched his temple.

"That's not my story to tell. I *can* tell you no one will ever lay a finger on him again."

McReedy nodded. "Y'all are married then? I saw the ring on his finger."

"We are. We've been together for just over a year now. It's not legal, but it's real. Real to us."

"So you met him in college?"

"Yeah. I never saw him coming, man." Justin laughed. "I was a goner, still am. He makes me happy. He loves me, and fuck, I love him so much it hurts."

"Explain this living arrangement, that whole leaving on the weekends."

"We live farther north at our real home. It's a long drive, but now, with this new place, he's thinking about staying here some during the week since it's more private and secure than the apartment was. If he agrees, I'd like you to come over, hang out, and get to know him. But if you're uncomfortable with that, I get it."

McReedy stopped. "I don't have a problem with it. I understand why you didn't tell me. And I know something bad happened to him. I can tell. I won't ask again, but something bad happened to my cousin, and Ethan has the look." McReedy motioned to his eyes. "It's in the eyes. This sadness that never goes away, even when they're happy. She has it too." He swallowed hard. "I'm sorry for whatever it was."

Justin nodded, choked up. "Me too. And for your cousin."

McReedy started walking again. "You bought *him* the kayak?"

"Yeah, and now he wants a fucking 'big boy' boat. Know anything about real boats?"

"A bit, probably more than your dumb ass," McReedy teased, having already witnessed Justin's horrible attempt at picking out the right kayak.

"Right. So, I'll put you on the security list."

"You better," McReedy said, rolling his hand, indicating they could stop talking and pick up the pace.

"I thought that would be harder," Justin said, starting to jog.

"You love him; I can tell. Just seeing how you look at him. I get it. As long as he treats you right."

Justin laughed. "He does."

"Good. Secret's safe with me."

Justin bumped fists with McReedy.

*

TWO MONTHS LATER, Justin shook his head as he tied his tie and looked out the back door at *The WAG* in her slip, gleaming chrome with a white deck and navy-blue bottom. Ethan had fallen in love with the trawler yacht on-site, with its cabin and kitchen, after an entire month of researching used boats with McReedy, yessing or noing ones they'd found. He'd even convinced McReedy to teach him how to operate and maintain it, along with *everything* boating.

They were also having a dock and slip built to accommodate her at their real home. The plan was to be able to take the boat between the houses when they had the time. Justin didn't care. Ethan was so happy over the boat, his new hobby, a new friend, and there'd been no mention of enrolling in school or boredom. "*A year off*," Ethan had said. There'd been no red flags, and while Justin worried about his selfish desires when it came to Ethan, he couldn't deny that Ethan was thriving. He was finding himself again, and for that, Justin would accept that being selfish wasn't always a bad thing.

"You ready?" John asked, and Justin nodded.

"You look good; don't be nervous," Bethany said, and Justin and Ethan both laughed.

"That's the second shirt." Ethan said, telling on him. "Sweated right through the first one."

"Kick ass, son," Nathan said.

"And don't get sacked." Missy hugged him tight.

"They'll all be out of here if you win," Ethan said and coughed.

"Ethan," Justin said as his face went bright red.

"Well." Ethan shrugged.

"Ok, ok, not for parents' ears. We've got our tickets. Give 'em hell," John said.

Justin nodded and checked one more time he had everything. He kissed Ethan in the garage and then got in his truck.

This was it, the dream he'd had since he was seven, in the backyard, throwing the ball with his dad. Justin coughed away the lump of emotions and started his truck.

Chapter Thirty-Five

Justin

"ASSHOLES!" HOLCOMBE YELLED and pointed to the whiteboard: *forty-six days since sacked*. "I swear to God, if this isn't forty-seven tomorrow, I'm asking Coach for an extra day of practice for the rest of the season."

The sack board had become a strange team motivator that even the coaching staff had gotten behind.

"You look like you might puke," McReedy said, and Justin stood and headed to the bathroom as McReedy laughed his ass off.

After Justin swore he tasted his intestines, he knew McReedy would tell Ethan about this. When there was no way he had a thing left for the field, he cleaned himself up, brushed his teeth, and rejoined his team.

"Now that the QB has shared that sound effect with us..." Coach

Richardson said, and then he got serious. "We are better than they are. We've worked harder. We've got the right components on this team to go all the way. No stupid mistakes, no penalties. Play clean and by the rules. Trust the plan and the calls…"

The building began to rumble with the roar of the crowd. Justin looked up; the ceiling practically vibrated, and Miller bailed next.

"Anyone else?" Coach Nellis asked, then gave his pregame speech.

The crowd was insane, and Justin stared at the chaos, the sea of color and the screaming. At ten thousand times the college crowd, the noise was so powerful he could feel it through his feet and into his bones. Justin hoped like hell he'd be able to even hear the plays in his helmet. Then McReedy nudged him to go.

And without thinking, like it was second nature, Justin ran out onto the field. The crowd went deafening as they cheered. Justin made it to the sideline and realized he'd never find Ethan. He searched around for their section and the bright green neon waving posterboard with a big *E* on it. Justin held up his hand with a number one, their signal that he knew where he was.

Ethan looked like a dot, but he was there. Justin breathed and nodded to himself. *Now* he could play. And the screams turned into a hum, rain on repeat, and rolling waves. Thunder and the wind. Ambient noise he could detach himself from. Everything—the field, the opponents, the scoreboard, the play chart, his teammates—all became crystal clear.

Throw to Ethan. Justin repeated the internal mantra that had worked for him since the Combine and in every practice since then.

"We got this," McReedy said, and Justin nodded, too in the zone to speak at the moment. They watched the kickoff and return and then ran out onto the field.

The first play, straight out of the shoot, was what Justin had asked Coach Richardson for in their pregame meeting. Justin had explained he wanted to fire off a bullet from the start with a bold first move, scoring a touchdown with Jones. Jones, sitting next to him, had nodded. Justin said he wanted them to come out strong with a loud and clear message to the world. Jones had been a nervous wreck after the meeting, and Justin just threw an arm over his shoulder and told him he better catch it, hang on to it, and run like hell.

McReedy snapped, and Justin faked, stepped back as Jones broke away and got open. He fired it off, visualizing Ethan's goofy-ass running around wildly and having to put it in his palms. Justin waited as everyone took off downfield, and Jones, palms open, closed them around the ball and turned on the speed. The crowd was up and going berserk, and Justin held up his one for Ethan. He hustled off the field for the field goal unit, swallowing the fear that rose up in his throat, hardly believing they'd pulled it off with all the nerves.

"Holy shit!" Jones said, still holding the ball. "I'm keepin' this. This shit is mine. This is mine. My ball. They can't have it. Ain't nobody taking it away from me."

Coach barked out a laugh and shook his head at the ref. "First NFL game, first play, first touchdown. He's keepin' it. But you give it to the trainer, Jones. Let's play with another one for a while." He gave him a reassuring pat.

Jones, still heaving, looked at Justin. "It was just like you said. Just like you said."

Justin pointed to the trainer.

Jones turned. "This is mine."

"I got you, man, I swear." The trainer reached for the ball, and Jones released it, seeming to shake it off.

"Did that really just happen?" Jones asked Coach Richardson, who then pointed at the big screen and replay.

"You made your point," Richardson said to Justin, but he was fighting the smile so hard. "This is the next play…" and Justin dropped his head and nodded. "Don't forget what we talked about."

"I got it; saving it, Coach." Justin turned to their defense on the field, waving off the tablet held out for him to review the previous play. He didn't want to watch unless he screwed up.

The opponents came out playing smart, but they were intimidated, and that was just what Justin wanted in that QB's head. They went for a field goal, and then Justin put on his helmet.

Each time they scored, he held up his finger for Ethan. By the third touchdown, the crowd did it, too, and Justin knew Ethan was dying over it, knowing only *he* knew what it meant. That he was Justin's one love. His one and only. And Justin played hard for his love of the game and for his love for Ethan.

"I love this fucking game!" Justin yelled, and his offensive line *oorah*ed back as he called out the next play. Another long pass and Miller's helmet was an inch from his cleat as he held down the intended sack. Justin hauled him up, patted him, and watched as Chastain was taken down.

They raced downfield and got into position. Justin passed off the ball behind him and wasn't shocked by the pile up three yards from the line. Their defense was determined, *him*, their target. Justin could practically hear his offensive line growling; it wasn't going to happen.

Hernandez, with the highest vertical jump, other than Justin, understood as Justin called the play. He eyeballed Jones and nodded, and Jones nodded back. The offensive line shifted. Justin faked to Jones, who was already in the endzone, covered, and then threw high to Hernandez, also surrounded, who jumped with the defensive player, outreached him, and brought down the ball with a tuck and roll.

Justin roared. It sounded animal, and he shot his hand and single finger up before running in. The crowd was out of control as the offense surrounded Hernandez, who, like Jones, was not giving up the ball.

They were quick to get off the field, and Coach bitched, "Damn rookies." But he was riding the high over the three balls he would already be paying for.

"Call Wilson," Justin yelled out to one of the referees. "We're going to need some more footballs."

The ref fought his grin as special teams sprinted on for the field goal. It was good, and Justin breathed at the scoreboard. Their lead was impressive, and the half was already on them as they jogged down their tunnel screaming, hollering, and whooping like it was peewee league on a Saturday afternoon and not the NFL.

Jones, Chastain, and Hernandez all had a ball. Justin squinted at Miller.

"No, I can't handle it," Miller said, nearly begging him not to.

"But how cool would that be? Just block, get in the endzone, and catch it, man. We'll switch you to an eligible receiver. Whatever you do, don't close your eyes."

"Don't, Justin, I'm serious," Miller mumbled.

"Coach?" Justin said.

"Here we go," McReedy barked, and everyone quieted down.

"We got a play where Miller can score, so all rookies get a game-one ball?" Justin asked.

"Are you going to do the interview after?" Coach fired back, and Justin nodded.

Richardson turned to the board and scratched out the play. "We got it?"

They all yelled.

"It's all fun and games after this one," Justin said to Miller. "Just open your hands, and I'll put the ball in them. Just remember to hold that ball, and don't drop it."

"I hate you so much right now," Miller said.

"You are making my game-one NFL dream come true, man. *Do not* let me down," Justin said, and they went through their ritual, then headed back onto the field.

*

"JUSTIN, ARE WE missing something here? What was the objective tonight?" a reporter asked during the post-game press conference.

Justin grinned. "I just thought it would be cool if all the rookie players who played tonight got their first NFL game, first score, first ball. Jones got his, Chastain, then Hernandez, and I looked at Miller." Justin shook his head. "Who's about ready to kill me, but I said how cool would it be, and we made it happen. And I've got the game ball, so that's all five of us. It just doesn't get any better than that until we start talking about the Super Bowl."

Hands flew into the air.

"So you think a rookie quarterback can take this team all the way?"

"Watch me," Justin said, and pens scribbled.

"It was a brave move to come out with a long pass for the first play."

"I wanted to make an impression and show everyone what Jones and this team can do," Justin said. "Let every opponent know from the start that I'm here to win. No one loves this game more than me."

"It's been rumored that you aren't a fan of the media," a brave young reporter said, bolting up above another. She appeared to be barely out of college compared to the veterans in the room and one of only two other females.

"I'm not at all. I've made that clear. But thank you for your question, and I'll give you an answer I haven't given anyone else." Justin paused. "You ready?" She nodded. "I like good reporting and fair, professional journalists, not ones who chase me down after a class or yell at me in the grocery store parking lot. Ones who get aggressive. Those experiences in college turned me against the media. But I'll make you a deal; treat me with respect and professionalism, and I'll do the same and see if you can change my opinion."

She nodded again, mouthed a *thank you*, and sat down.

"Who are you with?" Justin asked.

"*Newsweek*," she said as she stood back up.

"Are you a good one?"

"I am," she said confidently.

"Talk to our media director if you want an interview, and I'll do it," Justin said, and she took her seat again.

Justin answered one more question about whether he missed being a receiver, and he said he was happy in his position. Then he tilted his head at Jones, and they got the point.

Coach Richardson seemed pleased.

Justin listened and observed all the reporters, picked out the ones he would never trust, and noticed the young reporter still writing and eagerly paying attention as Miller managed through his answer.

"One last question for Justin," a male reporter said. He held up his arm and finger, imitating Justin's score celebration. "The fans loved this, but what does it mean?"

"We're number one, THE number one team," Justin said as the flashes went off.

"Why do you refuse interviews?" His media director smiled like she could kiss him and kill him all at the same time as she escorted him down the back hallway.

"I'm giving the *Newsweek* newb one," Justin said.

"Oh, I know." She shook her head at him. "But you're also doing the interview with *Sports Illustrated*."

"What do I get?"

She just laughed as she pointed to the chair for him to sit. "I'm going to get your girl," she said, flustered but on a media high.

Chapter Thirty-Six

Ethan

RECLINING IN THE new poolside lounger, Ethan flipped the magazine open, showing Justin the picture of him yelling like a madman: *"I love this game!"*

"You look crazed." Ethan turned his attention to the other page and read out loud:

How I Scored the Most Sought-after Interview in the NFL, by Shelly Marksman.

I had just been hired at Newsweek, straight out of college, and my editor came rushing in. 'Stop what you're working on and get over to the stadium'. Our senior sports writer, Gary Moreland, had been in an accident. She pointed to my press pass, and I threw it over my head. My assignment is politics. I know embarrassingly little about sports. 'Get a statement from Justin Halstead, the new quarterback,' she yelled at me before leaving the building to follow up on Gary's condition. The only thing I knew about the team's new quarterback was that he hated the media, refused to do interviews, and was a starting rookie. That was it.

Ethan looked over and grinned at Justin, who rolled his hand, so he continued:

The game was intense. There are no other clever words to describe the immediate long pass and out-of-the-gate first score, nor the Bay's new hand signal, adopted over two more touchdowns, and the sheer presence of Justin Halstead and his team on the field. Like me, if you were there or watched on TV, it was as if we were all under his spell. And it only got better as he ensured that every rookie starter went home with a ball for their first NFL touchdown in their first NFL game. That is a new record established and set by Justin Halstead, who was awarded the team game ball for all his MVP firsts.

Five balls.

Halstead told a referee on the field to call Wilson—that the NFL would need more footballs. Just before the end of the game, I knew I needed to find the press conference room and get a seat, but I could not stop watching the game, the madness, the celebration. Like everyone else, I heard Justin Halstead yelling, "I love this game!" and his team's answering oorah before he called the play. Everyone heard it. You've seen the picture. That was the moment. And Justin has had other incredible moments: this, an impossible catch that won his college game, or this, the high school Hail Mary that won the state championship. For me, my incredible moment came as a brand-new reporter trying to hang on to my first job. I jumped up and asked the winning quarterback why he hated the media. And he knew. He knew I was new, inexperienced, a first-time player on an unfamiliar field, and Halstead threw me a pass.

He talked about less than favorable behavior by the media in the past, being hounded after a college class when student schedules are supposed to be confidential. Or when he was chased through a parking lot to his vehicle when he was trying to buy groceries. Or journalists showing up at his dorm asking for an interview when he'd just played a rough game and was trying to sleep through the chaos of a college football dorm. So, he refused. He wanted to play ball and be left alone.

But I asked, and he answered, threw me that pass, and then let me score the only interview he's given. I thanked him, and he shrugged with a, "Hey, I'm new too," and we had a laugh.

"Who's your girlfriend?" I asked him, and he said her name was Wilson, and they'd been together since peewee league. At my confused look, he threw his head back, and his laughter is loud, like him. "Wilson, football manufacturer," he said, leaving the room still chuckling. He came back and handed me a football. "Shelly, meet Wilson, Wilson, Shelly." And I understood. He's funny, and he's cocky. He's extremely

confident and has openly challenged all opponents that he's taking his team to the Super Bowl as a rookie quarterback. "We are number one. The number one team," he said. And I'm a believer.

Then he asked me if I wouldn't mind giving a shout-out to a high school team he worked with over the summer, to all the guys. He named every single one off the top of his head; they are listed here. What do you do in your spare time? I asked. He said he plays catch and is trying to learn how to breathe in a tropical climate. Who is your hero? And he chewed on his lip and thought for a moment. "My mom. She's a high school English and literature teacher who instilled a love for reading that has never left me. I own more books than any other possessions." Is there a charity you plan to work with? And he said he hoped to promote literacy, then added, "That ought to make my mom proud." I found myself out of questions, unprepared as I was.

"What made you want to be a reporter?" he asked me, and I told him I hoped the media could improve its reputation with fair and honest reporting. That's why I applied at Newsweek, wanting to work for an outlet that held and stuck to those standards. He nodded as if he approved. "Is Gary okay?" Yes, he's going to be fine. "Who's your boyfriend?" And I winked at him. "His name is Webster; maybe you've met him."

Then Justin Halstead stood, shook my hand, and autographed the ball, telling me it was his first NFL autograph. He handed the ball to me, then pointed at it. "That makes ball six in the firsts. Now go be number one, Shelly Marksman, with Newsweek. And I'll see you at the Super Bowl."

"Oh," Ethan said and nodded. "That was good."

Justin leaned over and shook his head. "I do look crazy."

"It's on a billboard Justin. People are doing it, fans on social media. *I love this game, arrrrh,*" Ethan tried. "It's a thing now."

"So is our finger thing."

"Such a slick response."

"They hear what they want to hear. That's you and me."

"I know that," Ethan said. "But it's still convenient."

Justin grinned.

"Wilson," Ethan scoffed.

"I think we should rename the boat to *Wilson,*" Justin teased.

"No, she's *The WAG*. She'll always be *The WAG*."

"*The WAG*." Justin snorted. "What about one of those vanity license plates for your car?"

"Now you're trying to get caught." Ethan shook his head. "Nice answer though."

"I thought so," Justin said. "But you do sound a little jealous."

"I'm not. It wasn't your first NFL autograph, was it?" Ethan pouted.

"I signed yours right after the game on my game ball. *Your* ball. But, yes, that was my first official one, in public, recorded or whatever."

"Fine." Ethan sighed. "You totally helped her out."

"I don't know. I think she kind of helped me."

"True," Ethan said.

*

ETHAN GOT OUT of the shower, put a towel around his waist, and rummaged through the dresser drawer, searching for a pair of sleep pants. He turned around and eyed Justin, stretched out on their bed, his big arms behind his head, wearing nothing but a cocky grin.

"Funny."

Ethan leaned back on the dresser and lowered his fingers to the tuck of his towel. "So you think if you hide my clothes, what?"

Justin clearly liked this game by the look he wore, his eyes fixed on Ethan's fingers as he teased the corner of the towel.

"No clothes equals a naked Ethan," Justin quipped.

"Ah." Ethan released the corner, smirking as the towel hit the floor. He sauntered to the bed, watching as Justin's hand slid down, and he gripped himself. "That's for me?"

"Always," Justin promised as Ethan climbed across the bed and over Justin.

Ethan kissed his lips once and rolled off him, lying on his side of their big bed.

"What?" Justin asked of Ethan's abrupt shift.

"I think it's time for you to stop carrying around that essay," Ethan whispered, swallowing down his fears. He looked at Justin, hoping his eyes conveyed what he struggled to say.

Justin shifted over until his face was closer to Ethan's. "I do love you like that—more than you know."

"I do know it." Ethan admitted what he'd struggled so hard to accept. He knew it now. Justin loved him, truly loved him, and would never hurt him or leave him.

"Ethan…" Justin seemed to breathe his name as if it was the one word in the world that mattered. Then, he eased in even closer.

Ethan nodded slowly as his shaky hand touched Justin's cheek, and Justin leaned in with his eyes closed and pressed his dampened lips to Ethan's. Ethan responded, matching each move Justin made to deepen the kiss. He breathed through his nose and slid his hand to Justin's shoulder, pulling him in as a tongue dipped inside his mouth and met his own. Justin inhaled hard and then inched in against Ethan, gaining more access as his knee nestled between Ethan's legs and his tongue tangled with Ethan's.

They adjusted, crushing their bodies even more impossibly together as the kiss grew from a slow tempo to gradually more passionate, and the sound of their breathing filled the room. Ethan ran his hand down Justin's back, and Justin's hand slid across Ethan's bare side and squeezed there. *This* was the kiss Ethan had written about.

They were a tangle of heat and growing intensity. Ethan's need to fuse himself against Justin grew more demanding, and then a braver hand slid down to his ass and pulled. Pulled him in, encouraging the grind. Justin moaned, and Ethan finally accepted he could give himself to the man he loved.

They broke free, Justin panting, eyes lustful, and then they resumed, not missing a beat, skin to skin with hands exploring each other. The great weight of Justin on top of him settled in as they repositioned, and Justin's firm grip on Ethan's outer thigh as Justin ground into him made it clear Justin had an experienced sexual past, just not this version. Justin's mouth was against Ethan's ear, and he breathed hard as his hips rocked.

"This is going to be over fast," he panted when Ethan's hand joined them together and began to pump, gripping them tight against each other. Justin's mouth slid back to Ethan's, and the sounds he made into it had

Ethan's hips bucking up as Justin thrust his hips, and they found a rhythm to match Ethan's hand.

Ethan released them, reached for the tube, and passed it to Justin, then spread his thighs wider. He smiled at a wide-eyed Justin, who stared momentarily at the tube and further down between them at Ethan's new position. Justin's hesitation was quickly forgotten as a slick finger searched for unfamiliar ground, pressed against Ethan, and rubbed a slow circle.

"I've dreamed about this so many times," Justin said, his words gruff with strain as his finger pushed inside.

Justin's eyes were locked on him, but Ethan's rolled back at the sensation of Justin easing in timidly deeper and then pulling back slightly before braving in again.

"Too much?"

"No, keep going," Ethan said, finding it easier to relax than he'd thought he would.

"It's so hot inside you." Justin groaned as he found more confidence.

"More," Ethan decided; Justin's finger began to feel electrifying as it pumped with an undeniable rhythm.

And Justin was eagerly back with two fingers, patiently exploring as Ethan accepted the change. "I'm not sure I'm going to make it," he said, deadly serious. "I'm so close already, Ethan. It feels too good. You're like an inferno." He buried his face against Ethan's neck and groaned.

"Don't you dare," Ethan warned as Justin's body tensed.

"I can't help it." Justin lifted up and leaned back, jerking himself off, his eyes glued to his fingers pushing and pulling in and out of Ethan's body.

Ethan watched, mesmerized as Justin lost it so quickly, the way he did early on in their relationship, and reached down. His hand was knocked away; Justin settled in, replacing it with his lips, fingers still exploring as his mouth consumed Ethan.

"Okay," Ethan agreed, letting himself relax. This would work, too.

Justin seemed content to get lost in what his fingers were finally exploring. Ethan sensed the change in him as it became easier, with less resistance. Ethan absently searched for the tube and passed it down, whispering for Justin to add another finger. Ethan doubted he could come like this, his anxiety beginning to build. But Justin found that magic button inside him, and Ethan began to quiver as Justin moaned around him, and those two fingers massaged the switch that had Ethan firing off like Justin.

Justin leaned back, a satisfied victory on his face as he grabbed the tube, and then Ethan felt a slow expanding pressure as he was stretched. Justin checked on him, and Ethan confirmed he was good. He was more than good after the orgasm, and his anxiety faded as Justin took his time, got him ready, and was clearly rising to the occasion once more.

"I love you, Ethan," Justin said as he shifted up, kissed Ethan, and rubbed himself across Ethan's entrance. "I want you."

"Yes," Ethan whispered as Justin guided himself, rubbing again and pressing against him with uncertainty. Ethan exhaled hard and bore down at the stretch as Justin braved forward.

Like some raging restrained bull, Justin breathed hard as he pushed in, tested against the tight ring, backed off, and tried again. And while Ethan knew he should appreciate the snail's pace, he and his body searched for more as Justin danced around the pushing past. Ethan slid his hand down, helped Justin past the resistance, and went still as he allowed him some time.

"Fuuck." Justin forced out the word, and Ethan knew what he was feeling at that very moment. He'd experienced that overwhelming sensation himself the first time he'd been inside Justin.

Ethan withdrew his hand and pulled Justin's mouth to his, nodding slightly as they kissed. Justin tested with tiny pumps and sank in a little deeper as Ethan's body accepted him. It was easier than Ethan thought it would be, but it remained something to adjust and adapt to. He couldn't have asked for a more patient partner as their bodies were finally wholly joined.

"Ethan," Justin whispered, trembling above him, strong arms shaking with restraint, and glassy-eyed as he stared down at him.

"I know," Ethan agreed, just as choked up that they'd finally gotten here.

"I'm going to love you for the rest of my life," Justin said, and his hips pulled away, and he slid back in, slick, hot, and smooth like satin, tender inside Ethan's body.

Ethan slipped into a flashback; he struggled to stay with Justin, but his mind took him to his past, to a horrible, vile memory. The trauma would live with him for the rest of his life. But as Justin gently wiped away the tears, his body calmed, and he breathed to a count with Ethan as Ethan returned to the present.

"You are beautiful," Ethan whispered. "This is love."

Justin only nodded. Ethan knew Justin was too overcome with emotion to speak, his heart in his eyes.

"Don't stop," Ethan said, easing his hands down to Justin's hips, sinking his fingers into his flesh, and guiding him to move again.

"Are you with me?" Justin choked out.

"Yes." And Ethan was. Despite the flashback, he was with him.

"Stay with me." Justin kissed Ethan again, easily following the physical direction of Ethan's hands.

He'd known this wouldn't be easy, but he also knew how safe he was with Justin. Here was a man who would try to move mountains for him if Ethan wanted it, a partner who replaced horror with love as they struggled together through this first time, this impossible hurdle, a beautiful and simultaneously tragic milestone in their life together. Ethan knew after this, with his fear now diminishing, it would get easier.

Later, Justin's lazy hand stroked up and down Ethan's back as he held him. Ethan fought the urge to apologize.

"Shh," Justin soothed and laced his fingers through Ethan's, holding his hand.

"I'm okay."

"You are, and we are," Justin assured him.

Chapter Thirty-Seven

Ethan

ETHAN HELD UP his neon-colored posterboard sign. It was evident Ethan was no art major, but a giant bold single E in black was all he needed for this. He waited for the signal and sat down in his seat. Job done, Ethan rolled the poster, slid it underneath his chair, and turned to his dad. "Can you believe it?"

"Yes, I never doubted we'd be sitting here one day."

"Since when?" Ethan laughed.

"Since your ceremony," his dad said.

"Yeah, who puts the Super Bowl in their wedding vows?" Ethan recalled, shaking his head at the cockiness of his husband.

John enthusiastically recounted the line Justin had said in their backyard. "This is the first ring of many."

"Surely, he didn't mean that part about repeating the ceremony every time he won so he could put the ring on my finger."

"He told your mother to reserve the white arbor at the rental place."

"He's ridiculous." Ethan crossed his arms and pulled down his cap against the cold. They were in Baltimore, and Ethan inhaled deeply and exhaled, recalling Justin's relief over the easy breathing returning instantly when he'd played a northern team early on in their preseason.

"His breathing will be fine," John said.

"At least he doesn't have to use the inhaler as much here." Ethan was glad they'd finally had a team doctor recognize Justin's issue. How dumb they'd been to think it was only the climate.

"I should have caught that," John said with a sour tone.

"It isn't severe; none of us knew. And he's doing so much better now."

"That's true." John had to yell over the crowd's increasing volume as the opponents lined up for the kickoff.

"He's such a sore loser," Ethan said when the madness calmed.

"They lost two games all season. Was he really that bad?"

"The worst."

"Well, that's part of marriage. You gotta deal with the lows. And it sucks to lose."

Ethan knew this about his father as a player from his mother. He had seen it for himself, later when his dad became a coach with a struggling team, and now he was experiencing it firsthand with Justin. His high school and college careers in the sport had been nearly flawless, but two first-year NFL losses had been a hit on Justin. Of course, he only worked harder to ensure it wouldn't happen again.

"He's up," John said, leaning forward, and Ethan did the same next to him as Justin called the play, stepped back, and threw a pass under the pressure of a blitz.

"That's not going to bode well for them," Ethan mused. And sure enough, Justin pointed at someone on the defensive line and yelled something.

"Wonder what he said?" John asked.

"Something dumb like 'bring it' or 'try me,'" Ethan guessed. "He'll run it next. Watch. He does that when he gets irritated with someone."

Sure enough, Justin ran it, weaving and blowing past the defensemen, making his point before running it out of bounds to avoid the tackle. It had taken them thirty yards though.

"I don't know how you don't see it, Dad. He can be a real jerk out there."

His dad barked out a laugh. "Oh, I see it. That's just football."

"I know. Then they all shake hands and act like old friends when it's all over," Ethan said, still grasping that he might never fully understand the madness of this game his father and husband loved so much.

Then, Jones ran it in for a touchdown, and Ethan stood, cheering with 71,000 other people, some of whom booed around them. Ethan held up his finger to match Justin's and took in the sight of so many fans doing the same. They remained standing until the field goal was good.

John's knee bounced, and Ethan knew this wouldn't be another of Justin's easy wins. The opposing team was equally matched, and over the rest of the first quarter and the second, the two teams duked it out with a score-for-score fight. Justin scrambled to avoid another sack attempt and managed to get the ball to Chastain. Nick was taken down hard and had to be helped off the field, their first casualty.

When the next sack attempt came and Justin stiff-armed the player, he got a fifteen-yard penalty for unnecessary roughness, with the defensive player on his back from the unexpected move from the QB.

Ethan laughed, and John shook his head.

"Now he's pissed," Ethan said as Justin threw a long pass to make up for the penalty, and Hernandez ran it in. Ethan stood again, lifted his hand, and sat back down. "What do you want from the food court? I want to beat the crowd and watch the halftime show."

They headed down together to the confirming cheer of the field goal. Ethan used a card Justin had given him for food and swag, and they loaded up and headed back to their seats just as the crowd began to descend for the half. Ethan had gotten pretty good at timing this break from all the games he'd sat through. So far, he hadn't missed a single game, vowing he never would. He'd been flying to the away games and was thrilled over the miles he'd racked up over the season.

"What did you decide to do about school?"

"Justin wants me to consider the online program, but honestly, this is a full-time thing," Ethan said, motioning to the gridiron. "I can't imagine missing his games or not being there for him. I will probably do the online option part-time and still be able to travel to the games."

"Are you okay with that?"

"More than okay. Justin didn't save me, Dad, but he was a big part of putting me back together. I'll be there for him."

John nodded, not seeming bothered by the idea that his son wouldn't finish college as soon as originally planned.

"And I want to enjoy the off-season with him, not be worried about finals or writing papers."

They directed their attention to the show, which was as impressive as Ethan suspected it would be. Then, the second half began. Neck and neck, the two teams fought, getting a little dirtier and more desperate as they battled it out on the turf. Tempers got heated. There was a fumble, a Bay recovery, and a tackle at Baltimore's ten-yard line. Justin donned his helmet and returned to the field.

"Here we go," Ethan said, checking the scoreboard. He knew when Justin covered his ears over his helmet pretending to try to hear the call, he would do something unexpected his coach hadn't called. He'd only done it once before, in one of the earlier games in the season. Justin had been so shocked he hadn't gotten ripped a new one over his change in the play call. He'd later told Ethan he hadn't liked the call and couldn't believe he'd gotten away with it with Richardson.

Everyone in the stands turned as one in slow motion, tracking the unbelievable pass, which Justin had Ethan out on the beach each week to work on. The distance surpassed their greenspace at home, and Justin was determined to beat his best throw. It was easily a seventy-yard sailor as the ball seemed to float in the air before arcing back down and into Jones's hands. The twenty-yard run ended as the offensive line ran down the field to line up again.

Ethan glanced down to see if Richardson or Nellis were pissed, but they seemed to scramble, intent and just as much in this fight as they sent out the next play. Justin passed it off to the running back, and they gained five yards before the dogpile. The next down had them across that magical line, and the stadium roared as Ethan jumped up, spilling a few nachos along the way as he celebrated. They were in the lead again, and he had to tell his father to calm down before he gave himself a few more gray hairs.

"They're going for it," John said, seeming pleased with the decision to forego the field goal and increase their lead.

And Ethan wasn't surprised when his man ran it in, holding up the ball with one hand and flying the number one with the other.

"Guess he's bringing that one home," Ethan said, pleased.

"He was impressed with the shelf I helped you build," John said, looking just as satisfied with their shared effort building a football shelf to hold the numerous balls Justin had brought home to Ethan like a good grade on a report card. They'd constructed a cube-like shelf system in the game room, which was pretty much Justin's trophy case.

"This is over," Ethan said with pride as their defense destroyed every attempt at a comeback.

"Looks like Mom did the right thing reserving the arbor," his father said, amused and emotional as he looked down at the field at his son-in-law.

Ethan sighed, then finished his eleven-dollar nachos.

Chapter Thirty-Eight

Justin

"YOU DID IT," Shelly Marksman said into the microphone as confetti fluttered around a sweaty and victorious team.

"Thank you for flying down from Washington and being here with us today," Justin said.

"Last September, you told the world you'd bring your team to the Super Bowl as a rookie quarterback," she said.

"And you promised to be a good reporter." He nodded approvingly. "And we've both kept our promises."

"We have, and that's why I take pride in introducing the National Football League's World Champions today. Let's hear it for the Bay and for Coach Nellis." Shelley handed over the microphone and hugged Justin, posing for a picture with him holding the Lombardi Trophy and wearing a Super Bowl champion ball cap.

They stepped aside so others could make their way to the front, and Justin passed the trophy to Jones.

"Someday, I'll have a story for you when I retire," Justin said and glanced out to the stands where Ethan and his father still sat watching history being made.

"I'll write it," Shelly said, following his line of sight.

Justin held up his hand with the number-one finger, and Ethan stood, holding up his in return.

Shelly nodded slowly at Justin. "When you retire, I'll write that story."

"Good," Justin said and turned to the podium where Coach Richardson gave his Super Bowl victory speech with his son, Matt, next to him.

Justin gave him a thumbs-up, and Matt held up his, beaming with a grin that seemed to stretch from ear to ear.

Author's Note

Nothing in this story is meant to accurately depict the NHL, the NCAA, or the NFL, their players, process, or the sport. While research and knowledge were utilized to write this story, plot and character development took precedence over fact. This work is meant to be enjoyed as entertainment and is entirely fictional.

Acknowledgements

Special thanks to editor Elizabetta McKay, who makes the daunting task of editing for a writer not only a learning experience but frequently humorous along the way. I look forward to our continued hard-working fun with many more stories. And to the cover artist Jaycee DeLorenzo at NineStar Press.

Additional thanks to my graduate peers and writing instructors at the University of New Orleans Creative Writing Workshop, who ultimately contributed to this story through workshop. Barbara Ann Johnson, M.O. Walsh, Lauren Grey, Dixon Wingrove, Derek Direkx, Luca Van Der Heide, Micael Noldt, Annalia Hopper, Ali Householder, and Ryan Guenther.

And always, to my family for their endless patience, support, and love. No one else pretends to be nearly as interested in my wild story ideas as they do. I love them for it.

Lastly, to you, dear reader. Thank you for reading my work and the time spent in my worlds with my characters. I'll see you in the next story.

About the Author

GiGi DeGraham lives, plays, and learns in New Orleans. She is a proud southerner and enjoys fixing up old houses and writing. Most of her story and character ideas develop while sanding and painting. She loves to roller skate and has a favorite author-named cat called Irving, after Washington Irving. You'll always find her with an audiobook in her ear.

GiGi prefers the outdoors when the weather permits, going on rock and fossil hunts or visiting local rock shops. You could definitely find her at a hockey game. Otherwise, she's clacking away at her keyboard until the wee hours. GiGi firmly believes downtime should be spent on a porch swing. GiGi is a life-long supporter of the LGBTQ+ community.

Email

gigidegraham@gmail.com

Facebook

www.facebook.com/GiGiDeGrahamRomance

Twitter

@GigiDegraham

Instagram

www.instagram.com/gigidegrahamromance

Website

www.gigidegraham.weebly.com

Tiktok

Other NineStar books by this author

The Steele Pack Series

Prisoner

Fugitive

www.ninestarpress.com

www.facebook.com/ninestarpress

www.facebook.com/groups/NineStarNiche

www.twitter.com/ninestarpress

www.instagram.com/ninestarpress

bsky.app/profile/ninestarpress.bsky.social

www.threads.net/@ninestarpress

www.ingramcontent.com/pod-product-compliance
Lightning Source LLC
Chambersburg PA
CBHW060229100726
47907CB00003B/561